Wyrd Water

Jack Callaghan

Wyrd Water
Jack Callaghan

This edition copyright © 2025 by Oxford eBooks Ltd.
Published under the sci-fi-cafe.com imprint.

www.oxford-ebooks.com

Story copyright © 2025 Jack Callaghan
Cover Illustration by Ramiro Roman [SKINCUBE]

The right of the author to be identified as the author of this work
has been asserted in accordance with the
Copyright, Designs and Patents Act 1988.

ISBN 978-1-910779-52-1

#20251105-1

sci-fi-cafe.com

Chapter One

ANDRY ALWAYS FOUND the interior of her dad's Manchester office incredibly depressing, even though it changed almost every time she saw it.

He never seemed to be able to settle on a particular style, instead constantly refurbishing it, in order to fit with whatever was currently in vogue.

This year had come with the least inspiring change in decor so far. The entire space had been completely gutted, and new wallpaper and carpets had been put in, the floor now a dull, unpleasant beige, and the walls bearing an indecipherable tessellation of geometric shapes, black on a grey background, which was almost painful to look at. Her dad's previous, large oak desk had been replaced with one made mostly of plastic, and the deep cushioned, leather sofa was now a harsh, angular thing, the rigid cushions covered in rough, synthetic material.

When she'd asked him why he felt another redecoration was necessary, he'd explained that times were changing. It was 1979, almost a new decade, the start of a new era. All the tacky rubbish of the 70s had to be swept away and replaced with something more up to date. This wasn't down purely to his preferences, he'd said. Rather, it was what his clients would expect.

Andry's dad was a property developer, but all she'd ever been able to figure out with regards to what this meant was that he bought ugly, old buildings, 'Developed' them into ugly, new buildings, and then sold them for very large amounts of money. When she'd once repeated this description to him, he'd snorted with derision, told her it was much more complicated than that, and she was making him sound like some sort of lowly tradesman.

She leaned back into the unyielding sofa cushions and stared at the ceiling. Even the light fixture had been changed. A garish, lime green shade now hung around the bulb. It was nauseating.

She heard someone coming along the hall. She hoped it was her dad, who'd disappeared not long after they'd arrived, without saying anything about what they were doing for lunch, but it wasn't. Instead, Pat, her dad's 'Right hand man', strode into the office and looked around. He obviously knew she was there, but he was acting as though he didn't. He gave a puzzled hum and approached her dad's desk, like he might find him hiding behind it.

"Audrey," he said, finally acknowledging her presence. "I wasn't expecting to see you."

"Andry," she said.

"Huh?" said Pat.

"It's *An*dry," she repeated, placing extra emphasis upon the N in her name.

This was a common occurrence. Even people such as Pat, who'd known her for her entire life, often used the wrong name when speaking to her. She'd heard them all, more times than she could count, 'Audrey', 'Andy', 'Annie', 'Mandy', but almost never the right one. Her name was actually 'Andromeda', and even though her parents were now four years divorced, she, unlike her mum, still had her dad's surname of 'Watt', meaning the jokes practically wrote themselves. 'Androme-*what*?'.

"That's what I said," said Pat. "Your dad didn't tell me you were here."

"Yet, here I am," said Andry, pointing to herself with both thumbs.

"How's your mum?" asked Pat.

"Same as always," Andry replied. "Why do *you* care?"

She was right to ask. Pat had been one of her dad's chief references during her parents' divorce, assuring the court officials that her mum and dad's differences truly were 'Irreconcilable'. The court hadn't even questioned what made Pat such a reliable source. Had it done so, it would've been revealed that it was Pat, more often than not, who accompanied her dad during the liquid lunches and several days long 'Liaisons' with clients, which caused him to spend so much time away from his family that it seemed like he was allergic to them.

"No need to be like that," said Pat. "Whatever's happened between your mum and dad, we're still friends, aren't we?"

"*Are* we?" asked Andry. "Since you skulked up here with my dad, I only see you once or twice a year. You're more like an associate."

"Ouch!" said Pat with a laugh. "Sharp as ever, I see. I'd have thought you'd be happier. Six weeks off for summer. Last one you'll get, at your age. This time next year, you'll be kicked out into the big, bad world."

"Forgive me for not bursting with excitement," said Andry, "but I can think of better places to spend the 'Last one' I'll get than *here*."

Pat sat down on the armrest of the sofa by Andry's feet.

"Your dad thinks the world of you," he said. "You know that, right? He's always talking about you, and he's thinking about your future as well. This might not be the last summer holiday you get. Have you given any thought to staying on for A-levels? Your dad can get you transferred to Rossall. They're taking on girls now. He's already been making calls."

"I think I'd rather die," said Andry. "Besides, *has* he been making calls? Or have *you* been making calls on his behalf?"

"I do a lot of things on your dad's behalf," said Pat, "but this is one of the exceptions. I can pull strings, but I don't have the gift of the gab, like your dad does. That's why he's the boss, and I'm not."

"Are you happy with that?" asked Andry, sitting up and scooting back on the sofa. "Is this really how you saw your life? Dancing to whatever tune my dad decides to play, and fixing all his problems for him?"

Unlike her dad, Pat wasn't a property developer. All Andry had been able to deduce was that he was some kind of lawyer, and maybe even that title wasn't strictly correct. On the few times when she'd heard him give an explanation as to what exactly he was, Pat had said that he was her dad's 'Personal assistant'. He resembled a lawyer, in that he had the amazing ability to produce paperwork almost on cue, a lot of which supposedly had the power to cause a potential client's face to drain of its colour.

Andry had always thought that there were good lawyers and bad lawyers, or, that was to say, good lawyers and *evil* lawyers. Pat seemed to be somewhere in the middle. If her dad was trying to clinch a deal, and the client needed something sweet sprinkled on the top, Pat could provide it. However, if something sour sprinkled on the top was what was required to convince them, he could provide that with just as much ease. Either way, her dad rarely didn't get what he wanted.

Andry wasn't sure if any laws were being broken, and she didn't really care. This was a world that she had no desire to understand, never mind be a part of, hence why she had absolutely no interest in being sent to somewhere like Rossall, where her dad would, no doubt, 'Pull strings' to make sure her admittance came with the added bonus of her getting to study wretched subjects with '-ics' or '-ology' at the end of them, in a hope of encouraging her to enter the family trade. She also knew that 'Pull strings' probably meant 'Make a sizable donation', and the idea of her having been 'Bought' into a prestigious school filled her with revulsion.

"I'll dance to anything with a beat," said Pat. "As for problems, well, everyone's got those."

"How much longer is he going to be?" asked Andry. "It's two O'clock, and I'm starving."

"I *thought* he was here," said Pat, standing back up. "He called me ten minutes ago."

"He left at mid-day," said Andry.

"You've been sat here this whole time?" asked Pat.

"Nothing better to do," said Andry, swinging her legs over the armrest.

"You could've gone and bothered the girls downstairs," said Pat. "Learned to use the photocopier or something. It's a proper hi-tech one, sent over from the States."

"Fascinating," said Andry with a sigh and drummed her heels on the side of the couch.

"Why do you wear those?" asked Pat, looking at her feet. She was wearing her beloved pair of black Doc Marten boots, the intricate eyelets threaded with cherry red laces, their surfaces polished to a brilliant sheen.

"I like them," said Andry, raising a foot and turning it from side to side, admiring the shine job. "They're reliable."

"They're what yobbos wear," said Pat, wrinkling his nose in contempt. "You're not gonna go the full hog and get your head shaved, are you? Suspenders, Fred Perry and a bomber jacket?"

"I might," said Andry, flashing him a teasing grin. "Imagine how quick Rossall would turn me down *then*."

"Bah, a skinhead gang would eat you alive," said Pat, smiling back at her. "A young, middle-class girl, playing dress-up? Your feet wouldn't touch the ground, reliable boots or not."

"I think I stopped being middle-class when my parents split," said Andry, not taking this ribbing at all well. "Now, I just get a taste of it whenever I'm *here*, and I don't think too highly of it."

"Well, if you *don't* go to Rossall," said Pat with a shrug, "try telling me that again when your dad doesn't have to pay child maintenance anymore." Their eyes bored into one another for an achingly long moment, but Pat broke it with a click of his tongue and nodded at the door. "Speak of the Devil."

Andry leaned sideways on the couch and saw her dad coming along the hall.

His moods were always impossible to judge, even from up close. When he was annoyed, he *looked* annoyed, but this wasn't much help. When he was happy, he looked annoyed. When he was hungry, he looked annoyed. In fact, his face was permanently contorted into a mask of agitation, which seemed to be saying, 'I don't like any of *this*, and I'll kill whoever's responsible'.

"You took your time," she said as he entered the office.

He looked at her but then snapped his fingers when he saw where her boots were.

"Off!" he said, pointing at the offending footwear. "That couch is brand new! Why are you wearing those?"

"That's what *I* asked her," said Pat. "Apparently, she's a rude-girl now, as I believe they call themselves."

"Over my dead body," said her dad with a sharp, humourless laugh. "That's her mum's influence."

"I'm right here, you know," said Andry, taking her feet from the couch, but only to set them down on the floor with a thump. "Are you gonna feed me or what?"

"In a little while," said her dad. "I've got some things to go over with Pat first."

"But I'm—" Andry made to protest, but Pat cut her off, stepping in between her and her dad.

"I read the entire thing last night," he said, performing his trick of producing paperwork, seemingly from thin air. "It's not that you want to purchase it. It's about the renovations. The place is grade two listed. They won't sell if they think you're going to mess with it too much"

"To Hell with all that," said her dad. "If the price is right, they'll sell, and I can do what I want."

"Not that easy, I'm afraid," said Pat, sucking his teeth. "Since the resurvey in sixty-eight, they've gotten pretty strict on what you can and can't do. You know what the heritage people are like. If some fifteenth century nobleman's dog cocked its leg on a patch of land, they list it."

"Can't we get conveyancing solicitors in our corner?" asked her dad. "We can have those bloodthirsty gits from Bradstock-Wheeler handle it for us. They know what side their bread's buttered."

"We're dealing with a very different kind of property to what we're used to," said Pat with a shake of his head. "This isn't a pile of post-war concrete. The place is a local gem."

"If it's *my* name on the deed," said her dad, slapping himself on the chest, "then it's *my* gem. Think about it. How good will it look if I buy a property, with my *own* money, only to get bogged down by legislation? When we fit out that new shopping centre next year, how are we supposed to get contractors in if they think the guy running the show can't dodge red tape?"

"That's why I still think you should be more careful about this," said Pat, stroking his fingers through the sheath of paperwork.

"I don't pay you to think," her dad shot back. "I pay you to *do*. Find a way around it all. When I make my offer, I want it to look like they *bit* my hand off."

"Sure thing, Boss," said Pat, rolling up the papers and sticking them under his arm. He tipped Andry a wink as he left the room.

"How do you stand him?" she asked her dad. "He's like a pirate in a suit."

"He gets things done," her dad replied, "and he doesn't care how he does them." He frowned and turned to face her. "Anyway, what was it you wanted?"

"Food!" said Andry, holding her hands up at either side of her mouth. "I don't just sit here and look pretty. I need feeding every now and then."

"Fine," said her dad. "I'll get someone at reception to book us in somewhere."

"Oh, no, you won't," said Andry. "I'm not going to one of your fancy-pants places. *I'll* pick where we go."

Andry chose an Indian restaurant, much to her dad's chagrin.

"I left Leicester to get *away* from these kinds of places," he grumbled as they took their seats. "I would've thought you'd be sick of them."

"Not a chance," said Andry as she perused the menu. "I love it, always have. I hope they make the stuff properly, like back at home."

"Don't get your hopes up," said her dad with another of his mirthless chuckles. "This is the north. If it's not chips and gravy, it's too exotic. Didn't you notice it was a white bloke who seated us?"

"That doesn't matter," said Andry. "It's who's in the kitchen that counts."

"I hope it's *authentic* enough for you," said her dad, glancing around at the curtain draped walls and poking at one of the elaborately folded napkins on the table. "I'm guessing the plates get brought out by a guy with a bone through his nose, riding an elephant." He then placed his hands together, as though praying, and bowed up and down to Andry before putting on a ridiculous mock Indian accent. "Oh, thank you very much, please. Ding-ding-a-ling."

"That's not funny," said Andry, glaring at him over the menu. "The Indian people in Leicester are actually really nice. Maybe you'd have found that out if you weren't so keen to *get away*."

"I *got away*," said her dad, "because they were turning pretty much every building in the city into textile factories. Not very useful to someone in my business. Leicester may now 'Clothe the world', but it would've had the shirt off *my* back."

"Sorry," said Andry, returning her attention to the menu, "you aren't very good at jokes."

"Must be the way I tell 'em," said her dad, taking a look at his own menu. "I can't make hide nor hair of that," he said, dropping it back onto the table. "Besides, now's a good a time as any. About what Pat and I were discussing at the office."

"Something to do with a shopping centre," said Andry, having decided on a chicken Madras. The menu gave it a spice level of five, which was right up her street.

"No, before that," said her dad. He leaned forward, fixing her with a peculiar look. He was clearly trying to give an endearing smile, but the result was as though he'd only ever heard one described. "Back when I was little," he continued, "your grandma and granddad used to take me on summer holidays to the lake district. Do you know where that is?"

"I suppose it's a place with lots of lakes," said Andry, but she was being completely facetious. At school, they'd done a whole week on the 'Lake Poets', Wordsworth, Coleridge, etcetera, though this wasn't anything she thought her dad would be interested in.

"It's that, yes," said her dad. "As far as I'm concerned, it's one of the most beautiful places in the whole world. Lake Windermere is the largest in England. We used to go there and do boating, fishing, hiking, you name it." His smile had suddenly become more sincere, and Andry wasn't sure what to make of it.

"You?" she said. "Boating, fishing and hiking?"

"Is that so hard to believe?" asked her dad, his new, unnervingly genuine smile broadening. "I wasn't *born* in an office, was I?"

"Could've fooled *me*," said Andry. "Anway, what's this got to do with you growling at Pat?"

"There's a property up for sale on the shore of Windermere," said her dad, "and *I'm* going to buy it."

"Property developer buys property," said Andry. "Wow! Headline news."

"No," said her dad, his smile momentarily relapsing into his usual frown. "I'm going to buy it for *me*. I mean, for *us* to maybe go to."

"A holiday home?" said Andry, unable to stop herself from smirking. "Where's *this* come from? You're not having a mid-life crisis, are you?"

"Look," said her dad, setting his palms down on the table, "I know you hate coming up here, but it's the only time I get to see you. I *had* thought that, if I arranged somewhere more pleasant to go, these visits wouldn't be so awkward."

"What makes you think it'd be any less awkward there?" asked Andry. "It could be just as awkward, but in a more scenic setting."

"Seriously, Andry?" said her dad, sighing and leaning back in his chair. "It never used to be like this when you were younger. We had good times, didn't we? Remember Tenerife? Best week of your life, you said."

"This isn't exactly Tenerife," said Andry, "and the lake district probably isn't, either."

"You haven't seen the place yet," said her dad, trying to summon his smile back into action. "It's right on the edge of the lake, with a little jetty where you can moor a boat. The lake shore is practically a beach in its own right. Maybe I could buy a donkey, dress it up in a sombrero, and when the sun's blazing, you could almost imagine you *were* in Tenerife."

"What's the property like?" asked Andry, attempting to pronounce 'Property' in the same professional, yet utterly detached manner as her dad and Pat did. "Is it a thatched barn, with flowers around the windows, like something from the lid of a biscuit tin?"

"Not at all," said her dad. "Five bedrooms, two and a half baths, decked patio at the rear, all set in private grounds. I was thinking I could let it out for most of the year, but, for a week or so in the summer, it'll be just you and me."

"*Just* you and me?" asked Andry. "We'd be ready to kill each other after a few days."

"Well, there're things to do there," her dad insisted. "There's a town not fifteen minutes away, with shops and restaurants and everything."

"I guess that doesn't sound *too* bad," said Andry.

"See?" said her dad. "I *knew* you hadn't turned completely to stone." He drummed his fingers on the underside of the table. "How about we go this weekend? Friday to Monday?"

"I thought you said you were *going* to buy it," said Andry.

"It's as good as done," said her dad. "I'm just waiting for them to sign on the line. In the meantime, we could stay at a hotel and have a look at the place."

"I don't like hotels," said Andry. "That one you took us to in York last year, I hated it there. All the staff kept calling me 'Miss.'"

"How about a B&B, then?" said her dad. "Somewhere small and out of the way, proper rustic."

Even without the forced smile, Andry could tell that he was on the verge of pleading. As someone who was unaccustomed to not getting what he wanted, Andry could tell that this was foreign territory for him, and she couldn't help but feel a slight pang of satisfaction at having such power over him, if only in a small way.

"And it'll be *just* you and me?" she asked. "You won't have Pat staying in a room down the hall, waiting to swoop in if duty calls?"

"I think Pat can handle things here for a few days," said her dad. "I'd need to give him the number of where we're staying, of course." Andry rolled her eyes. "Only in case of emergencies," he added, obviously worried that he was potentially blowing the deal.

"Okay," said Andry. "Sounds like a plan."

"You'll love it, I promise," said her dad, his enthusiasm buoying. "You can get a nice bit of country air in your lungs. It'll do you the world of good. You look so pale these days."

"What's *that* supposed to mean?" asked Andry.

"Nothing," said her dad, stepping back from the precipice he'd suddenly found himself on. "Nothing at all."

"Whatever," said Andry, looking down at her hand and turning it over. *She* didn't think she looked pale. Well, maybe a little, but that was actually quite fashionable at the moment. If Siouxsie Sioux could pull it off, Andry felt that *she* could, too. "You'll have to let Mum know we're going."

"I don't see why," said her dad with a huff. "What we do is up to us. It's none of her business."

"What if something happens to us?" asked Andry.

"It's the lake district," her dad scoffed, "not darkest Asia. What could possibly *happen* to us?"

Chapter Two

ANDRY SHOULD'VE KNOWN her dad would want to get an early start on the Friday morning, but being roused at six O'clock seemed totally unnecessary.

She dragged herself out of bed and set about packing a few things for the trip. She'd brought more than enough clothes for the whole two weeks she was to spend in Manchester, but even this wasn't very much. She mostly lived in her boots, three pairs of jeans, and whatever top or band T-shirt she decided to fling on. Socks and underwear were a given, but she guessed she wouldn't need any more than two sets of each for just a long weekend. She only had to hope her dad didn't have anything unexpectedly formal planned. 'Proper rustic', he'd said, but that didn't mean he wouldn't spring something on her out of the blue that required her to be in some kind of dress. If he *did*, he'd be disappointed. Not only had she not packed a dress, but she wasn't sure if she still *owned* one.

Even at such an early hour, her dad was raring to go. He was clearly more excited than he'd let on. Mental images of his boyhood holidays were, no doubt, parading through his mind. He still didn't appear to be 'Happy', but his usual state of mild annoyance had been transformed into a fixation upon preparedness. He checked his suitcase, then checked it again. He made sure he had his keys, setting them on the kitchen counter, before remembering to check that the road atlas was in the car. When he couldn't get into it, he came back for the keys. Only, he couldn't remember where he'd put them, so he went to see if they were in his suitcase.

What had taken Andry about ten minutes took him until half past seven, which at least gave her enough time for some tea and toast.

"The roads will be choked if we don't get going," he grumbled as he came back into the kitchen, patting his pockets, as though he thought this would cause the keys to spontaneously appear within them.

"Won't get far without these," said Andry, scooping the keys from the counter and dangling them on the end of her finger.

"Give them here," said her dad, snatching the keys from her. "We've not got time for games."

"*You* put them there," said Andry. "Anyway, what's the rush? It's not like lakes *close*."

"We're supposed to be checking into the guesthouse at nine," said her dad. "If I'm paying for it, I want the whole stretch." He thrust the keys into his pocket, then looked more closely at Andry. "Really?" he said, his shoulders dropping. "Do you have to wear *that* one?"

"*This* one?" Andry replied, tugging at the hem of her shirt, which was definitely what he meant. "What's wrong with it?"

"You *know* what's wrong with it," said her dad. "Bands give themselves some pretty stupid names these days, but what exactly *is* a Sex Pistol?" Andry grinned and made to reply, but he stopped her with an upheld hand. "Forget I asked. Just put a jumper over it until we're at least checked in. Remember, we're going to a part of the country where they probably think The Banana Splits are too shocking."

They hit the road just before eight. Her dad said they had about an hour and a half of driving ahead of them, meaning they'd almost certainly arrive late, and he'd miss out on at least half an hour of the 'Stretch' he'd paid for.

Andry asked if they could work out just how much each wasted minute was going to cost, but her dad refused to disclose the full amount, which meant it was either not very much, or quite a lot.

Even though it was early August, the threat of autumn was already making itself known, and the roads were nowhere near as busy as her dad had feared, the main holiday season now being, if a little prematurely, well and truly over.

"What if it rains the whole time?" she asked as they hurtled along the motorway.

"It won't," her dad replied. He gave a shrug. "I mean, even if it does, it'll still be nice. Some places are worth seeing in any weather."

"As long as you can see them *through* the weather," said Andry.

"I still think you'll change your tune when we get there," said her dad. "Honestly, it's one of the loveliest places you'll ever see, and its right here on our doorstep."

"So, why haven't you ever wanted to buy a place there before" asked Andry. "Why now, all of a sudden?"

"Properties like *this* don't come on the market every day," said her dad. "There've been times before when I've looked, but either the asking price was too steep, or they were proper rat-holes that you *definitely* wouldn't see on a biscuit tin lid."

"What's the asking price on *this* one?" asked Andry, probing a little further.

"None of your concern, Madam," said her dad, looking from the road and raising his eyebrows at her.

"Oh, come on," said Andry, leaning over and batting him on the arm. "How am I supposed to follow in your footsteps if we can't even talk to each other about property prices?"

"Because *you're* an inside trader," said her dad. "Anything I tell you about my finances gets delivered straight to your mum."

"My lips are sealed," said Andry, miming a zip across her mouth. "Come on, spill the beans."

Her dad gave a groan and drummed his hands on the steering wheel.

"They *want* a quarter of a million," he said.

"*How* much?" cried Andry, causing her dad to wince.

"Keep your hair on," he hissed. "They *want* a quarter of a million, but it's not what they'll get. I'll make sure Pat sees to that."

"Even so," said Andry, "if you've got six figures to be throwing around at holiday homes, maybe I *should* tell Mum. I'm sure she'd love to hear about it."

"Okay, smarty-pants," said her dad, "if you do plan to follow in my footsteps, as you put it, can you tell me what transfer of equity means?"

"*No*," Andry drawled with a roll of her eyes. "I don't know what transfer of equity means. *Please* tell me."

"It means," said her dad, "at some point, I put your name on the deed. Then, when I eventually cark it, you get the whole thing."

"*I* get it?" asked Andry, quite taken aback.

"*You* get it," said her dad, pointing at her. "*You*. Not your mum. Not any other grubbing relative who comes creeping out from the woodwork. It's yours, and *only* yours. You can sell it, live in it, rent it out, whatever. Rest assured, though, I'll wrap the place up in so much legal barbed wire, anyone else who tries to touch it will lose their fingers. Inheritance tax might be a problem, but there're ways around it."

"Well," said Andry, leaning heavily into her seat, "thanks, I suppose."

"I was going to tell you after you'd seen it," said her dad, turning his attention back to the road. "I thought it'd be a nice surprise."

"It is," said Andry, sitting back up. "I mean, it's just …" She frowned at him in bewilderment. "A quarter of a *million*?"

"Not once Pat gives the owners a talking to," said her dad. "I won't go a penny over one-seventy-five. It's nice, but it's not quarter of a million nice."

"Why do I get the feeling there're strings on this?" asked Andry, narrowing her eyes at him. "What have I done to deserve such a fabulous gift?"

"Nothing," said her dad bluntly. "Not *yet* at least. It isn't a gift, it's an investment."

"Okay, *I* see," said Andry as realisation dawned within her. "I'm guessing this has something to do with Rossall?"

"To start with," her dad replied. "I *can* get you enrolled, but, if it's really not where you want to go, you still have to go somewhere. You're not marching out of school at sixteen. I won't allow it. Not even the first letter of your name goes on the deed until you've got at least a two-one degree in a decent subject. How does that sound?"

"It sounds like bribery," said Andry.

"I'd prefer to call it an incentive," said her dad.

"I'd need to get through O-levels first," said Andry.

Her dad rasped his lips.

"You'll *dance* through O-levels," he said. "You're not stupid, Andry. You're too rebellious to be stupid."

"Rebels aren't usually known for being good at school," said Andry.

"Actually, they *are*," said her dad. "All these morons

you see at the moment, dying their hair daft colours and shoving safety pins through themselves, they're not rebels. If you really want to stick it to the system, you beat it at its own game. You're a teenage girl. Society currently expects that the best you can hope for, if you don't end up in the dole queue, is to spend the rest of your life working as a receptionist for someone like *me*." He fixed her with a glare. "Are you gonna prove them right or wrong?"

"Right," said Andry.

"No," said her dad with a confused frown. "You're gonna prove them *wrong*, right?"

"No," said Andry, pointing at the road. "I mean, *right*. I think we just missed our exit."

The slight detour set them back by another half an hour, and they didn't reach the town of Windermere until gone ten O'clock.

"Where's this lake, then?" asked Andry, sitting up in her seat and peering through the windscreen. "You said it was big."

"Be patient," said her dad. "It stretches from north to south. We could've come up from the bottom and driven alongside it, but that would've taken too long. Isn't it nice here, though? Look at these houses. Nothing like that in Leicester."

Andry had to agree. In fact, almost every building they passed wouldn't have looked too out of place on a biscuit tin. There were no terrace houses or high-rise flat blocks. The roads were narrow and bordered by drystone walls. It was as though they'd gone back in time. She didn't think she'd ever want to *live* in a place like this, she was unashamedly a city girl, but the change in surroundings was certainly welcome.

"That man's got a goat," she said, pointing when they stopped at a junction.

"Oh, you'll see plenty of livestock," said her dad. "In these parts, eggs come straight from the nest, and milk comes straight from the udder."

It wasn't seeing the goat which had most caught Andry's attention. Rather, it was the fact that the man was coming *out* of a post office with it.

"Are we staying here in town?" she asked as they drove on.

"A bit closer to the outskirts," said her dad. "It's not quite a B&B, but it's a few steps down from a proper hotel. I doubt anyone will call you 'Miss.'"

"And what will they call *you*?" asked Andry, remembering the time at the hotel in York, when her dad had seemed pleased as punch whenever one of the staff had called him 'Sir'.

"I've been meaning to get to that," said her dad. "This little recognisance mission of ours needs to be kept as discreet as possible."

"Discreet?" said Andry. "Recognisance?"

"Word has gotten around that someone from out of town wants to buy the property," said her dad. "People in places like this can often be terrified of outside interference. I'm sure you heard Pat mention back at the office that the property is a grade two listed building. Some of the locals have worked themselves into a furious tizz, thinking this big city interloper wants to completely overhaul the building and turn it into some kind of modern eyesore."

"Only, they don't know it's you?" asked Andry.

"Not yet," her dad replied. "The current owners can't give any names until the deal goes through. So, if anyone asks, don't go blabbing about why we're really here. After all, it's not like I'm buying the property to turn it into a commercial business. Businesses are fine, they create jobs for the locals, but me wanting to just outright claim the place has ruffled more than a few feathers."

"You said you'd rent it out for most of the year," said Andry. "How's that not a business?"

"I'll rent it out to people I *know*," said her dad. "Self-catering, cash in hand. I won't be hiring *staff* for the place. I'm not John Marriott."

"And *are* you going to turn it into a modern eyesore?" asked Andry.

"Of course not," said her dad. "Like I say, it's grade two. I can't even *touch* the structure. What concerns me is it's got wiring from the sixties, plumbing from the forties, and it's been sat vacant and unmaintained for three years. I don't want to *change* it. I just want it to be liveable."

"Expensive, I'll bet," said Andry.

"You're damn right," said her dad with a huff, "especially if the council strongarm me into not bringing in my own contractors. I'll end up paying Bill and Ben from down the road to sit around drinking tea for God knows how long."

"Should we use assumed names when we check in?" asked Andry. "We could be Lord Wattington and his daughter … well, I suppose Andromeda sounds assumed enough already."

"You know what *I* wanted to call you," said her dad.

"Yeah," said Andry. "Anastasia." She stuck out her tongue. "Yuck! It sounds like something your doctor would give you a cream for."

"You can call yourself whatever you want," said her dad. "Just as long as you don't give away who we are. The last thing we need is to spend the entire time we're here being given the cold shoulder by every man and his goat. Or, even worse, coming out in the morning to find the car's tyres have been slashed."

"You said nothing would *happen* to us," said Andry.

"And nothing will," said her dad, "as long as you keep your gob shut."

It didn't take them much longer to reach the guesthouse, and Andry finally got her first view of the lake. Her dad hadn't been exaggerating when he'd said that it was big, and he hadn't been wrong about the shore being as good as a beach. The quick glimpse Andry got of it as they made their way around a bend in the road made the lake look almost as though it *were* an ocean. She hadn't been able to see the other side of it.

The guesthouse wasn't quite on the shore, but it was three floors tall, meaning the topmost rooms would have a decent view of the lake, and Andry kept her fingers crossed that she'd get one of these.

She wasn't surprised to see that the ground floor of the guesthouse was a pub. 'The Lychgate' a sign above the door declared.

"What's a lychgate?" she asked as they pulled up into the carpark.

"Not a clue," said her dad. "Makes a change from The Fox and Hounds or whatever, though, eh?"

"Yeah," said Andry. "I just hope it's *authentic* enough for you."

The inside of the pub turned out to be about as 'Authentic' as it got. Everything was wood and cast-iron, leather and stone. An open fire crackled away in the corner, apparently there to actually provide warmth against the sudden, autumnal snap which had descended, rather than for any aesthetic purpose. It was the kind of establishment that Andry had, of course, heard of, but she didn't think they still existed outside of some nostalgia tinted idea of what a rural pub should be like. She'd visited pubs in much further flung parts of the country than this, and even those had been unable to resist the encroachment of modern trappings such as jukeboxes and fruit machines.

Even at just gone ten in the morning, there were already a handful of patrons in the barroom. As Andry and her dad headed to the bar, she half expected these early drinkers to suddenly stop what they were doing and glance up at them, but their arrival caused no stir whatsoever.

The bar was being tended by a short but heavyset woman. Her reddish blonde hair was tied up into a torturous looking bun, and her face was caked with a layer of makeup which looked like the kind that was meant to be slept in.

"Good morning," said Andry's dad, setting his case down. "Martin Watt. Two rooms for three nights. I believe we spoke on the phone."

"Aye, that would've been me," said the barmaid, giving a smile which revealed notably white teeth. They were *so* white, in fact, that there was no way they were genuine. "Glad to have you. We were thinking of shutting the rooms down for the rest of the year, seeing as how foul the weather's gone. You're the only folks we've got in."

"A bit of cold doesn't stop us," said Andry's dad, taking an envelope from his inside pocket. The thickness of it meant it could only be money, and this also gave Andry an idea as to how much the 'Stretch' was costing. "I used to come here when I was a lad, and it was always worth it, rain or shine."

Andry couldn't help but notice the change in his accent. Or, rather, his choice of words. She'd never heard him use the term 'Lad' before, and she figured he was putting it on to try and blend in.

"I've put you both on the first floor," said the barmaid, taking the envelope. "Best rooms in the place."

"Can I have one on the top floor?" asked Andry. "I was hoping to see the lake from my window."

"I'm sure we can sort that out," said the barmaid. "Only, your fatha' paid for rooms on the first floor." She gripped the envelope, as though she thought it was about to be snatched back. "I can't change the fee around now it's been arranged."

"You said you're empty," said her dad.

"Oh, aye," said the barmaid, "but I've written it into the big book. Once it's in the big book, it's a done deal."

"I'd *really* like one on the top floor," Andry said to her dad, batting her eyes at him and watching the look on his face as yet more 'Wasted' money ran through his mind.

"Fine," he said with a forced smile. "Whatever you want."

"I'll need to have a top floor room turned over," said the barmaid. "If you'd like to wait here until it's done. Shouldn't take long."

"No rush," said Andry, taking her backpack from her shoulder and setting it down beside her dad's case.

"If you'd like to wait with her, Mister Watt," said the barmaid, "I can have your luggage taken to your room."

"I've just got the one," said Andry's dad. "I don't want to be a bother."

"Not at all," said the barmaid. She then looked over her shoulder. "Morgan!" she yelled. "Morgan! Come here and make yourself useful!"

A boy of about Andry's age came shuffling through the door which led to the interior of the building. He didn't look at either Andry or her dad, instead keeping his eyes on the floor. He had blonde but somewhat ruddy tinged hair, similar to the barmaid, long at the back and sides but shorter at the front, as though he'd had it cut just so he could see through it. He wore a powder blue shirt with long, pointed collar tips underneath a brown, sleeveless cardigan. He was also sporting a pair of stonewash, bell-bottom jeans. All of this combined made him look like the kind of kids at school who Andry often singled out for merciless ribbings. Who *was* this boy? A blonde Osmand brother?

"What?" he said, standing next to the barmaid with his head hung low.

"Take Mister Watt's luggage up to his room," said the barmaid. "Number three on the first floor."

"What about her?" asked the boy, pointing at Andry without looking at her.

"Who's *her*?" the barmaid snapped at him. "The cat's aunt? I need a room on second made ready, and you can take Miss Watt's things up when it's done."

"My name's Andry," said Andry. "I'm not *Miss* anyone."

"What?" said the boy, finally making eye contact through the curtain of his fringe.

"No, not Watt," said Andry, unable to resist the chance to play word games at the boy's expense. "Andry. Not Andy, or Mandy, or Annie. Andry. Call me anything else, and you won't get a tip."

"*What*?" said the boy, now completely baffled.

"Morgan!" the barmaid snapped again. "Don't be difficult!"

"Yeah, alright," said the boy, frowning at Andry. "*What*ever."

He picked up Andry's dad's case, then stalked towards a door at the other end of the bar.

"Can I get you some drinks?" asked the barmaid, giving another flash of her possibly counterfeit teeth.

"May as well," said Andry's dad. "What've you got on tap?"

"Bitter, mild, or stout," said the barmaid. "The mild's a local brew. Best in town."

"Sounds perfect," said Andry's dad.

"And for you?" the barmaid asked Andry. "Not *Miss*, you say. Andry, was it?"

"Yeah," said Andry, realising that the barmaid had hit the N in her name with pinpoint accuracy. "Wow, you got it in one."

"You pick up names fast in this game," said the barmaid as she set hands to the pumps. "Anyway, what'll you have?"

"Do you sell Coke?" asked Andry.

"Nope," said the barmaid. "None of that shipped in, Yank fizz. We do dandelion and burdock, though. Just as good as Coke, but it doesn't rot the teeth out of your head."

"I'll take your word for it," said Andry, earning a cough from her dad. "I mean, thank you, that'll be great."

With their drinks served, they went and sat by the fireplace.

"Look at that," said her dad, setting his drink down on the table and nodding at it. "Served in a proper pot with a handle. None of those slippery glasses, like back in the city."

"It's bit early, isn't it?" asked Andry, popping the top from her bottle and sniffing the contents.

"They're open, aren't they?" said her dad. "When in Rome, and all that."

Andry took a sip from the bottle.

"Hmm, that's actually not too bad," she said, pursing her lips in approval. "What *is* a burdock?"

"Prickly thing," said her dad, "sort of like a thistle. You've had it before, haven't you?"

"Not that tastes like *this*," said Andry, taking another sip.

"Ah, that's because it's all natural," said her dad. "No

additives or chemicals." He took a drink from his own mug and gave a sigh. "Yeah, this is the *real* stuff."

"Just like you remember?" asked Andry.

"I remember your granddad drank by the gallon while he was here," said her dad. "Hardly touched a drop for the rest of the year, not even at Christmas, but he more than made up for it on his holidays."

Andry didn't know much about her paternal grandparents, or her dad's entire side of the family, for that matter. They'd both died when she was still very young. Her mum had said something about them not liking the fact that she and her dad had gotten married. According to her mum, they were 'Snooty' and 'Bourgeoise' people who didn't approve of their son marrying someone 'Below his status'. Even Andry's arrival wasn't enough to win them over, as they'd been hoping for a boy, and there was nothing but bad blood between all involved. Her dad sometimes mentioned that she had an uncle somewhere, but he hadn't heard from him in years. This must have been who he was referring to when he mentioned 'Grubbing relatives' who might come sniffing around the lakeside property upon his own death.

She got on with her mum's side of the family like a house on fire. Her maternal grandparents were old-style, working-class types who'd lived in the Highfields area of Leicester when it was bombed during the war. Thus, they didn't really give a damn about anything, let alone 'Status'. She had an army of uncles, aunts, cousins, second cousins and everything in-between, who were collectively known as the 'Burnsley Clan'. After her parents' divorce, her mum *had* asked if Andry wanted to change her surname, but she'd decided against it, thinking that a name like 'Andry Burnsley' gave the impressions that she was destined to become a folk singer. Also, tacky jokes aside, the name Watt was a connection that she had with her dad, and she felt that dropping it would inflict a terrible wound upon him. As gruff as he could be, and how at odds they often found themselves, she had no real ill feeling towards him, and he obviously thought highly enough of her, and was so concerned about her future, that he'd dangled a not quite quarter of a million pound house within her reach, in order to keep her in school. She wasn't usually one to be swayed by such material things, but it was the thought that counted. At least, that's what she'd decided to tell herself.

"That little sod better not rummage through my case," said her dad, setting his drink down after another draught. "I've got a shaving kit in there that's probably worth twice what he makes in a month working here."

"I think he must be the barmaid's son," said Andry, "so I doubt he gets paid."

"All the worse," said her dad with a tut and checked his watch. "Taking his sweet time, too."

"Give him a break," said Andry. "She said they were thinking of closing for the year. All the usual staff must be off, and he's gotten roped in."

"Even so," said her dad, "you're not tipping him."

"Oh, come on," said Andry. "I want to see the look on his face."

"No," said her dad. "You've cost me a great chunk by not taking the good room. You want to tip him? Reach into your *own* purse."

"I haven't *got* a purse," said Andry, screwing her face up at him.

"Exactly," said her dad. "This is all being paid for out of *my* wallet, and *my* wallet says no tips to strange, country boys."

"He's not strange," said Andry. "In fact, he's the *opposite* of strange, which is what makes him so strange. Did you see his trousers? He wouldn't last five minutes in the yard at my school."

"No, I did *not* look at his trousers," said her dad, "and don't *you* look at his trousers, either. You'll give him ideas."

"What's *that* supposed to mean?" asked Andry.

"Let's just say it's not only my shaving kit that I don't want his grabby little hands on," said her dad. "He probably thinks you're a ditzy city girl who he can whisk off of her feet."

"I'd like to see him try," said Andry and kicked the table leg with the toe of her boot. "These things keep me pretty well grounded. Besides, he looked harmless enough."

"I think he looked shifty," said her dad, "so keep your wits about you. Remember, no-one finds out why we're here."

They were thinking about ordering a second round of drinks, when Morgan finally reappeared and came shuffling over to their table.

"You can go up now," he said to Andry's dad, again not making eye contact.

"What about me?" asked Andry.

"You can go up, too," said Morgan. "I've given you clean sheets and towels, but that room's been empty for the last week, so you might want to leave the window open for a bit."

As Andry and her dad got to their feet, Morgan made to leave.

"Aren't you going to take my bag?" Andry asked before he could escape.

Morgan looked around and spotted Andry's backpack.

"It's only small," he said. "Can't *you* take it?"

Andry turned to her dad.

"Is that the kind of service you're paying for?" she asked.

"Alright, calm down," said Morgan, returning and grabbing the backpack. "Wouldn't want you to trip on the stairs or anything."

They followed him through the door behind the bar and up the stairs.

"Number three, was it?" asked her dad when they reached the first-floor landing.

"Yeah," said Morgan, pointing along the hall. "Third from the end. Your key's on the dresser." He then started up the next set of stairs.

As Andry followed, her dad cleared his throat. She looked back, and he nodded after Morgan, tapped a finger below his eye, and then wriggled his fingers.

Andry stifled a laugh before heading up the stairs.

The top floor had six rooms. The first only had four, meaning they were definitely bigger and more lavish than those on this floor.

"My mum said you wanted a view of the lake," said Morgan as they walked along the hall, "so I've put you in number one. It looks right onto it."

"How very considerate of you," said Andry, putting on her best 'Ditzy city girl' voice.

Even though it was smaller, the interior of the room was perfect for Andry. When she and her dad had stayed at the hotel in York, she hadn't known what to do with herself, the room was so big. This room was much more to her liking. A perhaps not quite king-size bed took up most of the space, a small desk and chair taking up the rest, but it was the window that she was most interested in. Just as Morgan had said, it looked right out across the lake.

She walked over to it and set her elbows on the sill. It was certainly an impressive sight. She'd never been one for the great outdoors, the odd tree and bare, sprawling playing field being about as 'Outdoors' as things got in Leicester, but the lake was something else, especially when you got to look at it from the comfort of the great *in*doors.

The image she'd pictured in her mind had been something more like a caricature of a lake, a circular expanse of blue water, bordered by uniformly placed trees, and perhaps with a smiley-face sun hovering above it. The real thing was quite different. The water was dark, to the point that, from this distance, it appeared almost black. She could just make out the opposite shore, and there were, indeed, a great many trees running along it at the base of the steep hills which acted as a backdrop to the whole scene. She wouldn't go so far as to call it 'Breathtaking', but it filled her with a desire to see more, to go to the other side of the water and find out what was among those trees or on the tops of those hills, their appearance giving the sense that they were somehow forbidden.

"No lakes where you're from?" asked Morgan, tossing her backpack onto the bed.

"There's a few," she replied, "but nothing like this one."

Morgan stood in the doorway, folding his arms and leaning against the jamb.

"Do *all* girls from down south dress like you?" he asked, cocking his head to peer at her through his fringe.

"I'm not from down south," said Andry, turning to face him. "Do I *sound* like I'm from down south?"

"Yes," said Morgan. "You *look* it, too." He nodded at her feet. "Those are men's boots."

"They're unisex," said Andry, pushing herself up on the windowsill and knocking the heels of her boots together.

"Anyway, *you're* not one to dish out fashion advice. You look like you've just crawled out of a Littlewoods catalogue."

"So, are you part of a gang or something?" asked Morgan, tilting his head the other way.

"That's right," said Andry, giving him a sly smile. "You better watch it, or I'll pull out my flick-knife and shank you."

"You haven't got a flick-knife," said Morgan with a tut.

"*You* don't know that," said Andry.

"Okay," said Morgan. "Show it to me."

Andry dropped down from the windowsill and quickly sank to her haunches, sticking her fingers into the top of her right boot. Morgan gave a yelp and hopped sideways into the hall.

"You dithering wuss!" she laughed. "Come back. I *haven't* got a flick-knife."

"*I* don't know that," said Morgan, peeking around the doorframe. "You're crazy, you are."

"Give over," said Andry. "I was only pulling your leg."

"Maybe *you* should be the one to watch it," said Morgan, stepping warily back into the room. "You might not have a flick-knife, but *we've* got guns around here. Pull that trick on the wrong person, and you'll get blown away."

"Guns?" said Andry with a frown. "What do you have guns for?"

"For shooting," said Morgan.

"Yes, of course, for shooting," said Andry. "I mean, what *for*?"

"Shooting," Morgan repeated, miming that he was holding a rifle. "*Game* shooting. Pheasent usually, but sometimes grouse. They're even doing clay pigeon shooting over at the Graythwaite estate. They *call* them pigeons, but they're just plates. I've never seen the point in it. I think it's so you lot from down south can pretend like you're the real thing, only you don't have to get your shoes dirty."

"Do *you* get to shoot guns?" asked Andry.

"Yeah," said Morgan, puffing his chest out a little. "All the time. My dad's a …" He trailed off and bit his lip, as though he'd spoken without thinking. "I mean, he's a gamekeeper."

"So, why are you stuck getting my room ready for me?" asked Andry. "Why aren't you out gamekeeping?"

"Mum needed my help," said Morgan, narrowing his eyes at her from behind his fringe. "We *were* going to close down for the season, until *you* showed up."

"Well," said Andry, "I'm terribly sorry to have brought all of our lovely, down south money to put through your till."

"You can't have *that* much money," said Morgan. "If you did, you'd have stayed at one of the fancy hotels."

"I'll have you know …" Andry made to reply, but *she* trailed off this time, having spoken absolutely without thinking.

"I don't care *what* you'd have me know," said Morgan, coming unwittingly to her aid. "You lot reckon you're the bee's knees, and you think you can treat us locals like muck, as long as you're paying for it. My favourite part of the year is when you *stop* coming for a while."

"Hey, that's a bit harsh," said Andry, stung by the assumption. "You've only just met me."

"And I've already seen enough," Morgan shot back. He then raised his voice to a mocking falsetto. "I want a top floor room. I want a view. Carry my bag for me. I'll *have you know*."

They stared at each other for a moment, Morgan's eyes sending daggers at Andry, but she broke into laughter.

"You don't think I was being *serious*, do you?" she chuckled, walking over to him and slapping him on the arm. "You need

37

to relax, mate. Since when does a gun-toting gamekeeper let himself get wound up by a girl?"

"You *didn't* wind me up," said Morgan, a deep blush spreading across his cheeks. "It's just that …"

"Oh, come off it," said Andry. "You *knew* I wasn't being serious. If you didn't, you wouldn't have mouthed at me like that. I could tell my daddy how rude you are and get you sacked."

"I wish I *could* get sacked," said Morgan. "I always end up doing stupid stuff around here when school lets out, and it's all women's work. I'd much rather be in the woods or on the hills with my dad."

"*I'll* bet," said Andry, her face lighting up. "Do you get to go when there aren't any guests here? Could you take *me* there? I'd love to see woods and hills."

"I guess I could," said Morgan with a shrug, his cheeks growing redder by the second. "Do you think your dad would mind?"

"Probably," said Andry. "He says you look shifty, and I'm to keep an eye on your hands."

"I'd *never* hit a girl," said Morgan, shock joining the blush on his face.

"I don't think he's worried about hitting," said Andry, "and I suppose he doesn't have to know about it. I can just say I'm going for a wander by myself. Shouldn't be a problem if it's during the day. You don't go gamekeeping at night, do you?"

"Oh, no," said Morgan, shaking his head vigorously, his blush quickly draining. "Never. I don't *ever* go out at night, especially not at this time of year."

"Why not?" asked Andry.

"I just *don't*," said Morgan, "and you shouldn't be nosey.

You're only here for a holiday. You don't have to put up with local trouble."

"Trouble?" asked Andry, her interest firmly piqued.

"Forget about it," said Morgan. "If you want to go sightseeing with me during the day, that's fine. We're not going *anywhere* at night, though."

"Okay, okay," said Andry, holding her hands up, palms out. "No need to be like that."

"I'll let you get settled in," said Morgan, turning towards the door. "The bathroom's at the end of the hall. The hot water gets turned off at seven."

"Hey," said Andry, following after him. "I honestly didn't mean to upset you."

Morgan was already on the stairs, but he looked back at her before going down.

"You shouldn't even be here," he said. "We should've closed up when the weather started turning. An early autumn is bad news."

Andry spent a little while longer staring out across the lake and wondering what could have put such a scare on Morgan. Where *she* came from, 'Local trouble' usually meant gangs of unsavoury young lads going around mugging people. True, this *did* tend to happen mostly at night, so maybe Morgan's trouble was something similar, though Windermere didn't strike her as a 'Gangs' kind of place, especially if Morgan was an example of the town's youth.

She eventually decided to go down and check out her dad's room. Just as she'd expected, it was much bigger than hers, but the window looked directly onto the beer garden at the rear of the pub. She discovered this after pulling the curtains open, not understanding why her dad had drawn them at this time of day, only to find that one of the benches was occupied by three men, all of whom raised their pints and waved to her when she looked out.

"I opened it to let some air in," said her dad, coming up behind her and closing the curtains again. "Not two minutes later, one of them called up and asked me for a cigarette."

"He probably thought you had lots," said Andry. "Fancy, down south ones, in a gold foil packet."

"Down south?" asked her dad with a frown.

"That boy," said Andry, nodding towards the hall. "He thinks we're rich southerners."

"Hang on," said her dad, his frown deepening. "You've not been saying anything you shouldn't, have you?"

"No," Andry sighed. "He just, sort of, assumed. It says a lot about the kind of people they usually have as guests."

"Maybe this isn't going to be as easy as I thought," said her dad. "We stick out like sore thumbs. I mean, why is the place empty? It was mid-summer only the other week. If there were more 'Rich southerners' here, we'd have an easier time going unnoticed."

"Morgan said something about an early autumn," said Andry, sitting on the edge of the bed. "The bookings must've dried up when it looked like the weather was going to be bad. More fool *us* if we've picked the wrong weekend."

"Morgan?" said her dad, raising an eyebrow at her. "It was 'That boy' a moment ago."

"He's alright," said Andry, dropping backwards onto her elbows. She gave a snigger. "I spooked him good and proper by telling him I had a knife on me."

"*Do* you have a knife?" asked her dad, giving her a look which seemed to say that he wouldn't be surprised if she said no *or* yes.

"No," said Andry. "Why *would* I?"

"Shame," said her dad. "If you did, and he laid one finger on you, you'd have my permission to stick him."

"I don't think he's like that," said Andry.

"*All* teenage boys are like that," said her dad. "Trust me, I used to *be* one."

"I think he's too scared of me now," said Andry. "Seems like he's scared of a lot of things. He says he never goes anywhere at night."

"We used to when I was young," said her dad. "Night-fishing's the best time to catch bream. You use a lure that floats on the surface, and they practically *jump* into the boat."

"Was that during the summer, though?" asked Andry. "Morgan said it was something to do with the time of year."

"He's just telling you stories," said her dad with a sniff of contempt. "You spooked him about having a knife, and he's trying to spook you right back. They're notorious for it in these parts. Everywhere has ghosts, black dogs, fairy rings, will-o'-the-wisps, you name it."

"His dad's a gamekeeper," said Andry.

"Damn, you won't shut up about this boy, will you?" said her dad. "Have I got it wrong? Should I be warning *his* parents about *you*?"

"I don't *fancy* him," said Andry, poking her tongue out. "He's just interesting, is all. He's not like the stupid boys back at home, who just lumber about and fight each other all the time."

"Yep," said her dad with a nod. "'Interesting' is how it usually starts. That's why I ended up with your mother. She was 'Interesting' enough for *both* of us and look how *that* turned out."

"Well, maybe you can send me to a nunnery, instead of Rossall," said Andry. "Keep me away from anyone 'Interesting'."

"Don't think it hasn't crossed my mind," said her dad with a half-smile. "Come on. Let's go back down."

"Where are we going?" asked Andry, hopping up from the bed.

"Nowhere, for now," said her dad. "I'm thinking late breakfast or early lunch. Whatever they've got on offer."

Unfortunately, they'd missed breakfast, and it was still far too early for lunch, but the barmaid offered to make them some sandwiches, which turned out to be more than enough. The bread came in thick slices with cheese, cured ham, and a jar of pickle with a hand-written label. Once again, Andry's dad was greatly pleased with how 'Authentic' everything was, and he wolfed it down like he hadn't eaten in days, along with another pint of mild.

"Don't these people have jobs?" asked Andry in a hushed tone as she looked around at the other patrons. A few who'd been there when she and her dad had arrived were *still* there, and others had now joined them.

"They must make their own hours," said her dad, "or they were up early. If you've been at it since dawn, now's as good as afternoon. It's not exactly nine to five around here."

"Or we've just landed in the place where all the drunks come," said Andry.

"No-one's drunk," said her dad as he delved a spoon into the pickle jar, seeming determined to empty it. "The beer's good, but it's hardly strong."

"I should hope not," said Andry, tapping his mug with her butterknife. "That's your second before mid-day."

"Sorry, *Mum*," said her dad, pulling a face at her as he slopped pickle onto another slice of bread. "Hold up." He nodded across the room between bites. "Would you look who it is."

Andry turned and saw Morgan coming towards them, his head lowered, his hands in his pockets.

"Is everything to your liking?" he asked, speaking as though from a script.

"It is," said Andry's dad, wiping his fingers on a napkin. "What's this I hear about not going out at night? Scared of the dark?"

Morgan shot an accusing glare at Andry.

"We don't …" he mumbled. "Well, we *can't* …"

"Speak up, lad," said Andry's dad. "If you're going to frighten my daughter with your tall tales, you may as well try them on *me*. I used to go night-fishing here all the time. I wouldn't mind a bit of it while I'm here now."

"You heard him!" a voice from across the room cut in. It was one of the day drinkers, part of a trio, all of whom now had their eyes fixed on Andry's dad. "We don't go near the water at night, and *you* shouldn't be thinking about it, if you know what's good for you."

"I was just asking," said Andry's dad, a slight hint of nervousness hiding behind his defiance.

"Well, you *shouldn't* be asking," the drinker replied. "This time of year, when it gets cold, but the sky's still clear, all boats are off the lake before sunset. If any get spotted, the police go out and drag them back, then those in them spend the night in the cells." He took a drink from his pint and smacked his lips. "That's *if* they get spotted. Woe betide you if them from the other side spot you first."

"Shut up, Terry," the man next to him hissed, kicking him under the table.

"It's true, though, ain't it?" said 'Terry', kicking him back. "You know what happened that time in fifty-seven." He raised his pint at tapped it about halfway up. "What was left of them, you could've fit it in *there*."

"What are you talking about?" asked Andry's dad.

"Nothing, Sir, nothing," said the man who'd delivered the kick. "He's just had one too many on an empty stomach. It sets his brain wandering and his mouth running. He's not far wrong, though. It's fierce dangerous, going on the water at night, so you shouldn't do it. The coppers *will* tow you back and lock you up."

"They can't keep watch on the *whole* lake," said Andry's dad.

"No," the man replied, his tone deadpan, "they can't. Meaning, if you find yourself in trouble out there in the pitch dark, there's no-one coming to rescue you. I wouldn't like to imagine your young lady there going overboard, and you not being able to find her. Doesn't bear thinking about, does it?"

"When you put it like *that*," said Andry's dad.

"That's exactly how I'm putting it," said the man with a quick nod. "So, you stay safe, eh?"

Throughout all of this, Andry had kept an eye on Morgan. She'd expected him to slink away as soon as he was given the chance, but he'd stayed rooted to the spot, a look of ever-increasing horror engulfing his face as the supposedly 'One too many on an empty stomach' Terry had rattled off his spiel.

"Are you okay?" she asked him.

"What?" he said, blinking at her, as though awaking from a trance. "Oh, yeah. *Yeah*, I'm fine. I mean, do you want anything else?"

"We're good, thank you," said her dad, shooing him away with a flap of his hand. He tapped the pickle jar with his spoon. "Only, ask you mum where I can buy more of this."

As Morgan hurried off, Andry watched him until he was out of sight, then turned to her dad.

"See what I mean?" she asked.

"It wasn't *him* I was watching," said her dad, lowering his voice and cocking his head towards the trio of drinkers. "Maybe we should get out of here for a while."

They got up from the table and grabbed their coats. As they headed for the door, 'One too many' Terry shifted in his seat.

"Didn't catch your name, friend!" he called out.

"Martin," Andry's dad replied.

"Martin what?" asked Terry.

"Yep," said Andry's dad, holding the door open for her. "That's the one."

Once they were outside, Andry's dad headed straight for the car.

"You're not driving after two pints," she said, grabbing him by the arm as he fumbled with his keys.

"I'm fine," he said, shrugging her off. "Unlike our new friend, I ate on top of it."

"What do you think he was on about?" asked Andry as she went around to the passenger side.

"Meaningless, country rambling," said her dad, opening the driver's door and getting in.

"He sounded pretty serious," said Andry, climbing in next to him and fastening her belt. "Can the police really drag people off the lake and arrest them?"

"It's the first *I've* heard of it," said her dad. "That's more of a coastguard thing on the sea. I guess it makes sense, though. If they let party animal tourists go on the water on rough nights, there'd be bodies washing up by the dozen."

"You said *you* used to go night fishing," said Andry.

"Yeah," said her dad. "Thirty-odd years ago. They've obviously gotten a bit tighter on the old health and safety."

"He mentioned people from the other side," said Andry, "and not wanting to get spotted by them."

"There's nothing on the other side," said her dad, starting the car. "Well, I mean, there *is*, but you have to go over a few miles of nasty terrain before you reach it. Another thing you've got to understand about places like this is they can be *very* insular. If you ask what the people in the next town are like, they'll say they're rag-tag barbarians who eat children."

"I'm starting to wonder whether you actually like this place at all," said Andry as they rolled out of the carpark. "You're certainly not giving *me* a good impression of it."

"It'll be different once the sale goes through on the property," said her dad. "We won't have to worry too much about the locals. It can be our own little world."

"Until they come with pitchforks," said Andry, "and drive us out like Frankenstein's monster. I think we'd have to worry *then*."

"Nah, we'll be alright," said her dad. "We've got your new boyfriend to put in a good word for us. I saw him stare at you. Sharing secrets already, eh?"

"I *thought* you said you weren't watching him," said Andry with a sneer.

"I can watch more than one thing at a time," said her dad. "It was that third bloke who I most had my eye on. Did you see how his hands went under the table when the other two started talking to me?"

"I didn't," said Andry, thinking back to what Morgan had said about guns. "Do you think he was armed?"

"I dunno," said her dad. "Probably not. Only, your granddad always used to tell me not to trust a man who keeps his hands under the table, and he didn't *just* mean figuratively."

"Are we going to see the house now?" asked Andry as they pulled onto the first lane.

"I thought we could drive by it," said her dad. "If we get seen stopping and going up to it, we'll be rumbled, but a quick pass won't look too suspicious."

"Great," said Andry with a tut. "You can very quickly say, 'One day, all of this will be yours. Angry locals included.'"

"There'll be no bother by the time *you* own it," said her dad. "It's *me* who has to spend however many years convincing the locals *not* to be angry."

"Maybe you don't *have* to," said Andry. "I kind of like the idea of being the crazy lady who lives in the old lake-house." She pointed through the windscreen, her finger bent into a claw. "Ooh, no. We don't go near *that* house. It be cursed, I tell thee."

"Whatever suits you," said her dad with a snort. "Just remember you'll need planning permission to put up gargoyles and a widow's walk."

"Does it have a name?" asked Andry. "These kinds of places usually have fancy names."

"I don't think so," said her dad. "At least, one wasn't mentioned to me. Maybe *you* can give it a name."

"You'd let me do that?" asked Andry with a grin. "Anything I want?"

"Within reason," said her dad. He reached over and tugged at the shoulder of her jumper. "Your band names are bad enough as it is."

It didn't take them much longer to reach the house. The first Andry saw of it was the highest part of the roof, the apex jutting up from behind a row of sycamore trees.

She was eager to see what a quarter of a million pounds worth of house actually looked like, but the fact that two out of the first three windows she spotted were broken caused her to wonder whether she'd overestimated what that kind of money could really buy.

It was built mostly from what looked like sandstone and wood, painted a pale green, though this was cracked and peeling all over. The surrounding grounds were completely unkempt, the grass tall, the hedges having grown to monstrous size due to years of neglect.

"It …" she began as they rounded a bend and more of the house came into view, but she stopped and had to think for the right words. "It looks like it needs a bit of sprucing up."

"I told you it does," said her dad. "Don't let the outside put you off. That can be sorted in a couple of weeks. It's the inside that's impressive. See? Look at that." He pointed as they slowed down and passed the front gates. "That conservatory goes all the way around to the other side. Imagine what it'd be like on a blazing summer day."

Andry was forced to 'Imagine' quite hard. Just like the windows, several of the conservatory's roof panes were missing, while those which remained were almost totally opaque with dirt and algae.

"Pat said it's a local gem," said Andry. "You'd have thought the owners would take better care of it."

"It's tough to take care of a place like this," said her dad, "especially when you're as skint as *these* owners are. They'll take one seventy-five and thank me on their knees for every penny. If I bare my teeth, I could probably get it down to one fifty."

"How can you be so sure?" asked Andry.

"I've got a surveyor who lives *here*," said her dad, patting his trouser pocket. "When he comes and practically writes the place off, *asking* price goes out the window. From what I hear, the owners *have* had offers higher than mine, and the silly sods turned them down, holding out for the full quarter mil, because they don't understand that a 'Gem' is just a dirty rock if you don't keep the shine on it, and *that* costs money."

"I had no idea that you're so ruthless," said Andry, twisting around in her seat to get a final look at the place as they continued along the road.

"You don't get to where *I* am by being fair," said her dad. "I don't know how much of your mum's hippy, commie stuff has infected your brain, so I'll tell it to you like it really is. If someone's got something you want, but they're keeping it just out of your reach, what do you do?"

"Let me guess," said Andry, scratching her chin in mock contemplation. "You reach out and *take* it?"

"No," said her dad. "You stamp on their foot, so that they *drop* it, then you pick it up at *your* leisure."

"Is that another of granddad's pearls of wisdom?" asked Andry.

"Nope," said her dad. "That's a Martin Watt original."

"Sounds a lot like cheating to me," said Andry.

"It's not cheating," said her dad. "It's just knowing the rules of the game better than those you're playing against."

"How many feet do you think you'll have to stamp on to get your mitts on *that* place?" asked Andry, nodding back towards the house.

"Not too many, if I play it right," said her dad. "Buying it is only stage one. I need to get the council and the heritage cretins on my side before I think about renovating it."

"That's the bit I don't get," said Andry. "Won't they be happy if you're buying it to make it look nice again?"

"They're worried that I'll make it look *too* nice," said her dad. "What's the point in having a historic building if I end up making it look like it was built last year? One new rooftile or lick of paint too many, and they'll say I'm tampering and call a halt on the whole project. The last thing I want is any of *their* surveyors coming too near the place."

"Especially if they find out *your* one was bent," said Andry.

"He's not bent," said her dad. "He's on the take. Big difference."

"Is that legal?" asked Andry, narrowing an eye at him.

"Yes, *your Honour*," said her dad. "It's illegal to pay a surveyor to overlook issues. What *I'm* doing is paying this guy to zero in on them and maybe make them sound worse than they are. If the heritage people say I can't mess with the roof, but my guy says it's structurally unsafe, then I get to do what I want, as long as it doesn't 'Alter the character of the building', whatever *that* means."

"So, no gargoyles or widow's walks?" asked Andry.

"I dunno," said her dad, tilting his head from side to side. "Perhaps we could have *one* gargoyle. Just a small one, above your bedroom window. It'll let everyone know which room the crazy lady lives in."

"What about a swimming pool?" asked Andry. "Would that be 'Altering the character'?"

"It's next to a lake," said her dad. "Why would you want a swimming pool?"

"Just so we can say we've got one," said Andry with a shrug.

"Nah," said her dad. "Putting in a pool on a high-water table? It'd collapse in a week."

"I was only joking," Andry chuckled. "No need to get all technical on me."

"Sorry," said her dad, letting go of the wheel with one hand and dragging it down his face. "These things have been on my mind a lot lately. Shopping centres, flat blocks, business parks, they're *my* area of expertise. Grade two listed 'Gems' are new to me, and I'm worried that I'll mess it up."

Andry didn't think she'd ever heard her dad say that he was worried about anything, let alone that he might mess something up. What she'd seen of him while he had his business head on gave the impression of someone who was far too assertive to worry, and who could skilfully shift the blame if something got messed up. She, of course, understood that there was a real human being beneath his professional exterior, but she'd never seen it come to the surface like this.

"It'll be fine," she said, giving him a reassuring bat on the arm. "We're getting on good terms with the locals, aren't we? When we have to, like, pull off our masks and say, 'Ah-hah! It was *us* buying the place all along', I'm sure everything'll turn out okay."

"We aren't exactly off to a good start," said her dad. "I'm not looking forward to going back to the pub and finding the three stooges still there. Maybe I *should* buy some fancy, gold foil pack cigarettes to start handing out."

"No," said Andy, wagging a finger at him. "You can't *buy* people's trust. We just need to be on our best behaviour. If you can get someone to like you, to *really* like you, then it doesn't come across as so harsh if you have to do something they aren't too keen on."

"Is that an Andromeda Watt original?" asked her dad with a smirk. "You should write a book. You could call it 'How to win friends and *manipulate* people'. It'd fly off the shelves."

They spent the rest of the morning and early afternoon exploring the main town of Windermere. It was actually more of a village, but it possessed enough shops and points of interest to keep them occupied. It was the souvenir shops that Andry was most taken in by. She'd always had a love for trinkets or curios, and she quickly came away with three fridge magnets and a polished lake-stone pendant.

They passed by several more pubs, but Andry refused to go into any, insisting that they stop off in a café instead. They took a seat by the window, and as they were waiting for their drinks, they saw the goat man again. He walked right up to the front of the café and stopped to converse with another man. At one point, the goat turned its head and looked through the window, directly at Andry, its bizarre, horizontal pupil scrutinising her with an almost human interest. The strangeness of the moment was, however, broken when the goat raised its stumpy tail and pooed on the pavement.

"I hope he's got bags," said Andry, trying her best not to burst into laughter.

The café owner, Andry wasn't sure if he could technically be called either a waiter or a barista, came over and set down their tray of drinks, frowning through the window at the goat.

"He's a menace," he said.

"Who?" asked Andry. "The goat or the man?"

"Both," said the café owner, crossing his arms over his chest. "When I moved here, I knew it was going to be a bit more rural than I was used to, but I wasn't open an hour before he came waltzing in, dragging that creature behind him, sat himself down and asked what beers I serve."

"You're not a local, then?" asked Andry's dad.

"Nah," said the owner. "I'm from Bradford originally. I owned a restaurant there for the best part of ten years, but I sold up and moved here in seventy-four."

"Had enough of the city, eh?" asked Andry's dad.

"Pretty much," said the owner. "I thought it was time to slow down a bit. No evening rushes, no army of staff, no stuck-up, wannabe socialites, losing their rag because the salmon soufflés have run out."

"How accepting were the people here when you arrived?" asked Andry's dad.

"Oh, nice as you like," said the owner. "I had regulars within a month." He shot another glare at the goat. "No-one told me about the fauna, though."

"I suppose farmers sometimes need to take their animals with them," said Andry, twirling a spoon in her coffee and watching the goat. "Maybe it's sick."

"Farmer?" said the owner with a frown. "He's not a *farmer*, love. He lives off the dole. That thing's just one of his *pets*."

"The unemployment's hitting here, too, is it?" asked Andry's dad.

"It's getting there," said the owner with a nod. "It's mainly the tourist trade that keeps things running. If you're not in the service industry, you either *get* into it, or you're out of luck."

"We need a good war," said Andry's dad, spooning sugar into his mug.

"No, we *don't*," said Andry with a gasp. "What an awful thing to say."

"One half of the population in uniform," said her dad, waving his spoon back and forth, "the other half *making* the uniforms. Problem solved."

"I don't know about *that*," said the owner, "but I know we've got more than a few people around here who aren't best pleased when the tourists show up and start throwing their money around. Those who don't *see* any of it, I mean. There's talk of this place on the lakefront getting sold to some rich bleeder from down south, so he can turn it into his own, private palace, instead of making good use of it. Half a million, I'm told. Can you *imagine* having that much money to play with?"

"Who is he?" asked Andry's dad, raising his mug to his lips and flashing her a look over the rim. "This rich bleeder."

"They say he's some kind of glorified estate agent," said the owner. "Probably thinks he can come here and pretend at being a country lord or something. We get a lot of them, but they never look into *buying* places. They've got pairs of wellies and tweeds that they crack out for the occasion, but it's all a charade. Once they've had their fill, they're back in business suits."

"And the locals don't want this guy buying the lakeshore place?" Andry's dad probed a little further. "What's the harm in it?"

"Well …" said the owner and sucked at his teeth. "Now, this is just gossip, but strange things go on down by the water, and that place is smack-bang *on* it."

"Strange?" asked Andry, her ears pricked by the word. "What sort of strange things?"

"I'm not entirely sure," said the owner. "As I say, I've been here over four years, but I'm still not totally accepted by the fold. It took me long enough to convince anyone to sell me *eggs*. I had to go all the way to Staveley and buy them in. All I know is there're folks who get a bit odd about anything to do with the lake. Apparently, there was a right stink back in the day, when they first started running engine powered boats on it."

"Worried about pollution, I'll bet," said Andry's dad.

"I guess so," said the owner, "but it doesn't explain why, on *some* nights, if you go anywhere near the water, there'll conveniently be a bunch of lads down there already, threatening you with a good kicking if you don't push off. Not *young* lads, either. Old ones, like *him* out there." He nodded at the goat man, who still hadn't moved.

"He threatened you?" asked Andry's dad. "Do you think he was serious?"

"He certainly *sounded* serious," the owner replied with a nod.

"He doesn't look that threatening," said Andry.

"That's the thing," said the owner. "Most of the time, they're happy as Larry. Only, it's like a change comes over them. I've had tourists in here, complaining about being mouthed off at by some old boy for going near the lake at night, then that *same* old boy comes in, not five minutes later, and wishes them good day, like nothing'd happened."

"We heard about that," said Andry. "We were told not to go *onto* the lake at night, but what's wrong with just going *near* it?"

"I don't have a clue, love," said the owner with a slow shake of his head. "One telling off was good enough for me. I don't envy this southern estate agent. What's going to happen to *him* on these special nights? A bunch of fellas knock on his door and tell him to clear off out of his own house until morning? I don't think he'll like *that*."

"No," said Andry's dad, eyeing the goat man with a new suspicion, "he won't." Andry gave a low cough, and he checked himself. "I mean, I don't imagine he would."

"You pair here for long?" asked the owner, seeming not to have picked up on Andry's dad's slip.

"Until Monday," said Andry.

"Make sure to stop in again," said the owner. "I do a cracking full English, but you've just missed it. Locally sourced, free-range eggs, I promise you."

As he headed back towards the counter, Andry leaned towards her dad.

"You better watch your tongue," she growled.

"Turfed out of my own property by dole claiming bumpkins?" he muttered, his eyes still on the goat man, who'd finally ambled across to the other side of the road. "I'd like to see them bloody try." He took a big gulp from his drink, set it down heavily on the table and got to his feet. "Come on. Let's get back to the guesthouse."

"Why?" asked Andry. "Are we hiding there for the rest of the weekend?"

"No," said her dad, tugging his jacket on. "I need to make a call to Pat."

"I *thought* you said that was only in an emergency," said Andry.

"Listen," said her dad, leaning in close as she got up. "A flash, southern bleeder? A glorified estate agent, buying the lake property for his own use? That's hardly guesswork. The sellers have been talking, after we explicitly told them not to. I don't know about an emergency, but it's breach of contract, which is close enough."

They arrived back at the Lychgate just before two, and Andry's dad immediately went up to his room to make the call, leaving her to mull over another bottle of the dandelion and burdock. The first had been nice, but the second started to sour her stomach before she was even halfway through it.

Her dad's 'Three Stooges' were no longer there, but others had taken their place, so she decided to people-watch for a while. Two men were sat at the table by the fireplace, playing what, at first, Andry thought were dominoes. However, as she edged a little closer, she saw that the pieces were marked with strange symbols, rather than dots.

She watched as one of the men scooped the pieces into a pile and slid them from the table into a cloth bag. He juggled the bag between his hands a few times, then took out three of the pieces, setting them down across from his companion, who leaned over and scrutinised them.

"Come on," he said. "That's easy. You already *know* about this."

"Give me a moment," said the other man, peering intently at the pieces. "Uruz inverted? That doesn't sound like you."

"Yeah," said the first man, "but look at *this* one." He tapped at the piece on the right of the three. "Othala. Think about it."

"*Right*," said the other man, nodding and scratching his chin. "With Ehwaz in the middle." He looked up and grinned. "You've decided, then?"

"I have," said the first man, leaning back and folding his arms. "It'll be here before spring. I don't know why I dragged my feet for so long. I've been pulling Ehwaz like you wouldn't believe, and I should know to always trust them when they're not subtle."

Andry took the opportunity to scoot her chair a little closer.

"What're you playing?" she asked.

"Never you mind!" the second man snapped back, grabbing for the pieces and dragging them towards him.

"Here, calm down," said the first man. "You shouldn't mouth at a young girl."

"Yeah," said Andry. "I was only asking."

"It's not a game, love," said the first man, turning to her. "It's a … well, what would you call it?"

"It's an ancient means of divination," said the second man, snatching the cloth bag from the table and dropping the pieces into it. "Something fancy southerners don't know owt about."

"Ah, you mean like tarot cards," said Andry. "I know about those."

"Hark at *her*," said the second man, cocking his head at Andry. "Like tarot cards, is it? What does she think we are? Hippies?"

"*Her* name is Andry," said Andry, frowning at him. "I'm not a southerner, and I don't know *what* I think you are, apart from rude."

The first man broke into a deep laugh.

"That's *him* told," he said, tipping Andry a wink. "Well, Andry, who isn't a southerner," Andry noticed that, like the barmaid, he pronounced her name as though he'd said it a hundred times before, "I'm Dennis, and *this* miserable git," he nodded to his companion, "he's Bernie."

"*She's* not calling me that," 'Bernie' protested. "She should respect her elders. It's Bernard, or Mister Cunnigham."

"Oh, give it a rest," said Dennis. "You don't want to be antagonising the tourists, southerners or no. You'll be chucked out on your ear by Carol." He pointed across the room to the barmaid, who was busy setting out fresh pint mugs. "We can't scare the punters away."

"I don't care what Carol says," said Bernie. "She might stand behind the bar, but it's Dirty Harry who owns this place, and me and him are like *that*." He raised a hand, the index and middle fingers crossed over each other.

"Dirty Harry?" asked Andry.

"His name's Lewis," said Dennis, "but we call him Dirty Harry because he's always got this sneer on his mush, like Eastwood in the film."

"So, he's Carol's husband?" asked Andry. "Morgan's dad? The gamekeeper?"

"That's right," said Dennis. "I feel for that lad. A young man his age should be out learning the trade with his fatha', not stuck here, dusting doilies and folding bedsheets. It'll turn him strange, it will."

"Morgan told me that he goes out with his dad all the time," said Andry. She glanced around and lowered her voice. "He said they shoot guns."

Bernie gave a shrill cackle.

"Yeah, right," he said. "If *that* boy shot a gun, it'd knock him on his backside." He held up the bag of pieces and shook it. "You don't need *these* to see *his* future. Doilies and bedsheets, that's his lot."

"Don't be cruel," said Andry. "Maybe gamekeeping is something you have to grow into."

"Nah, it's something you're *born* into," said Bernie. "Gamekeeping's not all shooting guns and galivanting about. You've got to know the way of the land. You've got to have the soil and the water and the air flowing in your blood. That's how Dirty Harry keeps things the way they are, as did his fatha' *and* his grandfatha'."

"How does that make sense?" asked Andry, feeling insulted on Morgan's behalf. "If he's this Dirty Harry's son, then they have the same blood, don't they?"

"Well, yes and no," said Bernie. "You can be born *in* a place but not be born *of* it."

"You don't half prattle on," said Dennis. "The lass is right. Give him time, and I'm sure Morgan will learn the way of things." He gave a short, chuntering laugh. "*In* it but not *of* it. Weren't you born in Middlesborough?"

"We're not talking about *me*, though," Bernie retorted. "What's it gonna be like when Dirty Harry's not fit for it anymore, and there's no-one to deal with those from the other side? You know how they've been getting in recent years. Last October, Dave Lampard went out one morning and found a quarter of his flock gone. It cost him a fortune."

"That's enough," said Dennis, his voice stern as he glared at Bernie. "Don't want to frighten the young lady."

"I'm not frightened," said Andry. "Tell me more. Are you saying people steal sheep? Isn't that something the police should deal with?"

Dennis looked at her, then reached over and took the cloth bag from Bernie.

"Stick your hand in there," he said, undoing the drawstring and offering the bag to Andry. "Pull one out."

"Why?" asked Andry, eyeing the bag, like she thought it might've suddenly grown teeth.

"Indulge me," said Dennis, rustling the pieces.

Andry dipped her fingers into the bag, plucking out the first piece she felt.

"What did you get?" asked Bernie, leaning across the table.

"I think it's a dud," said Andry, holding the piece up to the light. "There's nothing on it."

"Ooh-er," said Bernie. "*That's* not good. You say you've never handled them before, and you pull a Wyrd on your first try. *Very* ominous."

"What does it mean?" asked Andry, turning the piece over in her hand.

"It means the unexpected," said Dennis, taking the piece from her and dropping it back into the bag. "So, you should be careful while you're here. When are you leaving?"

"On Monday," said Andry.

"I can't imagine you'll find yourself in much trouble between now and then," said Dennis. "Best not to worry about it."

"I'll *try* not to," said Andry, but it was more the tone of his question which had worried her. The owner of the café had asked pretty much the same thing, but 'How long are you here for?' and 'When are you leaving?' could be said to have two, very different meanings.

"Where's your old man gone?" asked Dennis. "I saw him come in with you, but that must've been half an hour ago."

"He's up in his room," said Andry, "laying into this guy from his office."

"Ah, an office man," said Dennis. "That'll be his office man motor out front, then?"

"It's a Ford Cortina," chuckled Andry. "It's hardly a Rolls Royce."

"Aye," said Dennis. "A Rolls Royce wouldn't do very well around here, especially on the narrower roads." He raised an eyebrow at her, "Like the ones near the old lakeshore place, eh?"

"I …" said Andry, breaking eye contact. "I don't know."

"I'm sure you don't," said Dennis. He dropped the bag back onto the table. "*These* things have convinced me to buy a new Range Rover. My old one's still got some life in it, though. If your Ford Cortina came up against *that* on one of the narrow roads, you'd never get by it. You'd have to turn around and go back, wouldn't you?"

It was strange. Andry sensed no real menace in his voice, but she knew a threat when she heard one. She also guessed that Dennis, or someone he knew, had spotted her and her dad during their brief pass by the lake property. Her dad would want to go there again during their stay, so she had to warn him that, even if they weren't being actively followed just yet, they were definitely being watched.

"I suppose I'll leave you to it," she said, trying her best to summon up a smile as she got to her feet.

"And we'll leave *you* to it," said Dennis, matching her smile and giving a nod. "Take care of yourself, Miss Watt."

Andry was about to give her usual reply that she wasn't 'Miss' anything, but she suddenly remembered that she hadn't mentioned her surname.

After heading straight for her dad's room, Andry found him in there, still snarling at Pat over the phone.

"I don't *care* what their solicitor says!" he snapped. "He can say anything! I only care about what's on the paperwork, and the paperwork says no disclosure! You call *them*, every thirty seconds, until they answer, and you find out if they've been talking! My bloody *daughter* is with me, in case you've forgotten, and I don't want to have to be looking over my shoulder the entire time we're here!"

"Your *bloody* daughter?" said Andry, coming into the room and closing the door behind her.

"Figure of speech," said her dad, placing a hand over the mouthpiece of the phone. "What do you want?"

"I think we've got a problem," said Andry.

"You're damn right, we've got a problem," said her dad. "Looks like I'm dealing with people who sign things without reading them."

"I'm talking about something a bit more immediate," said Andry, but her dad had already turned his attention back to the phone.

"Yeah," he said, "I'm still here. What? Intermediaries? When did these back-country creatures learn a word like *that*?"

"Dad!" said Andry, striding towards him and making a grab at the phone. "Listen!"

"Just give me minute," said her dad, dodging out of her way. "I'll sort this out and come right down. Go and … I dunno. Go for a walk or something."

"Fine!" said Andry. "Maybe I *will*!"

She went back into the hall, slamming the door behind her, and headed down to the barroom.

"Hi," she said, approaching the barmaid. "Carol, is it?"

"That's me," said Carol. "Is your fatha' alright? He looked fierce angry when he came in."

"Just problems with work," said Andry. "Do you know where Morgan is?"

"Probably in his room," said Carol. "What's up? Do you need more towels?"

"No, thank you," said Andry. "Can I go and see him?"

"Can if you want," said Carol. "I suppose you'll get fed up of being around adults all the time." She pointed towards the back of the room. "Door after the toilets, along the hall, his is first on the right."

Andry thanked her and went to find Morgan. She didn't even bother knocking on his door, and simply threw it open and barged right in. He'd been sitting on his bed, but he jumped in shock at her sudden entrance and scrambled to his feet.

"What're *you* doing in here?" he demanded. "This is the private part. No guests allowed."

"We're going for a walk," said Andry, marching up to him and grabbing his arm.

"No, we're not," said Morgan, twisting against her grip.

"Oh, yes, we *are*," said Andry, trying to drag him towards the door. "You said you'd take me for one."

"Yeah, but not right now," said Morgan. "My dad gets back soon, and I'll need to help him with things."

"That's not what *I've* heard," said Andry. "If you've not got any sheets to fold, and you're not too busy with …" She looked around the room. It was strangely bare. There was the bed, a table and chair, a bookshelf, and that was about it. "With whatever you're doing in here, you can accompany me, so I don't get into any trouble."

"*Get* into any trouble?" said Morgan, finally yanking his arm free. "*Find* any trouble, you mean. I'll bet you've got a nose for it."

"Okay," said Andry. "Let's put it this way. Your mum knows I came to find you. So, If I go off on my own, only to fall into a hole or something, then *my* dad will want to know why you weren't taking care of me."

"Oh, alright," said Morgan with a resigned sigh. "We're not going far, though."

"We won't need to," said Andry, standing in the doorway and beckoning him forward. "Come on. Shake a leg."

They left via a side door in the residential part of the building, Morgan stopping to pull on a waxed coat and a pair of knee-high wellingtons, both of which made him look ridiculous. Andry half expected him to produce a flat cap and a shepherd's crook to complete the ensemble, but she was left disappointed.

They headed across the carpark towards the road. Andry wanted to go straight to the lake, but Morgan urged her to follow him to the right, where the road disappeared into some trees.

"What's your name again?" he asked as they walked along the roadside.

"Andry," Andry replied. "Well, actually, it's Andromeda, but I don't tell many people that. Think yourself lucky."

"What kind of a name is Andromeda?" said Morgan. "Sounds like southern, hippy stuff."

"Andromeda was the wife of Perseus, son of Zeus," said Andry. Even though she didn't reveal her full name to just anyone, she always had this mythological explanation ready at hand for when she did.

"And what did *she* do?" asked Morgan.

"Her mother said that she was more beautiful than the Nereids," said Andry, "they were, like, ocean spirits. So, Poseidon sent a horrible sea monster to attack the coasts of her country. Her father decided to sacrifice her to the monster, so Poseidon would call it off, but Perseus came, and he had the head of Medusa, her with all the snakes for hair and could turn you to stone by looking at you, and he used it to kill the monster and save her. He then married her and made her his queen."

"Right," said Morgan, seeming a little bemused by this sudden lesson in the classics. "So, she was some lass, who got dropped in it by her mum, had the dirty done on her by her dad, and then this Percy bloke had to come and save her." He clicked his tongue. "Yeah, she sounds like *proper* fun to be around."

"Well, what kind of name is Morgan?" Andry shot back. "It sounds like a *girl's* name?"

"Shall we go and find that hole for you to fall into?" asked Morgan, scowling at her.

"Maybe later," said Andry. "Where *are* we going?"

"Just a little farther," said Morgan. He nodded at Andry's boots. "Those aren't just for show, are they? It might be a bit muddy. Why didn't you bring any wellies?"

"People don't own wellies *down south*," said Andry. "They're not the style."

"How about *that* stile?" asked Morgan, chuckling to himself and pointing to the drystone wall which bordered the road. Three stones had been set sticking out from the wall, so that it could be climbed over.

"Very funny," said Andry as they approached the wall. She mounted the first jutting stone while Morgan watched, his hands in his pockets.

"Go on," he said. "Shake a leg."

"Hang on," said Andry, stopping before she raised her foot to the next stone. "There's not, like, a bull in this field, is there? You better not be trying to get me splatted."

"There's no bull," said Morgan with a laugh. "I just wanted to see if you're as rough and tumble as you want me to think you are."

"*I'll* show you rough and tumble," said Andry, grabbing hold of the top of the wall. Instead of swinging her leg over it, she hauled herself on top of the wall and started walking along the section leading into the field. She waved for Morgan to follow. "Come on, gamekeeper boy. Let's go."

Morgan also scaled the wall, and they set off again. This was a completely pointless endeavour, as the wall was only around four feet high, and some sections were so narrow that they were forced to inch across them like a balance beam, but it was more entertaining than trudging across the fallow earth on either side of it.

"If Dave Lampard sees us doing this, he'll go mad," said Morgan as they traversed a particularly narrow section, using the lower fronds of an adjacent willow tree to keep their footing. "He helped build a lot of these walls himself, back when he was our age."

"It's just some old rocks," said Andry. "If any fall off, we'll put them back."

"You wait until you see where we're going," said Morgan. "People here take old rocks very seriously."

When they reached the top of the field, Morgan hopped down from the wall. A dirt path led towards a thick copse of trees, a wooden gate standing before the outmost trunks.

"What's through there?" asked Andry as she, too, dismounted the wall.

"That's what I'm going to *show* you," said Morgan as he started along the path. "If I *tell* you, it won't be a surprise."

As they approached the trees, Andry saw that the gate wasn't attached to a fence. Even so, it was secured with a padlock and chain, meaning that it was meant to keep vehicles out, rather than people on foot, and they were easily able to pass through the gap between the gate and the nearest tree trunk.

"I'm not sure I like surprises," she said, looking up at the canopy. Even at this time of day, the higher branches were blocking some of the sunlight, so that it felt as though they were at the entrance of a cave or tunnel.

"There's nothing to worry about," said Morgan. "This is a safe place. It always has been."

They carried on through the trees, and the path soon narrowed, so that they had to walk in single file, the ground to either side thick with moss and bracken.

"What're we looking for?" asked Andry. "If you're taking me to a clearing, so you can drop to one knee and sing me a ballad or something, you can think again."

"There *is* a clearing," said Morgan, "but I promise I won't sing."

Before long, they reached an area where the trees thinned out, but it wasn't a natural clearing. Instead, many of the trees had been felled, leaving only their stumps, at the centre of which stood a stone. It'd obviously been set there by hand, as there were no other stones in the area, standing or otherwise. It was tall enough so that Andry had to look up to see the top of it, but it was only about four feet wide. More bracken and tufts of grass grew around its base, suggesting that it was firmly planted into the ground.

"What do you think?" asked Morgan, nodding at the stone.

"Yep," Andry replied. "Just like you said. It's an old rock."

"Not just *any* old rock," said Morgan. "This is a bauta stone. It's been here for thousands of years. Yeah, I know it's not Stone Henge or anything, but-"

"I've *seen* Stone Henge," said Andry, cutting him off, "and *that* wasn't very impressive, either. My mum took me there a few years ago. Supposedly, it was for a festival, but all that happened was a bunch of guys with long beards, and women with not enough clothes on, banged drums for a while, and then they all got drunk."

"I don't think anyone's ever done that with *this* stone," said Morgan. "At least, not that *I've* heard of." He looked up at the stone, disappointment passing across his face. "I've always liked it, is all."

"Oh, okay," said Andry. "I'm just being cheeky. Go on. Tell me what's so special about it."

"Come here," said Morgan, approaching the base of the stone and beckoned for Andry to follow. "Look at this."

They knelt among the grass, and Morgan pulled aside some of the taller bracken fronds, revealing markings around the lower part of the stone. At first, Andry assumed that they'd simply be bits of graffiti, 'So-and-so woz 'ere 1940' or the like. However, as she looked closer, she saw that the carvings were clearly much older than that. A string of harsh, angular glyphs ran around the circumference of the stone. Some looked like letters, an R, an S, and what was maybe a T, but they didn't appear to spell out words. It took her a moment to realise that they were very similar to the markings she'd caught a glimpse of on Dennis and Bernie's playing pieces.

"What do they mean?" she asked, wrapping the sleeve of her jumper over her hand and rubbing at the stone.

"These are symbols of the old magic," said Morgan. "People put it here, ages ago, because they thought this was a special place, or they did spells here, or made sacrifices."

"Sacrifices?" said Andry. "You mean, *human* sacrifices?"

"No," said Morgan with a chuckle. "If they had a good harvest, or if they wanted something they were planning to go well, they'd leave offerings by the stone. Some of the old blokes still do it. If all the spring lambs grow up strong, they'll leave a prime cut by the stone, so it happens again the next year."

"Do they really think it works?" asked Andry.

"Depends how you look at it," said Morgan. "Let's say you had to do something important, but you were feeling anxious about it. You leave an offering by the stone for good luck, and if doing that gives you the extra oomph to get the thing done, then, yeah, I suppose that means it worked."

"It can't help with crops and lambs, though," said Andry. "Tricking yourself into feeling confident makes sense, but what if the lambs are all strong one year, and then they all die the next?"

"You'd just have to accept that it wasn't meant to be," said Morgan with a shrug. "That's the thing with this kind of stuff. People pick and choose. If the lambs are strong again, the stone did it. If they die, it wasn't meant to be."

"Sounds like a bit of a scam," said Andry.

"Maybe it is," said Morgan, standing up and brushing the dirt from his trousers, "but it keeps people happy."

"Okay," said Andry, also getting up. "Now we're here, I think we're far away enough."

"Far away enough for what?" asked Morgan, taking a half step backwards from Andry and looking her up and down, possibly worried that the fabled flick-knife was about to make an appearance after all.

"Far away enough," said Andry, "so that, if *you* try and run off, *I* can catch you."

Morgan gave a gasp.

"If you beat me up," he said, turning his shoulder to her and cringing, "my mum'll go spare. You won't get your deposit back."

"I won't *have* you beat you up," said Andry, taking a step towards him, "if you speak to me plain."

"About what?" asked Morgan, taking two, long strides backwards, trying to get behind the stone.

"What's going on here?" asked Andry, pursuing Morgan around to the other side of the stone. "How do people know our names? Why are they spying on us?"

"They must've just *asked*," Morgan replied, making another

turn around the stone and almost stumbling as he tried to keep Andry in front of him. "Your dad's name is in the big book."

"Do people *usually* ask who's in the big book?" Andry continued her interrogation as they completed a full circle of the stone.

"You're the only ones here," said Morgan. "Are you surprised people got curious?"

"Yeah," said Andry, speeding up a little, "I *am*. Also, what's the deal with the lake? Why does everyone act so strange about it?"

"It's the time of year," said Morgan, trying to match her pace, even though he was still going backwards. "There shouldn't be any tourists here when it starts getting colder."

"Why not?" asked Andry, quickly closing the distance between them.

"Those from the other side," said Morgan. "They can tell if someone's not from around here." He gave another gasp, his eyes widening, and stopped in his tracks. "I shouldn't have said that."

His hesitation allowed Andry to grab him by the front of his coat and push him onto the ground, where she promptly sat on his legs. She understood that this wasn't the best way of getting someone to '*Really* like you', but she felt she could make an exception with Morgan.

"Who are they?" she demanded, tugging up a handful of bracken and holding it over Morgan's face. "Tell me, or else it's feeding time."

"They've always been here," said Morgan through tightly pressed lips, "but they've been showing up a lot more."

"*Who*?" said Andry, stroking Morgan's nose with the bracken leaves.

"What's all this?" a voice suddenly rang out from behind them. Andry looked over her shoulder and saw a man coming from between the trees. He wore a long wax coat, similar to Morgan's but much more weatherbeaten, though it was the shotgun, hanging with its breech open over the crook of his elbow, which most caught Andry's attention.

"Dad!" cried Morgan as Andry dropped her handful of bracken.

"What're you doing?" asked the man. Andry wasn't sure which of them he was addressing, but she thought it best to release Morgan.

"We were just messing about," he said, scrambling to his feet. "This is Andry. She's staying at the house."

"I thought we'd closed up," said the man, looking from Morgan to Andry.

"It was a late booking," said Morgan, his eyes downcast. "Mum said there was no harm in it."

"That's for *me* to decide," said the man, coming closer. When he reached the stone, he leaned against it, closing the breech of the shotgun with a snap and sliding it into a scabbard bag at his hip.

Andry quickly decided that he was more than worthy of his 'Dirty Harry' nickname. She wasn't sure if she was truly a 'Punk', but she could easily imagine this man pointing the business end of his gun at her and asking if she felt lucky.

"I thought she must've told you," said Morgan.

"She didn't," said his dad, looking at Andry again, giving her a pure Eastwood style squint. He then looked back at Morgan. "What're you doing, getting put on your arse by a girl?"

"Like I say," said Morgan, his cheeks reddening with the same blush which Andry had seen during their first encounter, "we were just messing about."

"Well, maybe you should do a little *less* messing about," said his dad, "especially here. This isn't the kind of place for acting the fool."

"He was just showing me the stone," said Andry.

"And you decided to throw him to the ground and climb on top of him," said Morgan's dad. "I suppose I shouldn't expect anything less from a southerner."

"I'm *not* a southerner!" snapped Andry. She was getting seriously fed up of this.

"Really?" asked Morgan's dad. "Where're you from?"

"Leicester," Andry replied. "Hardly the south."

"For me," said Morgan's dad, sticking out a foot and scraping a line in the mossy ground before him, "the south is anything below *that*. How many of you are staying at the house?"

"Two of us," said Andry. "Me and my dad."

"I see," said Morgan's dad. "What does your fatha' do for work?"

"What's it to *you*?" asked Andry, thrusting her hand into her pockets. 'Dirty Harry' or not, she wasn't going to let herself be intimidated into spilling the beans so easily.

"It's *nothing* to me," said Morgan's dad with a slow shake of his head. "I was only asking."

"People around here seem to do far too much asking," said Andry. "There's asking, and there's being nosey."

"You're quite the fiery thing, aren't you?" said Morgan's dad, stepping away from the stone.

"That's right," said Andry, stiffening her stance.

Instead of coming towards them, Morgan's dad walked sideways towards the trees. As he passed Morgan, he nodded to him.

"Be careful with that one," he said, now nodding at Andry. "Fire and water don't mix."

With that, he strode away into the trees.

"What's *his* problem?" Andry asked Morgan when she thought they were out of earshot.

"*His* problem?" said Morgan, turning on her. "What's *your* problem? Actually, I *know* what your problem is right now." He pointed after his dad. "He's gonna go back to the pub and put the squeeze on your old man. You rough me around and start asking questions, but you clam up firm when anyone asks *you* something. Who *are* you? Why are you *really* here?"

"My *old man* used to come here when he was kid, so he's in love with the place," said Andry. "He's brought me here, hoping I'll fall in love with it, too. That's all *you* need to know."

"So, there's more?" asked Morgan. "If that's all I need to know, then what do I *not* need to know?"

"Don't get tricky with *me*," said Andry, jabbing a finger under his nose.

"Hang on a moment," said Morgan, batting her hand away. He narrowed his eyes at her. It wasn't quite as effective a squint as his dad's, but there was clearly something working its way through his mind. "Is your dad the one buying the empty house?"

"I didn't say that," said Andry, not missing a beat.

"I don't believe you," said Morgan.

"We're *not* here to buy some crumbly old lake-house," said Andry.

"Now I *definitely* don't believe you," said Morgan.

"Why not?" asked Andry.

"How do you know it's crumbly?" asked Morgan. "And how do you know it's by the lake?"

"I …" said Andry, realising she'd put her foot in it. She jabbed a finger at Morgan again, poking him in the chest this time. "Look, you better shut up!"

"Or else what?" Morgan retorted.

"Or else *I'll* dish the dirt on *you*," Andry growled at him. "I'll go to my dad, and he'll get police here. Proper police. *Southern* police."

"What dirt?" asked Morgan, but there was a hint of nerves in his voice.

"I can say it was the other way around," said Andry. "You brought me all the way out here and threw me down on the ground. 'Just messing about', you said, but that's not what it felt like to *me*. In fact," she snatched out a hand and seized hold of Morgan's, pulling it towards her and pressing it against her chest, the soil from Morgan's fingers leaving a streak down the front of her jumper, "see? You just touched my boob! How *dare* you!"

"Get off!" cried Morgan, yanking his arm back and clutching his hand, as though she'd bitten it. "No-one'll believe you."

"The people who matter will," said Andry. "My dad's got this guy called Pat. He can make *anything* stick. I somehow don't think you'd do very well when you're locked up in a borstal for getting grabby with a girl."

"You're crazy," said Morgan.

"So you've said," said Andry. "Do we have a deal?"

"You can't blackmail me with something I didn't do," said Morgan. "That's just wrong."

"Watch me," said Andry. "Now, are you gonna start playing ball, or do I turn on the waterworks and run back to my dad? Seriously, mate, I can turn them on and off like a tap. It's one of my many talents."

"Alright," groaned Morgan. "I won't say anything."

"There are a few things I *want* you to say," said Andry. "Who are these people from the other side? No more riddles. Who are they?"

"We don't really know," said Morgan, glancing around nervously. It didn't seem like he was looking for a way to escape, or even that he thought there might be someone else in the trees listening. Instead, it was as though he felt that simply speaking these words would bring on a sudden calamity. "They come every year, but we don't know where from."

"Not good enough," said Andry. "I'm told they take sheep. So, they're like… I dunno. Rustlers?"

"The sheep are only half of it," said Morgan. "They'll take anything." He screwed his eyes shut and shook his head vigorously. "You honestly *don't* want to know. It's none of your business. Best to keep it that way."

"It *will* be my business," said Andry, "if my dad *does* buy the lake-house, and we're here more often. He's leaving it to me when he dies. When that happens, and if I've gotten sick of living *down south*, you and I might be neighbours one day." She pointed off in the general direction of the lake. "If you're telling me that this place gets visited every year by people who come and steal stuff, then I want to know about it."

"They're *not* people!" said Morgan through gritted teeth. "If you saw one, you wouldn't have to use your talent of turning on the waterworks, because you'd bawl your eyes out on the spot!"

"What are you talking about?" asked Andry. She'd been shocked by his outburst, but he wasn't making any sense.

"They come every year, when the weather turns," said

Morgan. "Like I said, we don't know exactly where from. My dad's the gamekeeper, so he has to watch out for them. If we *do* end up neighbours one day, *I'll* probably be the gamekeeper by then, and I can't be coming to the old lake-house to protect *you* every cold night."

Andry stared at him for a long moment.

"You're just trying to scare me," she said.

"That's right," said Morgan, looking her dead in the eye. "I hope it's working. Why do you think the lake-house has been empty for so long?"

"Not a clue," said Andry. "Ask the owners."

"The people who *own* it have never *lived* there," said Morgan. "They had it left to them by the *old* owners. They were like you, thought they knew it all, didn't take the warnings when they were given. Ask me what happened to *them*."

"What happened to them?" asked Andry.

"You don't want to know," said Morgan. "It'd give you nightmares."

Andry stared at him again, a smile tugging at the corners of her lips.

"You're loving this, aren't you?" she said.

"What?" said Morgan with a frown.

"Is this the routine?" asked Andry. "The little story you've all come up with?"

"I …" stammered Morgan. "I don't …"

"No, no, it's good," said Andry, giving him a patronising grin. "You've got your act down. My dad can deal with legal problems like they're nothing. A decent horror story, though? What's better for keeping rich, city folks away than a proper bogey tale? I like that you didn't go with saying the lake-house is haunted. That'd be too on the nose."

"You think I'm making this up?" asked Morgan, his previous thunder collapsing into confusion.

"Of course you are," said Andry. "Don't worry. Me and my dad can keep it going when he buys the house. If anyone ever wants to, I dunno, build a shopping centre near the lake, just come and give us a knock, and we'll play along."

"You can't tell your dad," said Morgan, striding towards her but stopping just short of trying to grab her. "If you do that, then *my* dad will know that I told *you*, and I'll be in a whole world of trouble."

"And you'll squeal about who my dad really is," said Andry, raising a hand to her chin. "Hmm, looks like we've got a stalemate. If either one of us moves, both of our covers get blown."

"*Your* cover might get blown before the end of today," said Morgan. "My dad has a way with words, when he decides to use them. He'll figure out that your dad's the lake-house buyer in no time."

"Well, you better stop him," said Andry. "Don't forget, I've now got *two* ways that I can stitch you up. Grabby hands and a wagging tongue."

"Just as I was starting to like you," said Morgan.

"Oh, we don't have to fall out," said Andry, slinging an arm over his shoulder and pulling him along. "When this is all over, and we get the lake-house set up, you can be my occasional best friend."

They made their way back across the fields, forgoing any wall climbing this time. Andry hoped it'd make the journey quicker, but the state of the ground didn't make for easy going.

"So," said Morgan, breaking a silence which had fallen

between them, "where's your mum?"

"Back in Leicester," said Andry, as she trudged over a particularly difficult tuft of grass.

"Your dad really wants to buy somewhere so far away?" asked Morgan. "Aren't there any nice holiday places in Leicester?"

"Doesn't matter," said Andry. "My dad lives in Manchester."

"Ah, right," said Morgan. "Like *that*, is it?"

"Like *what*?" asked Andry, turning around to glare at him.

"My mum says *all* rich couples split up in the end," said Morgan. "They try to run their families like businesses, but all it does is make their kids hate them. We get that sort staying with us sometimes. You can spot them a mile off."

"I'm not *rich*," said Andry, gesturing down at herself, at her tatty jumper, her hole covered jeans, her Doc Martens, both now thick with mud. "Do I *look* rich?"

"You look like someone who's trying very hard not to *look* rich," said Morgan. "Maybe a little *too* hard. I'll bet you've got whole wardrobes at home, full of frocks and fancy shoes and …" He paused, thinking of something else. "*Tiaras*, or whatever."

"Okay," said Andry, "we'll play it *your* way. Who says I'm not *so* rich that I don't *need* frocks and shoes and tiaras? Perhaps I'm so *unspeakably* rich that wearing those would just be showing off."

"I know you're not," said Morgan, "because you just said *that*. I take it you haven't met many unspeakably rich people?"

"A few," said Andry. "Have *you*?"

"Yes," said Morgan with a nod. "We see them from time to time. They usually stay at the big hotels, but they wander into town to visit the lake. One summer, this guy brought his own *boat* with him. Stupidest thing you ever saw, with flags and a bell, and him wearing a little captain's hat, waving at everyone he passed and yelling, 'Good morning!', but what he was *really* saying was, 'Look at my boat!'. He got all annoyed when my mum told him we didn't have prosecco behind the bar. Now, *that* was unspeakably rich showing off."

"Sounds awful," said Andry as they started walking again.

"It was," said Morgan. "I'm not the biggest fan of tourists at all, but the rich, stuck-up ones do my head in." He bit his lower lip and looked away. "That's why I was, you know, a little sharp with you back in your room. I'm sorry about that."

Andry couldn't help but feel touched. Here was Morgan, not ten minutes after being assaulted and threatened by her, and he was apologising for being 'Sharp'.

"You don't have to be sorry," she said. "I shouldn't have teased you. The boys where I come from have to be stood up to. I guess it's just wired into my brain."

"So, if you're not rich," asked Morgan, "how can your dad afford to buy the lake-house?"

"I didn't say *he* wasn't rich," said Andry. "He could probably buy a boat, but I don't think he ever would. It's not his thing. In fact, this is the first big, I suppose you'd say 'Unnecessary' thing I've ever known him want to buy."

"And he's buying it for you?" asked Morgan.

"Well, it'll be mine eventually," said Andry. "It's mainly going to be our private getaway until then. He says he might let it out to friends during the rest of the year."

"Friends?" asked Morgan. "What sort of friends?"

"Wretched people," said Andry, "with names that make up parts of law firms. I'm sure you'll love them."

"Hang on," said Morgan, stepping in front of her. "You said it was just you and your dad. You can't be sending people here whenever you want. Weren't you listening to anything I told you?"

"Give it a rest," said Andry, pushing by him. "Wait until the friends arrive, then spin *them* your yarn. I'll look forward to it. 'We're not going back *there* again', they'll say to my dad. 'We were told about monsters in the lake'. It'll be hilarious."

"This just gets worse and worse," said Morgan. "Do you think you could convince your dad *not* to send any friends? I can try and keep the lid on who you really are for now, but you need to help, too. In the long run, I mean."

"Who we are will come out eventually," said Andry. "That's the plan. We're here to start making a good impression. I mean, look at how well *we're* getting along already."

"I've heard people at the pub say they should burn down the lake-house," said Morgan, "with this new owner *inside*, if it comes to it."

"Okay. Now *you* hang on," said Andry, grabbing him by the scruff and spinning him around to face her. "Spooky stories are one thing, but I don't take threats like *that* so lightly."

"Neither do I," said Morgan, throwing his hands up in surrender. "I'm only telling you what you're dealing with."

"This isn't funny anymore," said Andry, giving him a shake. "If my dad hears rumours about people planning to murder us, he won't just be sending friends. Like I said, he'll be sending police. He *really* wants that lake-house, and if getting it means nailing everyone within ten miles of the place for harassment, he'll *do* it. That's what *you're* dealing with!"

"We need to work together, then," said Morgan, trying to pull away from her. "If you move into the lake-house, and everyone's still sore about you being here, they *won't* protect you when those from the other side come."

"Enough of this other side rubbish!" snapped Andry. "What's gonna happen is *you* keep your mouth shut and try to keep people off our tail. In return, *I'll* try and keep my dad in check, to make sure he doesn't do anything stupid. I'm not joking. He could get your pub closed down if you cross him, just to see the look on your faces."

"*Now* who's threatening?" cried Morgan.

"That's not a threat," said Andry, letting go of him, "it's a fact."

"I don't get *you*," said Morgan, tugging at the collar of his coat. "How can you be so nice one moment, and so nasty the next?"

"It's another of my talents," said Andry. "Come on. Let's go. If we're lucky, *your* dad won't have *mine* pinned to the wall."

Chapter Three

WHEN THEY GOT back to the pub, they were glad to find Andry's dad there waiting for them, and he didn't look as though he'd been pinned to the wall any time recently.

"*Here* they are!" he declared as they came through the door. "Been off sightseeing without me, eh?"

"We didn't go far," said Andry. "There's a standing stone in the trees across the field. Morgan wanted to show it to me."

"I've just been speaking to your old man," said Andry's dad, nodding at Morgan as he raised a pint to his lips. "Nice fella. The first local I've met who seems likes like the real deal. I knew from the moment I clapped eyes on him that he wasn't a gamekeeper."

"He *is*," said Morgan, perhaps a little too hastily. "What else would he be?"

"Ah, come on, lad," said Andry's dad, winking at Morgan. "He's no gamekeeper. He's a poacher. Someone who's business is keeping *other people's* game, am I right?"

"I … I don't know what you mean," said Morgan, sharing a look with Andry.

"Your secret's safe with me," said Andry's dad. "I'll just file it away in the back of my mind. As long as he shares some of what he brought in today, that is."

"What did he bring in?" asked Morgan, growing visibly more nervous by the second.

"Two, big rubber buckets," said Andry's dad. "I didn't see what was in them. He took them through to the back before he came and sat with me. I told him, if he happens to," he raised his hands and made air-quotes, "'Come across' any decent sized pheasants while I'm here, I'll pay him more than a butcher will, but I wouldn't mind some of what was in those buckets as well. Strangest smell. Eels, do you think?"

"Probably," said Morgan, scratching at the back of his head and attempting a smile.

"Got to be careful, going after eels," said Andry's dad. "They make great eating, but if the wildlife trust find out your dad's been taking them, I imagine he'd be in a bit of bother."

"The secret's 'Safe' with *us*, though, right?" said Andry, matching her dad's air-quotes. "We'll just 'File it away'."

"Far be it from *me* to grass anyone up," said her dad. "I'm not here to rock the boat."

"That's good to know," said Morgan, his smile growing but gaining no more sincerity.

"Can you give us a moment, lad," said Andry's dad, gesturing for her to sit down.

"Okay," said Morgan. "I guess I'll see you both later. Let me know if you need anything."

Andry's dad watched him as he scurried away, then turned back to her.

"Very smart," he said, tapping the side of his head.

"He's really not," said Andry as she took a seat.

"I didn't mean *him*," said her dad. "I meant *you*. Been putting on the charm, eh? What did you learn?"

Andry wasn't sure where to begin, or even if she should begin at all. Revealing that Morgan had figured out who they were could cause more harm than good. As for his story about monsters, Andry knew her dad would react to it with immediate ridicule, and Morgan's secret being mocked would likely result in *their* secret being spread around for all to know.

"The people who are selling the lake-house," she said. "Did you know they've never lived there?"

"Yes, I knew that," said her dad. "They inherited it. They're not even directly related to the previous owners, if I remember right. The probate documents were a mess, but Pat says they're essentially all in order, so don't worry. No long-lost relatives are going to pop up and try to claim the place before us."

"Do you know what happened to the previous owners?" asked Andry.

"That doesn't matter," said her dad. "They could've been struck by lightning for all I care."

"How did you call with Pat go?" asked Andry. "*Have* the current owners been talking about you?"

"They *claim* that they haven't," said her dad, "but they clearly *have*. What we're trying to figure out is why. Pat mentioned putting the scare on their solicitor by threatening to withdraw the offer and seeing how fast they dance."

"Why would they lie?" asked Andry. "What'd be the point?"

"That's what I've been puzzling over," said her dad. "If they're trying to be sneaky, by leaking just enough information about me without it breaking our confidentiality agreement, then it's like you say, why? You'd have thought a hundred and seventy-five grand would be enough to hold someone's tongue for a while. Once we sign on the line, it's not their problem anymore."

"Maybe they feel they need to warn the locals," suggested Andry. "Warn them *before* the deal goes through."

"Warn them about what?" asked her dad. "Granted, I'm being a bit rough and ready with all this, but I'm not being hostile. They want to sell, and I want to buy. What is there to *warn* anyone about?"

"What if they've already been reached by someone?" asked Andry. "Someone who *is* being hostile and has said, 'Nuts to confidentiality. You'll tell us everything you know.'"

Her dad gave her a strange look and leaned in across the table.

"What's that boy been saying?" he asked. "Are the locals planning something? If they're putting together some sort of committee, I'll *crush* it. I've done it before."

"It might be something like that," said Andry, wondering whether a mob of arsonists could be called a 'Committee'.

Before she could say anything else, her dad gave a cough and looked over her shoulder. She turned around and saw Dennis coming towards them.

"Oi-oi," he said. "It's the Wyrd girl."

"Charming," said her dad with a laugh. "She's a bit of an odd one, but I wouldn't call her *weird*."

"Not what I meant," said Dennis, "but there's nothing wrong with either."

"Hello again," said Andry. "Is Bernie not with you?"

"Nah," said Dennis. "You won't see him here this evening. He's not in Dirty Harry's good books."

"I thought they were like *that*," said Andry, crossing her fingers.

"That's what he *says*," said Dennis, "but it's not true. Him and Harry got into a spat over a brace of trout, and Harry says he's not to come in for the share until he feels better about him."

"Who's this Dirty Harry?" asked Andry's dad.

"The gamekeeper," said Andry. "Morgan's dad."

"He told me his name was Lewis," said Andry's dad.

"It's a sort of in-joke," said Andry.

"Aren't *you* popular," said her dad. "Making friends, getting in on jokes, even if you *are* a bit weird."

"The reason I came over," said Dennis, pulling up a chair, "is to tell you that tonight's a share night. You'll see people coming in and getting fed, but I'm afraid it's locals only. I didn't want you try asking for some and getting a mouthful from Harry. He can be a bit touchy about it, so I thought it best to tell you to keep clear."

"A share night?" asked Andry's dad. "You mean, he hands out whatever he's caught?"

"That's one way of putting it," said Dennis. "As I say, though, locals only. It's nothing personal, of course. It's just that the shares usually only happen when there're no tourists around."

"I can pay," said Andry's dad. "I've already told him I can. If he's willing to slip a bit of the leftovers our way, I'll make it worth his while."

"It's not to do with money," said Dennis, shaking his head. "The fact that you say you've already spoken to him, and he didn't bring it up, means you're not getting any, no matter *how* much you can pay." He leaned back and stuck his thumbs into his belt. "Most of the big hotels have got fine restaurants. You should take your young lady to one of *them* for the evening. You don't want to be scranning with the likes of *us*."

"I think we'll stay," said Andry's dad, also leaning back.

Dennis chuckled and cocked his head at Andry.

"I can see where *you* get it from," he said. He then reached into the pocket of his coat and brought out the cloth bag containing the strange playing pieces and set it on the table. "Should we let him have a go?"

"Have a go at what?" asked Andry's dad.

"They're like fortune telling things," said Andry.

"No," said her dad. "I don't go in for stuff like that."

"It's just a bit of fun," said Dennis, pushing the bag across the table.

"Oh, alright," said Andry's dad, grabbing the bag. "What do I do?"

"You pull a piece out," said Andry.

"Your mum was always into this," said her dad, untying the cord at the top of the bag. "Rattling bones, howling at the moon. It's all hocus pocus." He dipped his fingers into the bag, taking out a piece and holding it up. It bore a long central marking with two smaller lines at the top, almost like a trident.

"Algiz," said Dennis. "Not bad."

"Great," said Andry's dad, setting the piece down on the table with a snap and pushing it towards Dennis. "What do I win?"

"Algiz *inverted*," said Dennis, tapping a finger next to the piece. Andry saw that her dad had placed it down with the three prongs of the 'Trident' facing towards him. When she'd pulled her own piece, she hadn't thought about which way up it was supposed to go, because it had, of course, been blank.

"And that makes it *not* so 'Not bad', does it?" asked her dad, contempt plain in his voice. "Go on, Merlin, what does it mean?"

"Caution," said Dennis.

"Yeah, yeah," said Andry's dad. "Whatever you say." He lifted the bag and weighed it in his hand. "I was only stringing you along. I *know* what these are. Like I said," he nodded at Andry, "her mum's hippy friends play with them. Aren't there, like, ten different versions, and they all mean something different, depending on what you *want* them to mean?"

"A woman who reads the runes," said Dennis, taking the bag back, "then gives birth to a daughter who pulls a Wyrd on her first try? I'd say you should speak of your wife with more respect."

"She stopped being my wife quite a while ago," said Andry's dad, "and most of my respect went with her."

Dennis turned to Andry.

"After meeting *you*," he said, "I imagined your fatha' to be a bit more congenial."

"He's just being stubborn," said Andry, glaring at her dad. "It's his way of trying to be funny."

"I didn't mean to upset anyone," said her dad. "I suppose it's quaint that that these little traditions are kept alive."

"More alive than you might think," said Dennis, dropping the trident rune back into the bag and returning it to his pocket.

"Don't be like that," said Andry's dad. "Honestly, if you'd pulled out a Ouija board or something, I'd have been a *lot* less congenial, especially when I found out you'd tried roping my daughter into it without my knowledge."

"He wasn't *roping* me in," said Andry. "I'm not a baby."

"These sorts of things can be dangerous," said her dad. "I don't believe that there's anything real about them, but if someone *does* believe they're real, it can do serious damage. One friend of your mum's, she got diagnosed with breast cancer at forty, thought she could cure herself of it with spells and potions, but she didn't see forty-two."

"This isn't the same, though," said Andry.

"I wouldn't be so sure," said Dennis. "Your fatha's not entirely wrong. I've seen folks make very foolish decisions based on what they see in the runes. You should never willingly let magic make your life worse. You're supposed to let it tell you what it needs to, and then you move forward, perhaps a little more aware of things than you were before."

"What about your Range Rover?" asked Andry. "You said the runes helped you to make up your mind."

"*Helped* being the main word," said Dennis. "My mind was already made up. I just needed a push, to make me feel better about how much the bloody thing costs. I'd never ask the runes if I should put all of my savings on a horse at ten to one, nor would I, as your fatha' says, let them decide on something when my *life* is in the balance."

"I'm not sure I understand," said Andry. "Are you saying that you *do* believe in it? Or that you *don't*? Not *really*, I mean."

"I think that's a bit philosophical for this time of day," said Dennis with a laugh.

"She doesn't get it from *me*," said Andry's dad, raising his pint and draining it. "What're you drinking, mate? I'll get a round in."

"Very kind of you," said Dennis. "Mine's a stout."

Andry waited until her dad was at the bar, then turned back to Dennis.

"Are there books you can read to learn about these runes?" she asked.

"I imagine so," said Dennis. "Why? Are you thinking of trying your hand?"

"I might," said Andry.

"Just be careful, though," said Dennis. "Don't go dishing out ominous readings to your mates in the schoolyard. Like your fatha' said, they can be dangerous to the wrong people."

"They can't be any more dangerous than the stuff in the schoolyards where *I'm* from," said Andry. "One of the primary schools banned Clackers last year, because this boy hit his together too hard and they shattered. A bit nearly took his eye out. Maybe the runes could've warned him not to be such a pillock."

"It was Jacks when *I* was young," said Dennis. "I don't know about taking your eye out, but I once fell over with them in my back pocket and landed straight on one. It stuck a hole right into my behind. I wish the runes had warned me about *that*." He sucked his teeth and gave a wince. "Cor blimey, it hurt."

As they both laughed, Andry concluded that Dennis couldn't be one of the scheming, potentially murderous locals that Morgan had told her about. If they existed at all, they probably wouldn't be so ready to give out handy hints on how not to get on the wrong side of people. She mentally added Dennis to her list of trusted locals, even though the only other person on the list was Morgan, and she wasn't sure she entirely trusted *him*, given how their agreements had been reached through mutual threats.

Her dad came back over, carrying a tray with two pint mugs and yet another bottle of dandelion and burdock for her. She foresaw getting very sick of the stuff very quickly.

"Something back there is smelling *good*," said her dad as he sat down. He slid one of the pints towards Dennis. "I know you said they won't serve *me* any, but what if I sent *you* up for some?"

"*I'm* not breaking Harry's rules," said Dennis. "I enjoy my evenings in here. I'm not getting myself exiled, like Bernie."

"What if I was here regularly?" asked Andry's dad. "How much of a fixture do you have to be before you're allowed to take part in these shares?"

"It's not a matter of regular," said Dennis. "It's about being someone who Harry trusts. I've known the man my whole life, but after he took over this place from his fatha', it was the better part of a year before he let me back in on the share. His old man was laxer about it, but Harry's a stickler for tradition." He took a sip from his pint. "Plus, he's a hard arse. He once kicked a fella off the share for the crime of singing an Irish song in *his* English pub."

"So, is it like a charity affair?" asked Andry's dad. "A little something for free, given out to those who he *deems* are in need of it?"

"On the contrary," said Dennis. "Only upstanding members of the community get in on the share. If you're a scab or a scrounger, you've got no chance."

"You know you're only making me more curious, right?" said Andry's dad. "If you came over to *warn* us, you're not doing a very good job."

"I'm just answering what you ask," said Dennis. "Take my advice, though. If you want the rest of your stay here to be pleasant, don't bother."

By now, Andry had started to notice some of the smell that her dad had mentioned. It crept its way through the barroom, propelled, she saw, by a steam which issued from the door behind the bar. She'd never smelled a cooking eel before, but she got the feeling that it wouldn't smell quite like this. There was an earthy undertone to the scent, but she could also pick out aromatic spices which could easily rival those from her beloved Indian restaurants back in Leicester. It certainly wasn't something she'd ever have imagined smelling while in a country pub, there was something far too exotic about it.

The other patrons had also picked up on the smell, and they kept casting anticipating glances towards the bar. Andry could almost hear their mouths watering.

It wasn't long before more people began to arrive. Just the odd one or two at first, but the place was almost full within an hour or so. They all clamoured for pints, squabbled over seats, several had dogs, though Andry saw no goats, and one man even produced a fiddle, which Andry guessed was the next best thing they had to a jukebox.

She'd imagined that this 'Share' would be more of a secretive thing, with each person coming in to quickly receive what was being dished out and then hurrying away with it. However, an almost festive atmosphere had descended over the pub. Pint mugs were clinked, tables were thumped in time to the melody from the fiddle, and everyone seemed to be having a grand time.

None of the revellers appeared to notice Andry and her dad. Or, rather, if they *did*, their gazes didn't linger. An inquisitive dog ambled over at one point and sniffed around beneath their table, but its owner swiftly tugged at the long strand of twine attached to its collar as a lead, and the dog disappeared back into the throng.

"Doesn't get more authentic than *this*!" Andry said to her dad, trying to get her voice above the din.

"What do you expect on a Friday night?" her dad replied. "There aren't any discos or dancehalls in *these* parts!"

The tantalising smell had, by now, permeated the entire building, overpowering even the noxious cloud of tobacco smoke which the gathered patrons were producing. It wasn't like most smells, where you eventually get used to it once it's filled the room that you're in. Instead, it only seemed to grow in intensity with each passing minute, and the patrons were growing visibly restless. Andry watched several people approach the bar, but they came back empty handed and looking disappointed. Whatever was being cooked up apparently took precedence over beer, which was a rare thing.

It didn't take Andry long to start wondering exactly *how* all these people were going to be fed. Her dad had said that he'd seen two, big buckets, but they'd have to be pretty big to hold enough to feed everyone who'd shown up.

A banging then came from the bar, loud enough to cut above the noise of the patrons. Andry turned and saw that Morgan's dad had appeared and was rapping the head of a walking stick against the bar top. A hush fell over all those assembled as he set the stick aside and took hold of the wide lapels of his waxed coat.

"Tonight," he declared, as though he were an actor, or a politician preparing to give a speech, "we honour the tradition of the share. We tend the land, and the land provides."

"The land provides," a few from the crowd repeated in agreement. "Aye, the land provides."

"The land is also vulnerable," Morgan's dad continued, "and must be protected. A wound done unto the land is the same as a wound done unto our own flesh." Andry wasn't certain, but she could have sworn that his eyes flashed towards her and her dad for a split second. "When the land is threatened, I shall defend it. Come forward and see evidence of that defence."

Morgan and his mum then appeared from the door leading into the rear of the building, each holding the handle of a large stockpot, billows of the fragrant steam rising from it as they hefted it up onto the bar.

"Is it the good stuff?" someone from the crowd enquired. "I've not come out in this cold for sprats or coneys."

"Of course it is," someone else replied. "Didn't you hear

what he said? Besides, what else smells like *that*?"

Andry expected them all to suddenly rush the bar. The pot was large but hardly enormous, and she didn't think there was any way it could hold enough for everyone. She was surprised, however, to see that the crowd began to form into an orderly line. There was no shoving or cutting, even from those right at the back.

One by one, they made their way towards the bar. Morgan's mum had produced a stack of small bowls, *very* small bowls, more like teacups without handles, and Andry's question over how everyone would be served was answered. It appeared that no-one got more than a spoonful or two.

Most of them downed the contents of the tiny bowls right at the bar, immediately handing them back to Morgan's mum to be refilled for the next in line, but a few took them back to their seats, holding them up to their faces and inhaling the steam, as though it were some sort of narcotic.

"Anyone would think they were taking communion," Andry's dad said to her as one of these bowl sniffers passed by them and sat at the table on the other side of the fireplace.

"Must be *good* eels," said Andry.

"Here, mate," said her dad, raising his chin at the man who'd sat across from them. He took his wallet from his pocket and pulled out a note, holding it between his first two fingers and waggling it, like he was coaxing a skittish animal. "I'll give you a fiver for that."

The man looked at his bowl, then around the room, then at the note.

"I shouldn't," he said. "Aren't you not supposed to be here?"

"Yet, here we are," said Andry's dad, flicking the note against the edge of the table. "A whole fiver. One time offer. If *you* don't take it, I'll ask someone else."

"Alright. Go on, then," the man said, keeping his voice low as he continued to look around nervously. "Just get it down you sharpish, before Harry sees."

As the bowl was slid towards him, Andry's dad winked at her.

"So much for it not being about money," he said. "Quick, you try some first."

Andry looked at the contents. There was about an inch of thin, almost clear broth with a few pieces of some kind of meat swimming in it, pale and stringy, like overboiled chicken. There was a sheen on the surface of the broth, which glistened as she tilted the bowl, reminding her of petrol on a wet road. Just these two ingredients couldn't possibly be what was producing the wonderful smell, but there didn't seem to be anything else in the bowl.

"I don't think I want to," she said. "It looks dodgy."

"It's not dodgy," said her dad. "If you can stand that gut burning, Indian muck, you can stand this."

"I'd still rather not," said Andry, pushing the bowl away.

"Suit yourself," said her dad, scooping up the bowl in both hands and draining the contents in a quick gulp. He then set it back down and gave a hard exhale, puffing his cheeks out. "Oof, ya bleeder. It's a got a kick to it. It almost tastes like there's booze in it."

The man who'd sold them the bowl sucked his teeth and gave a 'Watch out' raise of his eyebrows. Andry looked around and saw Morgan coming towards them.

"Ivor," he said to the man. "Mum sent me to get the bowls. She says she's fed up of people pinching them."

He looked at the table and saw that the bowl wasn't in front if Ivor. Instead, it was in front of Andry's dad, who had a glistening, tell-tale trickle of broth running down his chin. He then snatched up the bowl, turned on his heels, and started back towards the bar. Andry's dad leaned over to her.

"Go and work your magic," he said. "Stop him from snitching."

Andry gave a sigh as she got to her feet. She pushed through the crowd and managed to catch up with Morgan, grabbing him by the shoulder.

"Not so fast," she said as she spun him around.

"Did you eat any?" asked Morgan, his eyes boring into hers.

"I don't see what all the fuss is about," said Andry.

"*Did* you eat any?" Morgan asked again, snatching her hand from his shoulder and squeezing it.

"Ow! Let go!" snapped Andry. "I *didn't* eat any. It smells alright, but it looks horrid."

"You promise?" asked Morgan, pulling her towards him.

"Yeah, I promise," said Andry. "Look, what's going on? What *is* that stuff?"

Morgan glanced around and pulled her in even closer, so he could speak into her ear.

"It's one of *them*," he whispered. "My dad sets snares. He got one last night, but it was only small. That's why there's not much in the pot."

"*Them*?" asked Andry. "You mean, your lake monsters? You're not *still* trying to play me with that, are you?"

"You need to start believing me," said Morgan, "and *I* know how to make you. Come to my room tonight after everyone's gone. Make sure no-one hears you."

"I'm not coming to your room in the night," said Andry. "What if my dad catches me? He already told me what he thinks of teenage boys."

"You won't need to worry about him," said Morgan, nodding across the room at Andry's dad. "In a little while, he'll be sick as a dog."

"Are you saying it's poisonous?" asked Andry.

"No, not poisonous," said Morgan, but he then seemed to reconsider. "I mean, not *really*. Let's just say he's lucky everyone only got a mouthful tonight. If he'd eaten a regular size bowl, it probably *would* kill him."

"I need to warn him" said Andry, tugging against Morgan's hold.

"No," said Morgan, pulling her back. "Don't cause a scene. It passes. He'll have a banging head tomorrow morning, but he'll be fine."

"You better have some bloody good proof," said Andry, "because I'm starting to get tired of your games. If one more thing comes out of your mouth that I don't like the sound of, then our agreement is over, no matter what it means for *either* of us."

"You'll get your proof," said Morgan, letting go of her hand. "Now, go and keep an eye on your dad. It looks like it's setting in already."

Before Andry could ask anything else, Morgan slipped away from her and back towards the bar. She looked over at her dad, expecting him to perhaps be showing signs of this supposed sickness, but the truth was quite the opposite. He had a broad grin on his face and had slung his arm over the shoulder of 'Ivor', who'd sold him the bowl.

"Are you all right?" she asked when she got back to the table.

"Certainly, I'm all right," her dad replied, turning his dopey looking smile on her. "In fact, I feel *great*! You really should've tried some of that stuff."

Andry had seen him like this a few times before. She'd attended Christmas parties back at his previous office in Leicester, and he usually ended up in this state before the night was over. There seemed to be a point, normally around the sixth or seventh drink, where his callous exterior was stripped away and, in its place, a whole new myriad of emotions were trotted out. At first, everyone was his 'Mate' and weren't they 'Having a fantastic time?' This then transitioned into posturing and grandiose declarations, 'I built this company up from *nothing*!'. The final stage took the form of morose introspection, bordering upon the depressive, 'You wouldn't *believe* the sacrifices I've had to make'.

Andry had no idea how the attendants at *this* particular party would take the second and third phases of her dad's performance, so she had to make sure he didn't get to them.

"Maybe you should go and lay down," she suggested.

"I'm not going anywhere," said her dad, leaning into Ivor. "We've got everything we need right here. Drink, music, good company." He gave Ivor a jostle. "Where else would I rather be?"

Andry smiled at Ivor.

"Could you give us a moment?" she asked. "I need a word with my dad, in private."

"Bah, there's no private around here," her dad scoffed. "Everyone's thick as thieves, all in each other's business, asking names and doing all manner of daft stuff."

"I'd *really* like a word with you," said Andry.

"I'll leave you be," said Ivor, taking Andry's dad's arm from around his shoulder, as it appeared he needed some help doing it himself.

"Okay, whatever," said Andry's dad as Ivor stood up. "Remember what I said, though. Owning the land is a dead end. *Leasing* it to someone else is a gift that keeps on giving. Actually, I've got a card somewhere." He began patting at his pockets. "You can call me if you change your mind."

"Have you gone mad?" hissed Andry as she slipped into Ivor's vacated seat. "You can't hand out cards."

"Why not?" asked her dad, looking at her through bleary eyes.

"Because they say what you *do*," said Andry, "in big, bold letters."

"Oh," said her dad, his eyes widening. "I forgot about that."

"I seriously think you should go to bed," said Andry. "It looks like the beer has done a number on you."

"I've only had *three*," her dad protested. "Besides, I can't leave you down here by yourself."

"I think I'll be alright," said Andry. "Dennis is over there, and he seems like a good enough guy. Morgan's still around, too. I'll stick with them."

"Did you get him to keep his gob shut?" asked her dad.

"What does it matter," Andry replied with a tut, "if you're handing out cards?"

"It just slipped my mind," her dad groaned. "I give cards to everyone. It's like a reflex."

"I convinced him to stay quiet," said Andry. "We'll know by tomorrow whether he kept his word."

"Don't think I didn't notice that handprint," said her dad, casting a wavering finger over the front of Andry's jumper. The print was almost unrecognisable now, but he must have spotted it while it was still fresh. "Like I said, if he's been getting handsy, I'll skin him." He gave a huff. "Runes, magic, standing stones, it's all hippy stuff, and it only leads to one place."

"And where might *that* be?" asked Andry with a roll of her eyes.

"I saw it with your mum's weirdo mates," said her dad. "All this hocus pocus malarky, it's a way for lecherous old fellas to get their leg over. One minute, they're telling your fortune. The next, they're telling you about ancient *fertility* rites. This one beardy bleeder, he told your mum that marriage is a modern way for men to enslave women, and that we all belong to the Earth mother, so it doesn't matter who we *lay down* with. He said he could see into the future, but he was talking rubbish, because he didn't see it coming when I found out what he'd been saying and chinned him."

"It was nothing like that," said Andry. "I tripped, and he helped me up. In fact, I reckon he grabbed me by the jumper because he was worried about holding my hand. Does *that* ease your mind?"

"A little," said her dad. He screwed his eyes shut and ran a hand across his brow. "Ooh, I think you might be right. Something's got its grip on me. They probably brew the beer with water from the lake. God knows what's in it."

"You'll feel better tomorrow," said Andry, taking him by the arm and helping him to his feet. "We'll go back to that café and see if those breakfasts are as great as we were told."

"Good idea," said her dad, swaying slightly as he straightened up. "You take care down here. If things start getting wild, go to your room."

Andry looked over the patrons. The fiddle was still going, and everyone still seemed to be in high spirits, but she didn't think they knew what 'Wild' was.

"I'll keep my wits about me," she said.

"Good girl," said her dad, patting her on the arm before staggering off towards the stairs.

"He should've eaten," said a voice from behind her. She

turned and saw that it was Dennis, standing with his hands in his pockets, a short pipe stuck in the corner of his mouth.

"You told us not to," said Andry.

"I mean, in general," said Dennis. "You should always eat before you start supping. The beer we have aren't like that fizzy stuff from down south. It might *taste* weak, but it creeps up on you."

"We ate earlier," said Andry, "but obviously not enough."

Dennis took the pipe from his mouth, leaned forward, and sniffed at Andry, both of his nostrils flaring.

"I can smell it on you," he said. "If *you* didn't have any, you were sat right next to someone who *did*."

"Well, everyone got some," said Andry, holding her arms out at her sides. "This place isn't reservation only."

"Right you are," said Dennis, setting his pipe back between his teeth and puffing on it, though his tone didn't sound like he was convinced. "You staying down here for a bit?"

"That's the plan," said Andry. "Does it get any more exciting than this?"

"We'll start with the songs soon," said Dennis. "It's customary to put in a song on a share night."

"Oh," said Andry. "I don't think you'd want to hear *me* sing."

"Nah, don't worry," said Dennis. "Only those who've taken part in the share have to sing."

Andry was greatly relieved. She'd always thought that her rendition of 'Oh, bondage, up yours' by X-Ray Spex was spot on, but she couldn't imagine the lyrics going down well with this audience.

Instead, she settled in by the fireplace and listened as each singer stepped forward and performed their offering. Not only did many of the songs sound very similar, but a few of the singers insisted that *their* version of the previous song was better, so it was repeated several times. Most of the lyrics were to do with bringing in the harvest, chatting up your sweetheart, or drinking. The only break in this monotony came when a woman got up to sing, their songs being about bringing in the harvest, your sweetheart getting killed, or drinking.

Before long, Andry wasn't sure how much more she could take of 'Fields of golden wheat', 'Top full firkins', or 'My dashing Charlie, who in the war was slain', and she considered slipping away, but her attention was recaptured when Dennis got up to sing, everyone else falling silent as he approached the fiddle player.

"Minor, please, Phil," he said. "And slow, mind. This ain't a Yank hoedown."

The fiddler set his bow to the strings and started up a long, dulcet note, switching on the backstroke, so as to provide a drone, more than a melody, over which Dennis began to sing. He had a deep, baritone voice, like a Gregorian chanter, but there was also a brightness to it, suggesting that he was capable of easily reaching higher notes, should he wish to.

He didn't sing in English, but even after a good few lines, Andry wasn't able to pinpoint the language. She'd never heard anything like it. It simultaneously possessed both a fluidity *and* a harshness, like both water *and* the rocks that it broke upon.

The song was woefully short, and Andry found herself unable to hold back applause when it came to an end. No-one else joined in, however, and her claps rang out overly loud until she realised.

"Sorry," she said, holding up her hands before they could give a further clap.

"You see," laughed Dennis, pointing the stem of his pipe at her. "At least *someone* appreciated it."

As another, more jovial singer took his place, he came over to join Andry.

"What *was* that?" she asked. "Your song, I mean."

"That was a song from a long time ago," said Dennis, lighting a match from the fire and using it to rekindle his pipe. "From back before the language got messed around with."

"Like, from the fifties?" asked Andry.

"A little longer ago than that," chuckled Dennis. "There's a power in those words, and I'm guessing you felt it."

"I think so," said Andry. "I'm not really into this kind of music, but maybe I've been missing out."

"Those four scousers with the silly haircuts played a few good tunes," said Dennis. "Well, before they went to India and turned all strange. Doesn't hold a candle to the traditional music, though."

"I suppose not," said Andry, mentally going through a list of her music collection, trying to perhaps find some more common ground. She definitely didn't own anything which sounded like the song Dennis had performed. If post-India Beatles was too much for him, she doubted he'd have heard of The Damned. "I'll have to hit the record shops when I get home."

"You won't find many records of *that* kind of music," said Dennis. "It's not exactly top of the pops. If you want to hear it, you need to find someone singing it in person. That's how it keeps its power. If you played it back on some portable spinner, it wouldn't be the same."

"How do you know all this stuff?" asked Andry. "Runes, old songs, things like that."

"I mostly picked it up as I went along," said Dennis. "It's not that hard. Pull yourself away from your records and your telly for a while, and you'll learn all sorts of things. Talk to the people around you, hear their stories. It's right there, but you need to scratch the surface to reach it."

Andry then decided to go out on a very perilous limb.

"Do you know what happened to the people who used to own the house by the lake?"

"They died," said Dennis, puffing at his pipe. He didn't even flinch at the question.

"*How* did they die?" asked Andry.

"Suddenly," said Dennis. "It's why the place is empty. What trouble is it of yours?"

"Me and my dad drove by it earlier," said Andry. "We saw what a state it was in and were wondering why such a nice house had been left to rot."

"Okay," said Dennis with a slight nod. "So, how do you know that something *happened* to the people who used to own it?"

"It's what Morgan told me," said Andry, feeling the perilous limb starting to crack beneath her. "I figured he was just trying to creep me out, though."

"Sounds about right," said Dennis. "You're probably the only other kid he's seen since the school let out, and boys *do* like telling tales."

"Doesn't he have any friends?" asked Andry, only realising how awful this sounded after she'd said it.

"I don't know the lad that well," said Dennis, "but he doesn't strike me as the *friends* type. It's for the best, really. He'll take over from Harry one day, and gamekeeper can be a lonely job. Helps if he's already used to it."

"I guess," said Andry, but she was only feeling more awful.

She understood the isolation that sometimes came with being an only child, but she never let it get to her. Even when school was out, she still had people who she regularly hung around with. Sally, Grace, that bonehead, Mitch, who'd once made his own shirt with a swastika on it, attempting to emulate Sid Vicious, and had come to hide at Andry's place after being chased up Narborough Road by a bunch of Caribbean guys.

The more she thought about it, she actually quite liked a bit of isolation every now and then, as it was self-imposed, but having it thrust upon you, with nothing to do but fold sheets and put up with difficult tourists, was something she knew she wouldn't be able to bear.

"I'm about done for the evening," said Dennis, tapping his pipe out against the brickwork of the fireplace. "Don't wait up too late. I promise you won't be missing much. This lot get moody and mopey as the night draws on. It's why I never stay"

"I think I'll go to my room," said Andry. "I'm feeling a little weird. You know, the *usual* kind of weird."

"Kip well," said Dennis as they both stood up, "and don't let anything Morgan says worry you. You're safe under Harry's roof, safest place in town."

"I know," said Andry. "I've seen his *gun*."

"There're better things than guns," said Dennis, wrapping his coat around himself. "When you go up, take a closer look at the top of your door. You'll see something you might recognise."

As she reached the exit, Andry was startled by a yelp. She span to see a particularly ugly pug dog squirming in the arms of a man in his twenties. The little dog continued to yell at Andry in a shrill tone that cut through the noise of the bar.

"Quiet Fou-Fou," the man stroked the little dog's head and it immediately became passive. His eyes connected with Andry's and a chill ran down her spine. This guy, the way he was dressed, the little glass of green liqueur on the table marked him as someone not from around these parts. She backed away, spooked and nearly knocked into a man carrying a tray full of drinks.

She shook her head. Fou-Fou? It sounded like what a southerner would name their dog.

She managed to slip upstairs without being noticed. Neither Morgan nor his dad were anywhere to be seen, and his mum was still busy at the bar. She wondered if she should go and check on her own dad, but she was intrigued by what Dennis had said and carried on to the top floor.

The hallway was in darkness, and she couldn't find a light switch, meaning she couldn't see any of the doors. When she got to her room, she opened the door wide and flicked on the light. Just as Dennis had said, there was a small mark right at the top if it, burned into the wood by maybe a branding iron or a hot wire. It was the same rune that her dad had pulled from the bag, only with the three prongs pointing upwards.

She'd already gathered that a rune turned upside down meant the opposite of its right meaning. So, if her dad's inverted one meant caution, then *this* one meant safety. At least, that was the best interpretation she could come up with.

She understood straight away that this wasn't some kind of gimmick, a ploy for the place to pretend to be more 'Authentic' than it actually was. If that had been the case, the rune would be a foot long, in bright red paint. Instead, this was something that wasn't supposed to be noticed.

Her mum had once mentioned something about sprinkling salt in front of a door to keep nasty things out, but the only nasty things that Andry could think of which wouldn't cross a salty threshold were slugs, so she just hoped that the rune was more effective.

She checked herself. Effective against *what*? Had she really let Morgan's nonsense work its way so deeply into her mind? He'd said he'd show her proof, but she guessed it'd only be more silliness, another rock, or a funny shaped piece of wood, most likely picked out by Morgan himself for just this sort of occasion. He'd probably played this same trick on dozens of southern, tourist girls and got a kick out of it. The moment she said anything about lake monsters, everyone would burst out laughing and say that they'd 'Got another!'.

She'd show him. When his 'Proof' came up lacking, she'd tighten the noose around his neck and find out what was *really* going on with the lake-house. With his part of the game over, the ball would be in her court, and she could make any demand that she wanted.

Judging what would be the best time to go and knock on Morgan's door was tricky. Several times, she walked to the staircase and listened, but she could still hear the occasional voice or scraping chairs, so some of the patrons were clearly there for the long haul. She assumed that Morgan would retire to his room before they left, and thought about joining him pre-emptively, but he'd said that no-one should see or hear her, and crossing the barroom unseen when it was less occupied would be impossible.

She took the polished stone pendant she'd bought at the souvenir shop out from her pocket and examined it. It was pretty nice, the stone attached to the ring with a tiny screw, rather than glue, and it was strung on a proper chain with a lobster clasp, instead of the tacky bead-chains that all her others had. She hung it around her neck and held the stone to the light, watching it glimmer on the pale surface.

"Yep," she said to herself. "Very authentic."

She then laid down on the bed and stared at the ceiling. She found it hard to believe that she'd only been here for such a short time, and already so much had happened. However, she was forced to check herself again. *What* had happened? When she really thought about it, a fat lot of nothing had happened. It was all talk and riddles and stupid secrets. She wondered how things might've played out if her dad *had* brought Pat along. *He* wouldn't have put up with any of this craziness. 'The previous lake-house residents mysteriously dead? That's not what *this* paperwork says'. 'That strange broth looks like it breaks food hygiene regulations. Should I ask the health inspector to pay you a visit?'. 'Anyone who talks about burning gets slapped with a restraining order. I'll see to it personally'.

It certainly would've made things simpler, but all it'd do was make enemies for her dad, and potentially for Andry herself. Like they'd been saying all along, who wants to go on holiday each year to a place where everyone hates you? The breakfasts at the café could be the finest in the world, but that wouldn't count for much if you were worried the owner was gobbing in your eggs.

No, she had to stick to the plan, and getting Morgan to drop his act was the first part of it. If she went to his room, and he didn't have a real-life lake monster in there, ready and waiting with a smile on its face, she could move to the next stage.

She sniggered to herself. She was *good* at this. She couldn't wait to tell everyone back home. What she'd thought was going to be a dreary long weekend had turned into a sort of mini adventure, though she doubted that anyone back in Leicester would believe her. Well, maybe Mitch would, but *he* also believed that David Bowie was an alien.

She made two more listening trips to the stairs but could still hear sounds of activity. She didn't understand adults and drinking. She knew there was a point where it stopped being fun, usually when you throw up, fall down, or both, but she didn't see why so much time was allotted to it. She could think of several better things to be doing on a Friday evening, and she started wishing that *these* people knew about them. Anyone who spent more than three hours a night in a pub needed to find a hobby.

On her third trip, she saw that the lights downstairs had been switched off, so she slowly began her descent, treading lightly to avoid any bumps or creaks.

Crossing the barroom in the dark took some doing. The tiled floor felt to have spontaneously grown terribly uneven under the cover of night, and she made her way forwards at a slight stoop, holding a hand out in front of her, so that she didn't run into any furniture. She reached the other side of the room and went along with her hand pressed to the wall until she found the hallway leading to Morgan's door. Thinking it'd be a very bad idea to knock, she instead slowly turned the handle and opened the door an inch or so. No light came from inside.

"Morgan?" she whispered. "It's me."

"I'm here," Morgan replied from out of the darkness.

Andry opened the door enough for her to slip through. Once she was inside, she saw that the moon had risen on this side of the building, and she could just about make out Morgan's outline as he stood by his bed.

"Why are you standing here with the lights off?" she asked.

Morgan took her by the arm and led her to the window.

"See over there?" he said. From here, Andry could see the rear part of the building. A single-story section was set at a right angle to the rest. "That first window is my mum and dad's room. They'd be able to see if I had the light on."

"Wouldn't want you to be up past your bedtime," said Andry. "*How* old are you?"

"Stop messing around," said Morgan, his voice blunt. "That shed, there. That's where we're going, but we have to pass their window. If you make one peep, we'll *both* be in serious trouble."

Andry pushed the curtains aside and spotted what looked more like a small barn than a shed. It was broader than it was tall, but she couldn't tell how far back it went.

"What's in there?" she asked.

"You'll see," said Morgan. "If I told you, you wouldn't come."

They crept into the hallway and went out via the same door they'd used earlier that day, Morgan setting a bundled-up coat in the gap to stop it from closing fully.

Crossing the gravel of the carpark was even trickier than the barroom tiles. It seemed that only the slightest movement of their feet caused loud crunches, and they made their way around the building with as much care and delicacy as they would if they'd been walking over thin ice.

When the shed came into view, Andry saw that there was a door on the side that faced away from the main building.

"Why don't we go in through there?" she asked, pointing at it.

"No way," said Morgan. "That door's on a rail. It slides sideways and makes a whole *lot* of noise. There's a smaller one at the back."

Just as Morgan had warned, getting around to the opposite side of the shed took them within only ten or so feet of his parents' window, and Andry even held her breath as they sneaked by it, her eyes fixed on what she could see of the curtains, expecting them to twitch at any second. She wondered why they couldn't have approached from the rear, but when they reached the smaller door, she saw that this route was blocked by a chain-link fence and some very stubborn looking hedges, which would've been hard enough to get through during the day, never mind at night.

When they reached the door, she saw a padlock attached to a hasp latch. The moonlight glinted from its brass casing, showing that it was regularly handled.

"It's locked," she said.

"Always," said Morgan, "but I grabbed the key earlier."

He produced the key from his back pocket and carefully inserted it into the lock, holding it away from the latch, so that it didn't make a sound when he undid it. He then slowly pushed the door inwards, standing sideways to the opening until there was enough room for him to fit through.

"Hold it for me," said Andry as she made to go next.

"You'll have to breathe in," said Morgan.

"Are you calling me fat?" hissed Andry. "Just hold it, so it doesn't bang shut when I'm in."

She got through easily enough, and Morgan closed the door behind them. The darkness inside the shed was almost absolute. Morgan rummaged in his pockets again and took out a small torch, flicking it on and dazzling Andry.

"We don't have to worry now we're inside," he said. "Look."

He turned the beam of the torch on the broadest wall of the shed, and Andry saw that, while it did have windows, they'd been covered up with piled sacks, stacks of loose bricks and sheets of corrugated metal.

"What's that stink?" she asked, tugging the neck of her jumper up over her nose.

There was an awful stench coming from somewhere. Not the damp, rotten smell that usually hung around in old outbuildings, but something which suggested freshness, like some creature, its innards racked with gripe, had recently come in here to do its shameful business.

"Not so nice when you smell it like *this*, eh?" said Morgan. "Come on. We better be quick."

"What are we looking for?" asked Andry as Morgan started towards the bottom end of the shed, the light from his torch casting shifting shadows as it passed over work benches, a pile of tyres, something draped with a tarp, and all manner of pieces of machinery in varying states of disrepair.

"Down here," he said, turning the torch back on her and getting her right in the eyes.

"Cover that a bit, will you?" she said as she followed him. "You won't be able to show me anything if you've already blinded me."

"Oh, sorry," said Morgan, pointing the torch at the ground as she caught up with him. "It's just over here. I had to show you tonight, because it'll be gone tomorrow morning."

"*What* will?" asked Andry. "I've already said that I'm through with your games. If you've got something important to show me, then show me, right now. And if it's not bloody impressive, I'll go back and wake the whole house up."

"This," said Morgan.

He raised the torch again and focused the beam on something right at the back of the shed. At first, Andry thought that it was large metal bucket, but as she looked closer and took a few steps towards it, she saw that it was an old tin bath stood on some stacks of bricks. She'd seen one before at her grandparents' house, but they'd repurposed theirs into a garden planter after having a proper bathroom installed. Her mum and all her aunts and uncles would often throw pebbles or cigarette ends at it, cursing the memory of having to wash in the wretched thing when they were children.

Unlike the junk which surrounded it, the bath was in good condition, its sides shiny and free of dents or holes. A tarp was hung over it, secured at each end with bricks. She approached it and placed a hand on the rim, giving it a slight shove. Liquid sloshed around within it, some even spilling from beneath the tarp. The smell which this produced was truly terrible. The bath was clearly the source of the stench, but only now that it'd been disturbed did its full pungency hit home.

"Eurgh, God!" she gasped, hopping backwards to avoid any of the foetid liquid getting on her.

"Keep quiet," hissed Morgan, "and don't push it like that. If you knock it over, we're finished."

"What *is* it?" asked Andry, covering her mouth and nose with her jumper again.

"Here, hold this," said Morgan, passing the torch to her. He then went to one end of the bath and used his foot to push aside the bricks which held the tarp down, sliding off half of the tarp as he did so.

If Andry had thought the smell was bad to begin with, then nothing could have prepared her for the full, eye-watering miasma which hit her when the tarp was drawn away. It almost *was* like a physical blow, a smell that you could taste, a smell that, in better light, you could probably *see*.

It took all of her resolve to go back up to the edge of the bath and look inside. She scanned the torch over it, seeing that it was around two thirds full of some dark liquid, the beam of light not fully penetrating it. As she turned the torch in her hand, she saw that the surface of the liquid possessed the same, spectrum splitting sheen that she'd seen on the bowl of broth.

"You're kidding me," she said, looking up at Morgan, her eyes wide, despite the sting from the vapours which rose from the tub. "This? *This* is what they were eating?"

"No," said Morgan. "This is what you *don't* eat. This is what's left." He glanced around and then went up to one of the piles of junk, returning with a snapped off broom handle. "Watch," he said, delving the handle down into the tub.

As he stirred the contents, Andry saw partially solid masses begin bobbing to the surface. She was no expert, but she knew guts when she saw them. Horrid, pallid sacks and snaking coils of tubes swirled around in the liquid, like the brew of a witch and a butcher who'd joined forces.

When Morgan stopped stirring, and the liquid slowed, Andry heard something bump against the side of the tub. Even though the smell was now almost completely unbearable, she managed to bring herself to lean over the tub and look straight down into it. A shape appeared on the surface for a brief moment, before being dragged back down by the still swirling eddies. Teeth. A crooked crescent, pale as moonlight.

Andry spat out a flurry of swearwords, leaping away from the tub and dropping the torch.

"Shh! Keep it down," said Morgan, holding his hands up, palms out.

"Keep it down?" said Andry, her throat tight as she tried to stop from shouting. "That's a skull in there. A *person's* skull. I saw it."

"It's not," said Morgan, coming around to the other side of the tub.

"I think I know what a skull looks like," said Andry. "There's no way it was big enough to be a grow-up's skull, either. It was a *kid's* skull."

"It's not," Morgan said again, picking up the torch.

"All this time," said Andry. "All of your stupid stories, and it turns out you're a bunch of bloody …" The word was right on her lips, but it took an extra bit of effort to get it out. "A bunch of bloody *cannibals.*"

Morgan looked at her. At first, he seemed shocked, but his face then broke into a smile, and he was forced to clap a hand over his mouth to keep from laughing.

"Cannibals?" he said through his fingers. "If only it were *that* simple."

"Well, I mean…" said Andry, her certainty wavering just a little. "I mean, who *else* keeps dead people in bathtubs and serves them up as an evening snack?"

"I've told you before," said Morgan. "They're *not* people. They sort of look like people on the outside, but they're different on the inside. Their bones are softer than ours."

"Hang on," said Andry. "You're saying that's one of your lake monsters in there?"

"I told you it was only a small one," said Morgan. "Not very monstrous, really. My dad cut it in half, so he could carry it here in the buckets. The big ones get hung from the beams, so they can drain." He pointed the torch up towards the roof, and Andry saw several hooks fixed into the wooden rafters. "You've got to catch all the blood."

"Okay," said Andry, running a hand across her face. "Let's just *pretend* that I believe you. Not only are there monsters on the loose, but you catch them and *eat* them?"

"Same as eating anything else," said Morgan with a shrug. "And they *have* to be caught. Imagine if one escaped and got run down on the big roads. Or, even worse, made it to another town. The last thing we need is people showing up *looking* for these things."

"They could *do* something about it," said Andry. "Police, or the army, I mean."

"And dozens of government eggheads, sticking their noses into things they don't understand," said Morgan. "This is the way it's been for years and years. Anyway," he nodded at the bathtub, "you haven't seen what else that stuff can do."

"*What* can it do?" asked Andry.

"You mix it into a crop sprayer," said Morgan, "at as little as one part in ten, and you'll have plants three feet high before anyone else's have even sprouted."

"You're joking?" said Andry.

"Works every time," said Morgan with another shrug. "How do you think this place manages to keep going? Tourists in the summer, and bumper crops in the autumn, that's how."

"Right," said Andry. "I suppose that makes sense."

"I must say," said Morgan, tilting his head and frowning at Andry. "I know we're still only pretending, but you're taking this pretty well."

"Actually, I'm *not*," said Andry. "I'm just very good at not showing it."

"Another of your talents?" asked Morgan.

"Something like that," said Andry.

Indeed, she *wasn't* showing it, but this didn't mean that she wasn't also trying incredibly hard to fight back the creeping panic that was building up inside her. Morgan had, when you looked at it plainly, shown her what appeared to be a dead body. Every rational part of her was screaming that she should get out of there as quickly as possible and sound the alarm to her dad. They had to leave, right away, and call the police, lake-house be damned. No doubt these mysteriously missing previous owners had met the same fate as whoever was in the bathtub, bumped off when they started 'Sticking their noses into things they didn't understand', as Morgan had put it, and Andry and her dad might find themselves hanging from the rafter hooks if they stuck around long enough for the locals to figure them out.

Despite all of this, there was another, much smaller part of her that was clouding her reason, but which spoke up none the less. If Morgan and the rest of the locals were a gang of murderers, then why would he be so eager to show her the evidence of their crimes? She'd already proven that she was more than a match for him physically, so he wouldn't have lured her out here to try and overpower her, and if he was planning to spring some sort of trap, he'd have surely done it by now.

There was also the fact that, as far as she knew, he'd held up his side of the bargain by not revealing her dad's true identity. What would be in it for him to continue lying? What if it was all true?

"This isn't enough," she said, shaking her head.

"What isn't?" asked Morgan.

"That could just be bits of any old animal," said Andry, pointing at the tub.

"You said you knew what a skull looks like," said Morgan. He scanned the torch over to the junk pile where he'd left the broom handle. "Shall I see if I can fish it out?"

"No," said Andry, loud enough to stop Morgan in his tracks. "I don't want to see it again. I want to see one."

"I don't follow," said Morgan. "I just *showed* it to you."

"I mean, I want to see one *alive*," said Andry. "If you want to convince me, then I need to see one for real, standing on two legs, or whatever they do. Also, let's get one thing straight. Remember that Pat guy I told you about? That wasn't a bluff. If me and my dad aren't back when he's expecting us, he'll be here in a heartbeat. You'd never get away with it."

"Get away with what?" asked Morgan, the confusion on his face so utter that it was almost funny.

"*Doing* anything to us," said Andry.

"We don't want to *do* anything to you," said Morgan. "I thought this was about keeping you safe. If you're going to be my occasional best friend, then I suppose you need to know these things, so your dad won't send any of *his* friends."

"It'll take a bit more than tub full of guts to win my dad over," said Andry. "For now, this stays between you and me."

"Getting to see a live one isn't that easy," said Morgan. "Even *I've* only seen them a few times. My dad says I'm not ready yet."

"Not ready for what?" asked Andry.

"For when they come," said Morgan. "He says he can tell just by looking at the lake, but I've never been able to figure it out." He passed the torch over the tub. "This means we're safe for tonight. The smell of a fresh dead one keeps them away. They can even smell it on someone who's eaten some. That's why the shares are so important."

"Did *you* eat any?" asked Andry.

"No," said Morgan. "I'm not old enough. The first few times can be really bad, especially for a kid. Even women who are nursing a baby aren't allowed any. It gets in through the milk."

"Okay," said Andry. "So, just *how* sick is my dad going to be?"

"I'm told it's like the worst flu you've ever had," said Morgan, "times ten. He only had a mouthful, though, so it shouldn't be *that* bad. Let's just say he won't want to be more than a few feet away from a toilet for a while."

"Okay," Andry said again. Her original plan of attack had been completely scuppered, and she was trying to think of a new one. "Can you get me inside the lake-house? I want to see what it's like in there."

"Not a good idea," said Morgan. "Everyone's been told to stay clear of that place."

"If it comes to it," said Andry, "you can say I forced you. We were just going for a stroll, and I, being a stuck-up, southern, gang member girl, decided I wanted to do a bit of breaking and entering. I'll take the full blame."

"There'll be a bit more than blame," said Morgan. "If we get caught, there'll be serious questions. Dennis keeps an eye on that road."

"Me and Dennis are mates now," said Andry. "He'll understand."

"It was *him* who said we should burn the lake-house," said Morgan. "He says that, ever since the old owners died, it's turned into a Wyrd place, and we should do away with it altogether."

"How did they die?" asked Andry. "Dennis was quick enough to say they had, but he wouldn't say how. He just said it was sudden."

"We don't really know how," said Morgan. "We think they might've done it themselves, but no-one's sure."

"And you don't want anyone else moving into the lake-house because…?" said Andry.

"Because of all of *this*," said Morgan, holding his arms out at his sides. "Haven't you been listening? Or are we still only pretending?" A look of cold concern passed over his face. "You're not going to tell your dad anything, are you? This isn't a game. This is for real. You have to believe me."

"Calm down," said Andry. "I won't tell him anything, because I'm still not sure if I believe it or not. Either way, him knowing could mean bad news for you, and I don't want to see that happen."

"Why not?" asked Morgan.

"Because I'm actually growing rather fond of you, you little screwball," said Andry, stepping up to Morgan and poking him in the chest. "If my dad takes a disliking to you and everyone else here, he'll move into the lake-house anyway, surround it with a twelve-foot, electrified fence, and say we're to have nothing to do with you."

"That *would* be bad," said Morgan. "For *you*, I mean."

"It doesn't need to happen," said Andry, "as long as you keep helping me. If there *are* monsters, I want to see one. In the meantime, let's take a look in the lake-house."

"If you see one," said Morgan, "you won't *want* to go into the lake-house."

"We'll do that first, then," said Andry, pouncing on the fact that Morgan had just tripped himself up without realising it.

"You know what?" he said. "It sort of feels good to say all of this out loud after so long."

"Can't be an easy thing to have trapped in your head for your whole life," said Andry. "Do you talk to anyone at school about it?"

"Sometimes," said Morgan. "They're not as in on it as I am. They only know what their parents tell them."

"I guess you must be pretty well respected, then?" asked Andry. "You being the gamekeeper in training and all."

She already knew what his answer would be, Dennis having said that he wasn't the *friends* type, but she wanted to hear how he'd phrase it.

"Not as much as you'd think," he said, tugging the tarp back over the tub. "I mean, the gamekeeper *is* respected, but that doesn't mean people have to *like* him. In fact, the other kids always seem to keep a distance from me, like they think there's something on me which might rub off."

"Well, *I* like you," said Andry, stepping forward and linking an arm through his, hoping to show him that she didn't care what 'Might rub off'. "Wait until the other kids find out that you're mates with the rich, city girl. They'll be green with envy, especially when I start mailing you mixtapes. You can be the only boy in town who knows who The Ramones are."

"The who?" asked Morgan as they headed towards the door.

"Yeah," said Andry, "them, too."

When they got back to the rear door of the pub, Morgan slowly opened it, pulling the coat from the gap.

"This was risky," he whispered, "but you can't open this door from the outside. All the big doors are like that."

Andry *had* noticed that the main entrance to the pub was kept open with a stop, a further, simpler door keeping the bad weather out, but this was normal for many establishments. She hadn't even thought to look at the locks.

"What for?" she asked.

"To stop *them* from getting in," said Morgan. "They'll try if you let them. We've got extra protection, though." He pointed to the top of the door. "You see that sign?"

Andry looked but couldn't make out the mark in the darkness.

"I've seen the ones upstairs," she said. "Dennis said to look for them. He's been telling me about runes."

"Really?" said Morgan. "He must've taken quite a shine to you. Did he do you a spread?"

"I don't think so," said Andry. "He let me pull one out of the bag."

"Which did you get?" asked Morgan.

"The blank one," said Andry. "The weird one."

"*Really*?" Morgan said again. "I guess I shouldn't be surprised. You're about as Wyrd as they come."

"Luckily," said Andry, pushing by him, "I already know that's not an insult."

"Can you get back to your room okay?" asked Morgan.

"I'll be fine," said Andry. "My sneaking skills are better than I thought."

"Another talent to add to the list," said Morgan. He carefully let the door snap shut and hung the coat back up. "I'll see you tomorrow."

"Yeah," said Andry. "Sweet dreams, eh?" She made to head into the barroom but heard Morgan shuffling his feet. She looked back and could still see him silhouetted in the hallway. She folded her arms and gave a sigh. "What's wrong?"

"You weren't joking, were you?" asked Morgan.

"About what?" said Andry.

"About being my mate, and sending me tapes and stuff," said Morgan. "Were you still pretending?"

Andry tried not to laugh. Of all the things that could be on his mind, *this* was what had stuck with him.

"No, I wasn't joking," she said. "To be honest, there's part of me that's hoping this *does* all turn out to be rubbish. You'll be much easier to be friends with that way."

"Just friends, though, right?" asked Morgan. "Nothing funny?"

"Believe me," said Andry with a tut, "you're not my type by a long shot."

"That's good to know," said Morgan. "My mum would go spare if she thought I was up to anything with a guest."

"What a couple we'd make," chuckled Andry. "I could go off and do the gamekeeping, and you could stay here and fold the sheets. Take *that*, gender stereotypes."

"You'd probably be a better gamekeeper than me," said Morgan. "You're not like other girls, are you? You're more like … well, you're not like *anything*."

"Carry on with silver-tongued blinders like that," said Andry, "and maybe things *will* get funny, Casanova."

"Ya what?" said Morgan.

Even though she couldn't see his face, Andry knew he must've donned his now almost trademark mask of bafflement.

"Never mind," she said. "Go to bed, before you get yourself worked up."

"Okay," said Morgan. "Goodnight. And don't be worried. The runes on the guest doors are really good ones. My great granddad put them there, and he *knew* his stuff."

"I'm sure I'll sleep like a baby, then," said Andry. "I'll see you first thing in the morning. I like my tea with two sugars."

When she finally got back to her room, she sat on the edge of the bed and frowned. Just like she'd told Morgan, not overreacting about things *was* one of her talents, she'd found that a near constant state of nonchalance could get you a long way, but even *she* was surprised at herself.

The rational side of her started to make its presence known again. There was no way she'd seen a real, human, dead body in the tub. If she had, then even her practiced calmness would've broken. What she saw had just *looked* like part of a human skull, that's all it was. Any carcass, when suitably mashed up and dumped into a tin bath, could look like parts of a person in the right light, and Morgan's torch had been *exactly* right for producing such an illusion.

What she couldn't figure out was why Morgan was so dedicated to the charade but also so hesitant about it. If he'd been trying to scare her, then he'd surely have been a bit more enthusiastic, insisting that she get close enough to the mess in the tub that she could bob for the giblets, while parading up and down and crying, 'Blergh! What do you think of *that*?'.

What if, she thought, there *weren't* any lake monsters, but Morgan was convinced that there *were*? This hadn't crossed her mind until now. Morgan could be just as caught up in all this nonsense as she was. Kids, even those her and Morgan's age, could go on believing in very implausible things for a long time. True, lake monsters weren't Father Christmas or the Tooth Fairy, but the principle was the same. If Morgan had been brought up believing in lake monsters, and no-one had stepped in to dispel this belief, instead only enforcing it through tales, folklore and strange rituals, then it was no wonder he still bought into it.

Yes, she pondered further, but he said he'd seen them. Just when she thought she'd worked it out, she was hit with another stumper. Hopefully, getting to see inside the lake-house would open up more avenues. When Morgan discovered that it was just another building, nothing sinister or dangerous, she could press him a little harder on what he knew about these so called 'Monsters'. *Was* the body in the tub that of a monster? Or had he just been *told* that it was? *Had* he genuinely seen one, with his own eyes? Or had she seen something peculiar, and simply *assumed* that it was one of these monsters he'd been brought up to fear? From what she'd learned of him so far, she imagined that a rustle in the bushes on a moonless night would have Morgan crying, 'Monster!'.

An odd feeling of pity washed over her. What an awful life Morgan must lead. Shunned by the other kids at school, mocked by adults like Bernie, ordered around by arrogant tourists, and spending the end of each year in constant terror of monsters which might not even exist. If anything, she hoped that the outcome of all this would be Morgan finding some backbone and learning to stick up for himself. She honestly did want to be his friend, but hanging around with someone who was scared of his own shadow and wouldn't say 'Boo' to a goose would likely become a drag pretty quickly.

She got into bed, but she lay there awake for a long time, her face turned towards the door. She wasn't worried that anything might burst through it. Instead, she was thinking about the rune on the other side. The last thing that went through her mind, before sleep finally took her, was, if the Wyrd rune, *her* rune, was blank, then how did you use it?

Chapter Four

She was awoken the next morning by a tapping at the door. At first, she thought she'd imagined it and rolled back over. Her sleep had been shallow and fitful, so she wasn't surprised that the slightest sound from downstairs would wake her, but the tapping then came again, quick but soft, like someone was using just a single finger.

"Who is it?" she asked, sitting up.

"It's me, Morgan. Can I come in? Are you decent?"

Andry looked down at herself. Sex Pistols shirt, still on. Socks and underwear, still on.

"I'm about as decent you'll get in the morning," she replied. "Enter at your own risk."

Morgan came in, but he did so backwards, pushing the door open with his elbows.

"You didn't lock it?" he asked.

"I thought the rune would be protection enough," said Andry. "And turn around, will you. What's wrong? Worried you might see my ankles?"

"No," said Morgan. "I've brought you this, haven't I?" Andry saw that the reason for his strange choice of entrance was that he was carrying a tray, a single mug set upon it. He gave her a smile as he nodded at it. "Two sugars, right?"

"You're hopeless," she laughed, flopping back down onto the bed. "If I'd known you were actually going to *bring* it, I'd have ordered the full continental."

Morgan set the tray down on the side table and frowned at her.

"Why does the Queen on your shirt have a safety pin

through her nose?" he asked. "I'm pretty sure that's illegal, like drawing on a pound note."

"That's kind of the point," said Andry, stretching out the hem of her shirt and looking at the defaced royal portrait. "It's a statement."

"About what?" asked Morgan.

"*You* wouldn't understand," said Andry. "Give it time, though. We'll make a proper terror out of you. We could dye your hair green and spike it up. I can show you this trick using egg whites that makes it stay rigid for days."

"I'd rather not," said Morgan. "Do you want this tea? I'll drink it if you don't."

"No, give it here," said Andry, sliding to the foot of the bed. "Has my dad made an appearance yet?"

"Not yet," said Morgan, handing her the mug. "I thought about knocking on his door, to see if he wanted one, too, but I decided I'd leave it to you."

"Probably for the best," said Andry, taking a swig of the tea. It was tooth-achingly sweet. If Morgan had only put two sugars in it, he must've been using a dessert spoon.

"You don't sleep in those, then?" asked Morgan, pointing at her boots, which she'd set next to the bed with her jeans draped over them. "I'm disappointed."

"I thought about it," said Andry, swinging her legs from the bed and kicking her feet in the air. "After all, I left my silk sleeping socks at home, right next to my tiara and my ballgown."

She'd only been joking when she'd mentioned Morgan being worried about seeing her ankles, but he flushed bright red none the less. She could, indeed, dye his hair green and spike it up with egg whites, but it'd obviously take a little more than that to knock the bashfulness out of him.

"If you want to go and look at the lake-house," he said, "it won't be until later. I have to help my dad out."

"Why don't I help, too?" asked Andry, setting aside the sickly tea and reaching for her jeans. "It can be a good way for me to see the local colour."

"That's not going to happen," said Morgan with a shake of his head. "He'd never allow it."

"You could at least ask," said Andry.

"Yeah, right," huffed Morgan. "If you're so sure, *you* ask him."

"Okay," said Andry, "I *will*."

"Hang on," said Morgan with a start. "No, you *won't*. Are you looking for trouble, or what?"

"If my dad's sick in bed, like you say he will be," said Andry, "then that's me on my lonesome. I can't be left unattended. Who knows what might happen to me."

"Fine," said Morgan. "You can ask, he'll say no, then he'll make *me* attend to you, only to give me a grilling later on for leaving him a pair of hands short."

"Sounds like a plan," said Andry, folding her jeans and hanging them over her arm. "I better check on my dad first, though."

"Do you want me to come with you?" asked Morgan.

"No," said Andry. "You make yourself scarce. I'm going down the hall for a wash, and I don't want you peeking at me." She stepped up to him and prodded him on the shoulder. "I'll bet you've got a spyhole in the room opposite, haven't you?"

"I *don't*!" gasped Morgan, his face turning redder than ever. "Where do you come up with this stuff?"

Andry chuckled as she opened the door.

"Wait for me downstairs," she said. "Go on. Now. I'm not

leaving you in here with my things. You might go through them, and I don't know where you've been."

Morgan appeared to finally grasp that she was messing with him, and he gave a sigh.

"Don't be long," he said. "Any more than half an hour, and I'll leave without you, save myself the hassle."

Andry washed up as best as she could using the sink. Not only was there no time for her to run a bath, but she didn't like the look of the tub. There was a suspicious ring around the inside. It was probably just limescale, she had no doubt that the water in this part of the country was as hard as a rock, but images from the previous night came into her mind unbidden. What if *this* tub had also been used for grizzly purposes?

She got her jeans on and went back for her boots, finding none of her things rummaged through.

She headed down to the next floor and knocked on her dad's door.

"What?" he replied after a moment, though his voice was oddly quiet.

"It's me," she said. "I'm coming in."

"No, don't!" said her dad, but she was already inside.

He was still in bed, rolled up in the covers, his clothes scattered around the room.

"Are you alright?" asked Andry.

"No, I'm not," said her dad. "I had to dash between here and the toilet about a dozen times during the night. Somethings got its claws in me. It's that rotten beer, I'm telling you."

"Front or back?" asked Andry.

"Both," groaned her dad, "if you *must* know."

"What about breakfast?" Andry persisted. She wasn't

exactly overjoyed to see her dad in this pitiful state, but if he'd only been feeling a tad groggy, it'd jeopardise her plans with Morgan.

"I think breakfast would kill me right now," said her dad, turning onto his back with a deep but trembling breath. "Go and see if there's anything you can have downstairs."

"Morgan mentioned helping his dad with something," said Andry. "I thought I'd ask if I could go along."

"Yeah, why not," said her dad, waving a dismissive hand at her before running it down his face. "I've just got to … you know … sweat this out. I'll be fine later."

"You don't think it was what you *ate* that's made you sick, do you?" asked Andry.

"Not likely," said her dad with a feeble laugh. "I've got a belly like iron where food is concerned. I ate that surströmming muck when I was on a business trip to Stockholm, and it didn't cause me any bother. Everyone else was hurling their guts up." He tensed and gulped back a burp. "It's the beer, I'm sure of it. I'm only going near bottles or cans from now on."

"Maybe you shouldn't go near *any* booze from now on," said Andry.

"Don't be a spoil sport," said her dad. "I know where my limit is. Got to admit, though, I've not had a hangover like *this* since I was a student. I must be losing my touch."

"Okay," said Andry. "I'll come and check on you later."

"Have fun," said her dad, rolling over to face away from her. He seemed to have another thought and rolled back. "Only, be careful around Morgan's old man. He's a nice enough chap, but I think he's figured out there's something strange about us. He asks a lot of questions but doesn't give a response to the answers. That's interrogation tactics lesson one. I've seen Pat do it. If he gives you any grief, drop a subtle hint that we know he takes game without a licence. It should shut him up."

Leaving her dad to 'Sweat this out', Andry went back to her room for her jumper, then headed downstairs to find Morgan.

He was waiting in the barroom, his waxed coat already on.

"Dad's out back," he said. "If you want to ask, now's your chance."

They left the pub and found Morgan's dad loading buckets into the back of a Range Rover. People around her certainly had a penchant for them. Andry sometimes saw them in Leicester, but she'd never understood why someone who lived in a city would want one. If you were stuck in an urban traffic jam, it didn't matter how big or imposing your vehicle was, it wouldn't get you anywhere any quicker. Also, the ones she'd seen were always far too clean, meaning they were never put to their intended use. *This* one, however, was dirty almost from the top to bottom and bore the scars of years of wear and tear.

"Would you look at that," said Morgan's dad when he saw them approaching. "It's the fire girl."

He raised the corner of his top lip, which Andry guessed was about as close as he got to a smile.

"I was wondering if I could come along," she said.

"Come along where?" asked Morgan's dad.

"Wherever you're going," said Andry. "Morgan said you need help. My dad's sick in bed, and I've got nothing else to do. Maybe you can find a use for me."

"Sick in bed?" said Morgan's dad. "That's no good."

"He says he'll be fine later," said Andry.

"Ah" said Morgan's dad, "I see." He raised a hand and mimed drinking. "Too much of *this*?"

"Looks that way," said Andry.

"Sorry," said Morgan's dad with a shrug. "Two people is all that's needed. Anyway, you don't want to come scrambling through the woods with us. Your fatha' might go mad if you wreck your clothes."

"They're pretty wrecked to begin with," said Andry, gesturing down at her tatty jeans and mud caked boots, "and scrambling through the woods sounds like heaven to me."

He looked her up and down, then turned to Morgan.

"What do *you* think, Squire?" he asked.

Morgan frowned and looked away. He obviously hadn't been expecting this. His dad was clearly hinting that he should say no.

"Maybe we could do a different trail," he said, though he still didn't meet his dad's eye.

"Could we?" asked his dad. "And which different trail might *that* be?"

"The back one," said Morgan. "The *easy* one."

"So, the main trail doesn't get done today?" asked His dad. "Is that *your* judgement?"

"Look, this was my idea," said Andry, feeling that she had to come to Morgan's defence. The poor boy was all but withering under his dad's scrutiny. "I only wanted to help, but I don't want to be a bother."

"No, no, it's fine," said Morgan's dad, shutting the boot of the Range Rover. "We can do the back trail." He shot a glare at Morgan. "The *easy* trail."

As they all climbed aboard, Andry was surprised to see that Morgan got into the back with her, rather than taking pride of place next to his dad. His decision to let her come along had clearly touched some sort of nerve, a previous agreement having been broken.

"So, what are these trails?" she asked, trying to lighten the mood.

"Routes that run along this whole part of the county," said Morgan's dad as he turned the Range Rover onto the road. "We check for gaps in fences, toppled walls, fallen trees blocking the lanes. The usual."

"Is that what a gamekeeper does?" asked Andry. "I thought it'd be more like taking care of animals and stuff."

"Amongst other things," said Morgan's dad. "My coat buttons up over a great many duties. Yes, I manage the fowl over at the estate, but I also need to make sure there isn't anything in the area that might come and take them, and that there's no way for it to get in if there is."

"Like a fox?" asked Andry.

"Amongst other things," Morgan's dad repeated.

"What do you do if you see a fox?" asked Andry.

"What do you *think* I'll do?" said Morgan's dad with a snort. "We're not in a storybook, fire girl. I'm sure you reckon all animals are cute and cuddly, but they aren't. If a fox gets into an enclosure, it'll kill every bird in there, even if it only takes one."

"I've seen it happen," said Morgan, speaking up at last. "One got into Dave Lampard's chickens, and it killed all of them, including his big, black rooster. He was furious."

"Aye, and you remember who he blamed," said his dad.

"You?" asked Andry.

"That's right," said Morgan's dad, sending another glare at his son in the rear-view mirror, "but he *shouldn't* have done."

Morgan wrung his hands together and stared down into the footwell.

"Do you think we'll see a fox today?" asked Andry, unsure how she'd feel about having to watch a fox get shot, even if it *wasn't* cute and cuddly.

"I doubt it," said Morgan's dad. "This trail runs along the outskirts. They don't like to be in the open. We set snares, but they're usually empty."

Andry couldn't tell if the word 'Fox' was being used to mean something else, but she wasn't going to ask. If Morgan's dad caught even a whiff of her being in on the secret, he'd likely turn the Range Rover around and take her back, or, even worse, dump her out right here on the roadside and tell her to make her *own* way back.

They turned a bend, and the lake came into view. The water caught the morning light as it pierced through the clouds, the surface looking as though it were a shimmering sheet of fire.

"Gosh," said Andry. "Look at *that*."

"Pretty impressive, eh?" said Morgan's dad. "Worth coming all this way to see?"

"Yeah," said Andry. "I've never seen water like this before. I mean, I've been to Tenerife, and the ocean there was lovely, but it was more just blue all the time."

"Tenerife," said Morgan's dad with a tut. "Hot Blackpool, from what *I've* heard. No, you can't beat a good bit of British scenery. It stays beautiful, because we protect it. If we let the wrong people have their way, there'd be speedboats ripping up and down the water, and shoddily built hotels every hundred yards."

"What wrong people?" asked Andry. She knew this was a gamble, but she pressed ahead anyway.

"People who think they know what's best," said Morgan's dad. "People who live in big cities and think they can rule the countryside from behind a desk, never having set foot on a patch of unpaved ground in their entire lives."

"You mean, the government?" asked Andry.

"Amongst other things," said Morgan's dad.

"What about people who want to come and be *part* of all the beauty?" asked Andry. "To *share* it?"

"It's not that simple," said Morgan's dad. "There are some things which are stronger than laws, so they don't abide by them. History, heritage, the way of the land. You can't just turn up in a place and claim it as your own. Some things need to be *earned*, through toil and sacrifice."

"Is that an original?" asked Andry.

"Pardon," said Morgan's dad.

"Nothing," said Andry. "Just a joke."

She'd said this mainly to break the tension. She had a feeling that Morgan's dad was swiftly heading to the point where he'd identify these 'Wrong' people as being, 'Like *you*', and she wanted to avoid it, her gamble having backfired.

"I don't get southern humour," said Morgan's dad. "Well, apart from Tony Hancock. Now, *he* was funny." He gave a chunter which was almost a laugh. "A pint? That's very nearly an armful."

Andry was surprised. She didn't think a word like 'Funny' would be in this man's vocabulary, but at least his mood appeared to have improved.

They drove on, turning away from the lake and onto the lanes which crisscrossed between the fields. They soon began to make stops, inspecting sections of fencing, oiling the counterweight on a self-closing gate, and even coming to the aid of a stranded sheep, which had gotten its legs stuck in a cattle grid. Andry volunteered to try and guide the poor thing free, but all she got by way of thanks was a smack in the shin from one of its filthy hooves, which Morgan found incredibly amusing, until his dad shot him a disapproving look. As the sheep had trotted away, Andry saw that there was a sign dyed red onto its fleece. Even though it hadn't been one which she'd seen come out of Dennis's bag, she immediately recognised it as a rune.

They then left the Range Rover parked up in a lane and headed towards the outer edges of the woods. Morgan's dad went in front, his shotgun hanging open on his arm.

"Can *I* try carrying that?" Andry asked him.

"No, you *can't*," he replied. "Mucky clothes are one thing, but you going back with a toe shot off is another."

"I think I know better than to point it at my foot," said Andry.

"Maybe you do," said Morgan's dad, "but you're still not touching it."

"It's the first real gun I've ever seen," said Andry. "How loud is it?"

"It's pretty loud," said Morgan's dad, "but my answer's no."

"No, what?" asked Andry.

"No, I'm not shooting it off for the sake of it," said Morgan's dad.

"Oh, *please*," said Andry. "There's no-one around. You won't hit anything."

"That's not the point," said Morgan's dad. "Shells cost money."

"I could take a practice shot," said Morgan. Until now, he'd been bringing up the rear, his hands in his pockets, his head hung. Andry guessed that he was still hurting a little from his dad's earlier admonishment. "You're always saying I need to get to grips with it."

"You told me you shoot guns all the time," said Andry, turning on him. "Have you been telling fibs?"

"*His* problem is he's frightened to death of the thing," said

Morgan's dad. "If you're scared of your weapon, your hand isn't fit to wield it."

"I'm not scared," said Morgan. "I'm just not used to it yet."

"Go on, let him," said Andry. "I want to see if he's as tough as he says he is."

"Alright," said Morgan's dad, taking the gun from his arm and snapping the breech shut. "I'll let you show off and impress the girl."

Morgan took the gun, which looked ridiculous in his hands. Or, rather, *it* made *him* look ridiculous. The weapon lost none of its deadly menace now that he was holding it, but just as Bernie had told Andry, it looked as though it would do more damage to *him* than *he* would to anything else. He slid his left hand down the forend and brought the butt of the stock to his right shoulder, but his arms weren't quite long enough to do both at the same time.

"Hold it properly," said Andry as she and his dad took a step back. "You're not Elmer Fudd."

"What would *you* know?" sneered Morgan.

"Eyes front," said his dad. "Take your time. And remember, you squeeze. You don't snatch."

Morgan shouldered the gun again, getting a better grip on it this time. He shook his hair out of his eyes and focused down the length of the barrel. The fact that he was aiming directly into the distance meant that this wasn't to be a test of his accuracy, which only bolstered Andry's suspicion about his claim of shooting guns 'All the time'.

She was just about to ask whether they should be wearing some sort of ear protection, when Morgan fired. 'Pretty loud' had been an understatement. She'd assumed that she knew how a gunshot sounded, but the reality was nowhere near what she'd seen in films. Rather than a

'Bang' or a 'Kapow', it was as though someone had cracked a leather bullwhip right next to her head. A few birds were frightened from the trees as the shot rang out, the report rolling across the field for so long that Morgan was able to open the gun's breech and eject the smoking shell before the sound finally faded.

"Here you go," he said, stooping to pick up the shell. "A souvenir."

He came over to Andry and dropped it into her hand. The primer cap was still warm.

"Thanks," she said. "I can hang it on a string and wear it around my neck."

"That was a good shot, Squire," said Morgan's dad. "Your stance was better. You absorbed the recoil. If I'd known that all you needed was a young lass watching you, I'd have found one ages ago."

Andry and Morgan looked at each other and laughed, but they were silenced by a sudden, terrible screech coming from the woods. They froze, and Morgan's face fell, but his eyes stayed fixed upon Andry's. The screech came again, not as loud this time, but no less dreadful. It was an anguished wail, feral and racked with pain.

"What the bloody hell was *that*?" cried Andry, looking towards the outer trees.

Morgan's dad grabbed the gun from him, pushing him aside as he did so.

"Stay here," he said, his voice stern.

"What *was* it?" asked Andry, following him and grabbing the back of his coat.

"I said, stay here," he said, brushing her hand away. "It's a fox caught in a snare. They scream blue murder when they're trapped."

He slid a fresh shell into the gun and started towards the treeline.

Andry continued to pursue, but another shriek rang out, and she stopped. Morgan came up behind her and took her by the arm.

"We should stay," he said. "Let dad deal with it."

"There's no *way* that was a fox," said Andry.

"No," said Morgan, "it *wasn't*."

"You mean …?" Andry began, but the look on Morgan's face was all the answer she needed. She looked back towards the trees, watching Morgan's dad disappear into them. "Right. We're skipping to stage two. I want to see it."

"No!" said Morgan, tugging at her arm. "He's not supposed to know that *you* already know! You'll ruin everything!"

"As far as he's concerned," said Andry, "I *don't* already know. I'm *finding out*."

She shoved Morgan away and carried on towards the trees.

"Stop!" Morgan pleaded, jogging to catch up with her. "What do you think he'll do when you *find out*?"

"Then why risk bringing me along at all?" said Andry.

"I thought he'd say no," said Morgan. "I didn't think he'd put me on the spot like that. When I was stuck between you and him, I didn't know what to do."

Andry finally stopped and gave a deep sigh.

"You need to learn to not be such a pushover," she said. "Look, here's what we'll do. We sneak in, to see what we can see, but not far enough so that we can't run back out if we hear your dad coming. How about that?"

Before Morgan could answer, the horrible wailing started up again, three, high-pitched cries, in quick succession. Morgan winced, screwing his eyes shut and clenching his jaw.

"I hate the way they scream," he said. "It makes my skin creep."

"It sounds like it's dying," said Andry, turning back towards the treeline.

"It *will* be dead in a minute," said Morgan.

"We better hurry up, then," said Andry. "The agreement was I don't believe you until see one *alive*. A fox and a monster might look very similar, once they've been blasted at short range."

When they reached the trees, Andry paused at the first trunk and listened. There were no more screams, but she could hear something scrambling around in the leaves not far ahead of them. Going carefully forward, she found that they were at the top of an incline, and it was tricky to start down it without making too much noise. She went a few strides at a time, stopping to grab hold of a trunk or low hanging limb whenever she felt herself slipping. Morgan followed behind her, his steps slower and more deliberate.

They were about halfway down when they heard another cry. From here, Andry could make out more than just its shrillness. Once it had died down, it was followed by a throaty rasping, like someone trying to cough up something they'd accidently swallowed.

"Over there," whispered Morgan, pointing to the left.

Andry looked and saw Morgan's dad about twenty yards ahead, his back turned to them. She dropped to her haunches and pressed herself against a trunk. She could only see him from the waist up, the rest of him being obscured by a thick gorse bush, but he was looking down at something in front of him, the gun slung across his shoulder.

"We just need to get a bit closer," she said to Morgan.

"No," hissed Morgan. "This is close enough."

"But I can't see anything," said Andry.

"If he turns around," said Morgan, "he'll spot us."

Andry was about to carry on anyway, but she froze when she heard Morgan's dad speak.

"What are you doing here?" he asked.

Andry thought that he must've had eyes in the back of his head, and he's seen them, just as Morgan had warned. She tried to think of a reply, some sort of excuse for why they'd followed, but another, new voice answered the question instead.

"Ga aweg," it croaked. "Forlaet me."

It was a thin, hideous voice, nasal and rattling, but there was also a hint of wetness to it, as though it were gargling out the words through a mouthful of water.

"I'm not going anywhere," said Morgan's dad, "and neither are you. I know you understand me, so I'll ask again. What are you doing here?"

"Me hyngreth," the awful voice replied, a keening, almost begging edge to its tone. "*Hyngreth.*"

"You've come a bit far for that," said Morgan's dad. "Fancied yourself a feast, did you? Been in someone's coops again?"

"Nese," said the voice. "Ne briddas. Haran. Anlic haran."

Andry stayed frozen as she listened. It'd never occurred to her that these 'Monsters' of Morgan's would be able to speak. She was so struck by the fact that it *did* speak, as well as by the horridness of its voice, that it took her a moment to realise that she'd heard these words before, or at least something very much like them. It was the same, strange language that Dennis had sung in back at the pub.

"That'd be easier to believe," said Morgan's dad, "if you didn't have feathers around your gob."

"Sar," said the voice with a rasping cough. "Rap biteth."

"I'll bet it does," said Morgan's dad. "That's a 22-gauge wire. It'll take your head off if I yank it hard enough."

"Nese!" cried the voice. "Nese! Aliesan me!"

"Not that easy, I'm afraid," said Morgan's dad as he swung the gun around from his shoulder. "Sorry, but this is it for you."

"Nese! Nese!" the voice continued to plead as Morgan's dad aimed the gun.

Andry saw a hand rise up from behind the gorse bush. It was thin and pale, the flesh almost translucent. Also, even from this distance, she could make out the same, oil on water sheen that she'd seen on the surface of the broth and the mess in the bathtub.

Morgan's dad fired, and the hand jerked backwards, a splatter of greyish brown liquid coating the tree trunk in front of him.

Andry used the cover of the shot to make her escape, not even checking to see if Morgan was following. Once she was out of the trees, she stopped and wrapped both arms around the back of her head.

Morgan *had* followed, and he came up behind her, grabbing her jumper and pulling her towards him.

"Calm down," he whispered. "Calm *down*. He'll know you saw."

"Calm down?" Andry snapped back. "It *spoke*. You didn't say they *speak*. You said they aren't people."

"They speak the old language," said Morgan. "They understand *some* of ours, but they can't get their tongues around it."

"What did it say?" asked Andry.

"I don't know," said Morgan. "I only know a few of their words."

They heard a rustling from behind them and turned to see Morgan's dad emerging from the trees.

"What're you pair playing at now?" he asked.

"Nothing," said Morgan, letting go of Andry and stepping away from her. "Did you get it?"

"Aye, I got it," said his dad. "Big bleeder, too. A vixen. And where there's a vixen, you're bound to find pups sooner or later."

"Where's the body?" asked Andry, trying her best to compose herself, even though her mind was reeling.

"I'll leave it there for a while," said Morgan's dad. "If there're more around, it'll stop them from coming any farther than here." He broke the breech of the gun as he approached, giving Andry a puzzled stare as he ejected the shell. "What's up, fire girl? You look like you've seen a ghost."

"I'm fine," said Andry. "It's just …"

"You didn't think it'd be this *real*," Morgan's dad finished for her. "Like I told you, we're not in a storybook. When things get caught in traps, they make a noise about it. And when I find them in the traps, I deal with them. Country living isn't all sunny days and green fields. Sometimes, it's muck and blood and stink." He snapped the gun shut. "And that's *far* from an original."

"I understand," said Andry, deciding it was best to run with this. "I suppose that, when you come from a world where animals arrive already in packets, you don't think about this kind of stuff."

"That's right," said Morgan's dad. "Only, don't tell your fatha' about it. Last thing I need is him thinking I've traumatised you."

"I'm not *traumatised*," said Andry, though she wasn't sure if this was entirely true. "It was just a shock, is all."

"Well, it's over now," said Morgan's dad. "Come on. I want to take a look at that fence down there, and then we'll go back."

The drive back to the pub was quiet and felt twice as long, even though they mostly took the same roads. Morgan kept glancing at Andry, as though he were about to speak, but would then pause and look out of the window instead.

When they pulled up in front of the pub and got out of the Range Rover, Morgan's dad nodded up at the first floor.

"If your fatha' still feels a bit rough," he said, "tell him I'll ask the wife to send him up a tonic. Chamomile and primrose. It fixes most troubles, especially a stomach made bad by ale."

"Thanks," she said. "I'm sure he'd like that."

As he headed inside, Andry and Morgan stayed on the carpark, Andry pretending to have something in her boot.

"I'm guessing that's done the trick, then?" asked Morgan, stooping down next to her.

"What has?" asked Andry. "What trick?"

"You won't want to see any more," said Morgan. "You believe me now, and you definitely won't want to go to the lake-house."

"Are you joking?" said Andry. "We're going there *tonight*."

"Are *you* joking?" said Morgan. "We're not going *anywhere* at night."

"We did last night," said Andry, tightening her boot laces and standing up.

"That was different," said Morgan. He pointed from the pub to the roof of the shed. "We went from there to there. The lake-house is a half hour walk away, and it's *right* near the lake. The clue is in the name."

"I'm still not sure what I saw back there," said Andry, looking across the fields towards the woods.

"You said you heard it speak," said Morgan. "What more do you need?"

"Yeah," said Andry. "I heard *something* speak, and then I saw your dad blow it away. Where I come from, the only things that speak are people, and shooting them is called murder."

"Do you really believe that?" asked Morgan. "Or are you just trying to convince *yourself*?"

Andry took a breath, ready to make some snarky reply, but she held it.

"I don't know," she said after a moment. "That's as far as I'm willing to go right now. I don't know."

"And what could be in the lake-house to help you?" asked Morgan. "It's been empty for ages. There's nothing in there."

"I want to know what we're working with," said Andry. "I mean, is it secure? Or is there a big sign outside which says, 'Hello, monsters, come on in'? My dad *will* buy the place, and if there's ever a time when he decides that we're going to spend Christmas there or whatever, I want to know what I can do to keep any unwanted carollers away."

"You're going to *have* to tell him at some point," said Morgan.

"Yeah, right," scoffed Andry. "My dad wouldn't believe in a monster if you sat one down in front of him. He'd just think that it was *you* lot up to no good, like, dressed in costumes or something."

"He'll believe it when one has him by the throat," said Morgan.

"Funnily enough," said Andry, "no. I still don't think he would. Are they really that dangerous? The one I heard sounded pretty pitiful."

"That's because it was caught in a snare," said Morgan. "*You'd* sound pitiful with a wire around your neck and a gun pointed at you."

"So, they take people's animals," said Andry. "I get how that can be a problem, but have you ever heard of one attacking a person?"

"Not in *my* lifetime," said Morgan, "but, yeah, it's happened."

"You mean, what happened in fifty-seven?" asked Andry, remembering what she'd heard one of the men in the pub say.

"Yeah," said Morgan with a weak nod. "These two tourists, they were here on their honeymoon and went onto the lake at night. They were trying to get over to Belle Isle, and no-one saw them. The next morning, the boat was spotted about a hundred yards out, covered in blood. My dad and a few others went over to the Isle, and they found what was left of them."

"And they just didn't tell anyone?" asked Andry. "If two people go missing, someone usually comes looking for them."

"They *did* come looking," said Morgan. "Only, this was after my dad and the others had gotten rid of what was on the Isle. The police searched everywhere. They eventually chalked it up as death by misadventure and called it a day."

"So, the police were in on it," said Andry. "We've been told that they'll drag people off of the lake and bung them in a cell, but they'll overlook tampering with evidence, too?"

"Seems that way," said Morgan.

"What about the people who used to live in the lake-house?" asked Andry. "You say it might not have really been suicide?"

"As far as I know, it *was*," said Morgan. "At least, that's what everyone says. If those from the other side had taken them, I reckon people would be a bit more worried."

"Why?" asked Andry.

"Because they lived there for years," said Morgan. "It'd be a funny thing if they suddenly allowed themselves to get snatched. My dad says they had a 'Covenant' with those from the other side, but I don't know what that means, apart from it's something you don't do."

"Okay," said Andry. "Do you have weapons?"

"Weapons?" said Morgan. "What for?"

"For *protection*, stupid," said Andry. "If we're going somewhere where there might be more of these things, then we're gonna want to be tooled up, aren't we?"

"Is there nothing I can say to talk you out of this?" asked Morgan.

"No," said Andry. "If you don't come, I'll go alone, and it'll be *your* fault if anything happens to me."

"What if something happens to *both* of us?" asked Morgan. "Whose fault will *that* be?"

"Mine, I suppose," said Andry with a shrug. "If it comes to it, I'll let you call me every rude name under the sun and slap me a good one across the face before we die."

"You shouldn't make jokes like that," said Morgan, crossing his arms. "And I can't get the gun, if that's what you're asking."

"I wouldn't trust you with it," said Andry. "If I stepped on a twig, you'd probably jump and shoot *me*. Just see what you can come up with."

She patted him on the shoulder and headed towards the door.

"Where are you going now?" Morgan called after her.

"To check on my dad," said Andry. "I'll find you later. I'm sure you've got some sheets to fold."

Chapter Five

HER DAD HADN'T gotten any worse, but he hadn't gotten a great deal better. He was still in bed, moaning as though he had the black plague, and almost bit Andry's head off when she tried opening the curtains.

He refused the chamomile and primrose tonic, saying that, if this was the state the local beer left him in, he dreaded to think what the local remedies would do.

"I said I'd call Pat again today," he groaned from within the quilt, "but I don't want him finding out that I've taken ill. He'll just say, 'I told you so. You never should've gone near the place'. Can *you* speak to him for me? Tell him I'm busy or something?"

"*I'm* not talking to him," said Andry as she sat down at the foot of the bed. "I hate the guy. You know I do. What could I possibly have to say to him?"

"You tell him we're having a fantastic time," said her dad, "the lake property is a veritable palace, and we're winning the incredibly friendly natives over one by one."

"He'll know I'm lying," said Andry.

"Well, tell him the truth, then," said her dad, rolling over onto his back with a laboured breath. "You're having a terrible time, the property's a hellhole, and everyone here is out to get us. Just make sure to pick some nice flowers when you've finished helping to dig my professional grave."

"Don't be so dramatic," said Andry, nudging him with her knee. "I'll use my charm to bend the truth. What's the number?"

"You can call him from here," said her dad. "I want to listen in."

"Oh, no, you won't," said Andry. "If I have to speak to him, I'm doing it privately."

"You've got a phone in your room?" asked her dad.

"I have," said Andry. "All mod cons here. Not very authentic, though."

"Typical," huffed her dad. "And there *I* was, forking out for the fancier rooms."

She grabbed a business card from his wallet and headed up to her own room.

It took her a little while to figure out how to get an outside line. She'd never been much good with phones, which called her dad's previous notion of her becoming a receptionist into question, but she eventually managed to get through to Pat.

"Martin?" he asked, answering after only two rings.

"Nope," said Andry. "It's the other one."

"Ah, Audrey," said Pat. "Lovely to hear from you."

"It's *Andry*," she growled.

"That's what I said," said Pat. "Anyway, how's tricks?"

"Not too bad," said Andry. "My dad asked me to call and let you know how we're doing. He's busy right now, but he didn't want you to get worried."

"Really?" said Pat. "What's he busy with?"

"This and that," said Andry. "He's, you know, *talking* to people."

"That doesn't sound like him," said Pat. "He decrees, he condescends, he obfuscates, he talks *at* people, but he rarely talks *to* them."

Andry should've known that this was a bad idea. She was less than thirty seconds into the conversation, and she already wanted to hang up.

"Whatever he's doing," she said, thankful that Pat couldn't

see the face she was pulling, "it seems to be going well."

"Have you seen the property yet?" asked Pat.

"I have," said Andry. "We drove by it yesterday."

"What do you think?" asked Pat, his tone suggesting that he already knew the answer.

"It needs a bit of doing up," said Andry. "I'm sure that, after some care, it'll be lovely."

"Right," said Pat. "So, either you *haven't* seen it, which means you're fibbing, or you *have* seen it, and you're still fibbing."

Andry didn't need to be able to see him to know what face *he* was probably pulling.

"What're you getting at?" she asked.

"I've seen photos of the place," said Pat with a snigger. "They were taken in sixty-eight, and it already looked like it was about to fall over. It doesn't just need care. It needs *intensive* care. *Palliative*, some might say."

"If it's that bad," said Andry, "why are you letting my dad go through with all this?"

"So that he learns," said Pat. "You've got to let people make some mistakes, so they realise where their strengths are. He'll never try anything like this again."

"Wait a minute," said Andry, moving the phone to her other ear, as though this would give her some sort of edge. "What're you hiding?"

"Hiding?" said Pat. "I'm not hiding anything. You want to see the stuff I've been *revealing*."

"Like what?" asked Andry.

"Like the fact that this listed building rubbish has nothing to do with the actual property itself," said Pat. "I'll let you see the documents when you get back. Nice bit of light reading, before you go off to Rossall. We get the sale done, your dad's happy, and we can go back to some proper business. I'm going to make your dad a *very* wealthy man, Audrey. You should thank me. When he inevitably loses interest in the place, he can sign the deed over to me, and *I'll* take care of it for you. There's no point in you having to fill your head with legal worries so early in your life."

"Does my dad know about this?" asked Andry.

"Not yet," said Pat. "But it's a good idea, right?"

"You want it for *yourself*, don't you?" said Andry, beginning to see through his wordplay

"Hey, steady on," said Pat. "You shouldn't make accusations like that."

"I just did," said Andry. "It'll never work. My dad says he's going to wrap the place up in barbed wire, to keep people's hands off."

"Yes," said Pat, "and who do you think he'll get to cosign the paperwork that does the wrapping? Your mum? I don't think so."

"He'll kill you if I tell him what you're scheming," said Andry.

"I doubt it," said Pat. "He won't believe a word you say."

"You smarmy git!" snapped Andry. "He trusts me more than *you*!"

"Yeah, keep telling yourself that, honey bunch," said Pat.

"Did you know that the people who used to live in the lake-house killed themselves?" asked Andry, trying her hardest to contain her anger. She could tell that Pat was having a whale of time getting to talk to her like this, but she wasn't going to give him the satisfaction of slamming the phone down.

"Not that it's anything to do with you," he said, "but, yes, I've heard something similar. What's the matter? Scared of ghosts?"

"Isn't that the kind of thing you should know *before* buying somewhere?" asked Andry.

"I don't see why," said Pat. "Does your dad know you've been snooping?"

"Oi," said Andry, "this little chat is confidential."

"Ooh, big word," said Pat. "Tell me, how did *you* find out how they died?"

"I have my ways," said Andry.

"I assume it was from this lad you've been mooning over," said Pat. "Your dad mentioned him. Scruffy looking oik, he says. Honestly, Audrey, skinheads and rude-boys are bad enough, but you want to stay away from rough, country youths. You don't know what you might catch."

Andry wanted to say, 'You'll catch my fist with your face in a minute!', but what would be the point?

"It's nothing like that," she said. "We don't *all* have our minds in the gutter."

"Damn, you're nasty when you get going," said Pat with a chuckle. "Look, as much as I'm enjoying this *little chat*, do you have anything important to tell me, or are we just going to sit here and spit nails at each other?"

"I'm not telling you anything," said Andry.

"So, you do have *something* to tell me," said Pat, "but you're not going to tell it. *Now* who's hiding things? I'll hear it all from your dad anyway, so you might as well spill it."

"You wouldn't believe a word I say," said Andry and set the phone down, making sure that it wasn't anything that could be taken as a slam. This done, she hopped away from the phone, pointed at it, her finger like a fixed bayonet, and proceeded to yell out every single swearword she could think of.

There wasn't a lot that Pat could directly do from back in Manchester, but he could easily speak poisonous words into her dad's ear and blow any plan that she might have. She also didn't know if Pat had been right about her dad trusting him more than her. Their paths had never crossed like this before, so her dad's trust had never been tested. She'd like to have thought that blood was thicker than water, but whether blood was thicker than money was another matter entirely.

The bombshell of Pat having designs on the lake-house deeds had also come as a tremendous shock. There was no way she was going to let *that* happen. Pat would probably sell off timeshares on the place to a string of hapless, unsuspecting people, and she could only imagine what the outcome would be.

She had to decide if going to her dad and revealing Pat's plan was the right move. At the moment, it didn't feel like it. If her dad were to confront Pat, he'd just counter with something along the lines of, 'I said no such thing', or, more likely, 'She's twisting my words', and that was only if her dad believed her in the first place. He probably wouldn't be willing to disturb the waters of a hitherto prosperous working relationship, just because his wayward daughter had taken offence at a bit of 'Teasing', as Pat would definitely call it.

She needed to think, to figure out exactly what she was hoping to achieve. If Morgan was right, and living in the lake-house was dangerous, she needed to come up with a way to make sure that no harm befell anyone. She had absolutely no idea how she was going to do this, but getting a look inside the lake-house was the next step.

After giving her dad a sanitised version of her conversation with Pat, she went down to the barroom. Morgan's mum, Carol, was mopping the floor, the stinging scent of bleach permeating the entire room as she slopped foaming water onto the tiles.

"Watch the cuffs of your trousers, love," she said when she noticed Andry. "They'll get stained."

"Bleached jeans are actually quite fashionable back home," said Andry. "Maybe not just the bottoms, though. Is Morgan in his room?"

"You two have gotten close," chuckled Carol, leaning on the stave of the mop. "Took you to the old stone, I'm told, *and* a trip out in the Rover. That's more than he's ever done with a guest until now."

"I kind of didn't give him a choice," said Andry. "I've found that you have to assert yourself with some boys."

"True, true," said Carol with a nod. "Anyway, no, he's not here. I sent him over to Dave Lampard's for eggs. If you get a shift on, you might be able to catch him."

"Which way is it?" asked Andry. "I've heard of this Dave Lampard, but I don't know where he lives. I wouldn't want to miss Morgan and get lost."

"You come out of here," said Carol, "second lane on the right, and it's a straight line to Dave's place. It's the only house up there, so you can't really get lost.

"Sounds easy enough," said Andry. "Hopefully, I'll meet Morgan on the way. I'm also liking the idea of eggs right now."

"Good ones, Dave's are," said Carol. "Brown double-yolkers, big as your fist, which is why he charges a bleedin' fortune for them."

"Does he only keep chickens?" asked Andry. "Or does he have other animals?"

"Chickens mostly," said Carol, "but he has a small flock of sheep." She gave a titter. "I hear you've already met one of his ewes."

"Have I already met *him*?" asked Andry. "Was he here last night?"

"Oh, no," said Carol. "Dave never comes for the share. He says it's beneath him."

Andry made to leave, but she stopped before she reached the door.

"If I *don't* meet Morgan," she said, "and he gets back here without me, can you ask him to come and look for me?"

"I can," said Carol. "He might not be pleased, though. Can't abide too much trekking, that boy, which is why I was surprised that he'd taken you all the way to the old stone *and* back. His legs must've been like lengths of yarn."

Andry left the pub and started along the road. The second lane led alongside the same field where she and Morgan had traversed the stone wall, but it soon took a bend and joined another path which went up a slight hill. There was no sign of Morgan, meaning he'd either set off shortly after they'd arrived back at the pub, or he wasn't as averse to trekking as his mum believed.

She wondered why he hadn't waited and suggested that they go together, but perhaps he needed a break from her. Just as she'd said to his mum, she *had* been asserting herself rather a lot. She considered heading back. If Morgan wanted some time away from her, then chasing after him everywhere he went might not be the best idea. She'd probably get sick of herself before long if their places were reversed. However, she'd already come this far, and she wanted to meet this famous Dave Lambard fellow. From what she'd heard of him, he sounded like a pain in the backside, but she was interested in meeting someone who was a respected member of the community, if 'Respected' was the right word, but who hadn't been present for the illustrious 'Share'.

When she got to the top of hill, she looked back over the landscape. From here, she could just about make out the lake-house, the upper parts of the roof and the panes of the conservatory visible through the trees, though she could now see the surrounding gardens quite clearly from this vantage point. She thought about how she and Morgan would be able to get in. It looked as though the wall went all the way around the grounds, and no doubt the gate would be locked. The only area which wasn't walled off was a sloping lawn which ended at the shore of the lake, where she could see part of a wooden jetty. Perhaps they'd be able to get around the wall at the point where it met the water. Either that, or ladders would have to be involved, and she couldn't imagine Morgan being up for climbing ladders.

She carried on along the lane, the land flattening out again now she was at the top, and she soon saw a house not far ahead. It was whitewashed all over, with a thatched roof and a low barn at the side of it. As she got closer, she began to hear the tell-tale sound of chickens coming from the barn, meaning it was actually a henhouse. A car was parked up next to it, and she was surprised to see that it *wasn't* a Range Rover. Instead, it was a snappy looking Morris Minor in British racing green, certainly not what she'd associate with chickens and sheep.

Wanting to get a better look at it, she walked along the drystone wall bordering the property and was able to get almost right up to the front of the barn. Her attention was quickly taken away from the car when she saw the barn doors. All across the panels, running from top to bottom, were what appeared to be hundreds of runes, daubed in what was probably the same whitewash that covered the house. Some of them looked fresh, while others had clearly been put there a long time ago. Far from being merely graffiti or haphazard scrawls, each of them had been painted with evident care and attention, their sizes uniform, their angles perfect. The whole front of the barn looked like the pages of an enormous book, only Andry had no idea in what order or which direction they were supposed to be read, if such things even applied to runes.

"Can I help you?" a voice rang out from behind her, causing her to jump.

She turned and saw that a man had appeared from behind the house. He wore the same kind of waxed coat as Morgan and his dad and was standing with his hands thrust deep into the pockets, rocking back and forth on his heels.

"Oh, sorry," said Andry, stepping away from the wall.

"Sorry?" said the man. "Why? What've you done?"

"Mister Lampard?" asked Andry.

"Aye," the man replied, "but Dave will do. Who might *you* be?"

"I'm Andry," she said. "I'm a friend of Morgan's. Is he here?"

"He *was*," Dave replied.

"But he isn't anymore?" asked Andry.

"Nope," said Dave, stopping his rocking with a crunch of his toes on the gravel path.

"Okay," said Andry. "Do you know which way he went?"

"Nope," Dave said again. "So, *who* might you be?"

"I already said," said Andry, starting to wonder whether Dave was, apart from being a pain in the backside, not entirely all there. "My names Andry. I'm staying at the pub with my dad."

"Ah, you're the *southern* chap's girl," said Dave. "Aye, Lewis told me about you. Sweet on his lad, eh?"

"I am *not*," said Andry.

"Really?" said Dave, giving her a sly grin. "You came all

this way looking for him." He sucked his teeth and walked towards her. "You're barking up the wrong tree, love. That boy's been raised doing too much woman's work, and he's turned out queer."

"What?" said Andry, a pang of anger sparking up within her. "Don't be daft. That's not how it works. You don't *turn* queer from doing a job. You either are, or you aren't."

"Says *you*," said Dave. "My uncle spent twenty years grafting at the Honister slate mine, after he came back from the war." He raised a hand to his head and twisted a finger into his temple. "Turned *him* queer as anything."

"Oh," said Andry, her thunder vanishing as quickly as it had arisen. "You mean, crazy."

"Aye," said Dave. "Why? What did you *think* I meant?"

"Never mind," said Andry, turning back to face the barn. "What's all this?"

"Protection," said Dave, coming to stand beside her. "Nothing gets through *that* lot."

"Why so many?" asked Andry. "The guest rooms at the pub only have one each."

"They only *need* one," said Dave. "One is enough for a bedroom, but I've got my livelihood in there." He nodded at the barn doors. "You know about this stuff, do you?"

"A little," said Andry. "This guy, Dennis, has been telling me about it."

"Dennis?" scoffed Dave. "That lump doesn't know what he's talking about. He casts the runes around like he's playing marbles, and he's got everyone convinced that he's a shaman or something, the silly sod."

"Do they work?" asked Andry. "Do they keep things away from the hens?"

"Not curious southern girls, it'd appear," said Dave.

"Actually, it was the car that caught my eye," said Andry. "Do you park it here, so it gets protected as well?"

"I'm not worried about anyone trying to nick the car," said Dave. "I park it here, so the doors won't open fully. The runes do their bit, but nigh on two thousand pounds of metal comes in handy, too."

"Morgan says something got in once," said Andry. "When was that?"

"Last year," said Dave, frowning at the thought. "The whole brood, gone! I had to start again from scratch. The idiot boy didn't lay down traps right. I keep telling his fatha' that we need more fences. Big fences. Those new, electric ones that you can make as long as you want."

"I'm sure he tried his best," said Andry.

"Well, he's going to have to try a lot harder than that," said Dave. He pointed down the lane. "You see there?" Andry followed his finger and saw that he was pointing towards the lake-house. "*That's* where they get through. I don't know exactly how, but there's a weak spot, I'm certain of it."

"Why not go and fix it for yourself?" asked Andry.

"You wouldn't catch me *dead* in there," said Dave with a chuckle. "There's a darkness to that place, and it's gotten worse since Tom and Beryl went. I can practically smell it from here. It's *everywhere*."

"You knew them?" asked Andry. "The people who lived there?"

"Of course I knew them," said Dave. "Everyone did. I used to chum around with Tom back when we were younger than *you*. That was when his fatha' looked after the place. Now, *he* knew what he was doing. We could go whole winters without a stitch of trouble."

"What did he do differently?" asked Andry.

"*He* fought in the *first* war," said Dave. "Proper nasty stuff. Nose to nose with the Hun in Flanders. You stick a trench spike into a man's face, and it prepares you for certain things."

"Like dealing with foxes?" asked Andry.

"We both know we're not talking about foxes," said Dave.

"Do we?" asked Andry.

"Aye," said Dave. "I saw it in your eyes when you said 'Something' had gotten into the henhouse. How much has Morgan told you?"

"Nothing," said Andry. "I mean … I don't know what you're talking about."

"You mutter and stutter a lot," said Dave, starting back up with his rocking, "for someone who's been told nothing."

"Why don't you take part in the shares?" asked Andry, wanting to simply derail the conversation as much as to hear the answer.

"I won't mix my blood with theirs," said Dave. "Everything has a price in the end. And I won't feed it to my fowl, either. You feed it to a hen, and it gets into the eggs. You hatch the eggs, and it starts all over again. It's like mercury, you can't get rid of it."

"Is it dangerous?" asked Andry.

"It can be," said Dave. "Why? *You* haven't eaten any, have you?"

"No," said Andry. "I was offered some, but I didn't like the look of it."

"Smart girl," said Dave. "You should always trust your instincts."

"Morgan says it gets sprayed onto the crops," said Andry. "Does that mean it's in those, too?"

"Small amounts, yes," said Dave. "Not enough to have an effect on someone, but it's in there."

"My dad ate some," said Andry. "I know we weren't supposed to be allowed any, but he paid this other guy. It was just a little bit, only it made him sick. Will he be okay?"

"Shouldn't do too much harm," said Dave. "Don't let him have any more, though. Once you start, it gets a hold on you."

"Why are you being so open?" asked Andry. "So far, it's been this massive secret. I pretty much had to threaten to *beat* it out of Morgan."

"Actually," said Dave, "this is me being tight-lipped. Besides, no-one listens to me. I could walk up and down the lakefront, with a sandwich board around my neck, screaming at tourists about those from the other side, and the rest of the locals wouldn't bat an eye. They'd just say, 'Oh, that's mad Lampard from up on the hill. Don't pay him any mind'. Either way, by the sound of it, I haven't told you much that you didn't already know. It's Morgan who wants to worry about being 'Open', threats of a beating or not."

"We've got a kind of pact of silence," said Andry, "which I guess I've now broken. You won't drop him in it with his dad, will you?"

"You can trust me," said Dave with a nod. "You've ended up with more than you bargained for, eh? The last thing I want to do is cause you more bother. I'll give you a bit of advice, though. You can't trust Morgan's fatha' like you can me, and you definitely can't trust Dennis. People can disappear around here, and it's folks like them who do the disappearing."

"Yeah," said Andry, "I've heard about that. The honeymooners."

"And the rest," said Dave. "*They* were just the ones who people came looking for. Make sure that you leave here safe, and no-one has to come looking for *you*. Go home and forget what you've learned. You don't want this sort of thing eating at your soul."

This was the point where Andry was done with being 'Open'. Despite what he claimed, she wasn't sure if she could trust Dave, and an admission of her dad being the one looking to buy the lake-house could turn 'Mad' Lampard into 'Very honest and believable' Lampard when he went running to Dirty Harry with the news.

"Everyone back at home would say I'm making it up," she said.

"That's what keeps these kinds of things in check," said Dave. "There've been plenty who grew up here and moved away, but we've never found ourselves inundated with people looking for those from the other side. You know why?" Andry shook her head. "Because there's no proof. We make *sure* there isn't any."

"I've seen one," said Andry. "I mean, I saw its arm, and I heard it speak, and Morgan showed me what he said was a dead one."

"Really?" said Dave, leaning towards her. "Prove it."

"I …," said Andry. "Well, I can't."

"Exactly," said Dave, straightening back up. "Prove *anything* that we've been talking about. Lack of evidence can sometimes be the greatest ally of the truth." He turned on his heels and started towards the house, waving for Andry to follow him. "Come on. I've got something for you."

Andry went after him, wondering what he could possibly have to give to her. Some sort of protection, perhaps? A charm, or a magic wand? A specially drawn up scroll of runes, delved from his knowledge of the arcane? No. In fact, quite the opposite. They went through the side door and into the kitchen, where Dave produced a jar of pickle. She instantly recognised the handwriting on the label.

"Oh," she said. "Thanks."

"Carol mentioned that your fatha' wanted more," said Dave. "I should've given it to Morgan when he was here, but I only remembered about it when you turned up yourself. Lucky, eh?"

"You say you don't know which way Morgan went?" asked Andry. "I thought I'd have met him on the lane."

"He must've gone another way," said Dave. "If you go around the back of the henhouse, there's a path that leads towards the old church. Don't know why he'd want to go there, though."

"To get away from *me*," said Andry with a half-smile as she passed the jar from hand to hand. "Maybe I should leave him to himself."

"Nah, go after him," said Dave. "He should get used to people giving him grief. He'll have enough of it when his old man isn't around anymore."

"Okay," said Andry. "I'll see if I can find him." She held up the jar. "Thanks for this, and thanks for the … you know, the talk."

"Think nothing of it," said Dave. "Do as I say, mind. Stay away from any trouble, and keep your eyes peeled for it. You've picked the *wrong* time to be visiting."

She went behind the henhouse and found the path. She could already see the spire of the church from here, and it didn't look like it'd take her long to get there, especially now that she'd be going downhill. She just had to hope that Morgan's hiking skills were as bad as his mum had said, and she'd be able to catch up with him. He hadn't put up too much of a complaint during their trip to the old stone, but that had been a walk to somewhere he'd *wanted* to get to. If he wasn't overly keen on getting back to the pub, then he'd be dragging his feet.

The path was bordered by thick hawthorn hedges, and she was forced to pick from several new paths which branched off from it. She kept her eye on the church spire to keep her bearings, but she ended up having to walk away from it for long stretches after a straight section of path took a turn or came to a dead-end.

It was while she was taking one of these detours that she became aware of voices up ahead of her. She was at a point where her only choices were to go straight on or turn back, so she decided to just stand there and wait, thinking that whoever it was might take another path and wouldn't even know she'd been there.

The voices grew steadily louder and closer, seeming to be right around the bend in front of her. She didn't much fancy trying to push through one of the hedges, they had thorns on them like knitting needles, and she wouldn't be able to retreat without being spotted, so it looked as though a crossing of paths was inevitable.

Two kids, a boy and a girl, both maybe a little older than her, appeared around the bend. Andry was relieved but also oddly shocked. It was almost as though she'd convinced herself that other kids, at least other than Morgan, didn't even exist in this place. The pair looked very alike. Perhaps not twins, but definitely siblings.

"Hang on," said the boy when he saw Andry, holding an arm out sideways to stop his sister. "Who's this?"

Andry saw that he was carrying a box under his other arm. This wouldn't have caught her attention, had she not noticed a few small, downy feathers poking out from one of the seams.

"That's just what *I* was thinking," she said.

"Where did *you* come from?" asked the girl, pushing her brother's arm down.

"From up there," said Andry, nodding over her shoulder. "I'm trying to get to the church. Am I going the right way?"

"For what?" asked the boy.

"To *get* to the church," said Andry. "You got wool in your ears?"

The boy screwed his face up and looked ready to fire back, but his sister stepped in before he could.

"Are you a tourist?" she asked.

"That's right," said Andry. "Tourist, noun, a person who likes to visit places. Old churches, for example."

"All by yourself?" asked the girl.

"At the moment, yes," said Andry. "I was supposed to have a guide, but he's gotten away from me. Maybe you've seen him. Small guy, silly hair, answers to Morgan."

"Aye, we've seen him," said the boy, but his sister hissed at him and punched him on the arm. "Ow! I mean, no, we've *not* seen him."

"Okay," said Andry. "What's in the box?"

"Nothing," said the boy, clutching the box to his chest.

"Pretty big box to keep nothing in," said Andry. "How many nothings have you got in there? I'll hazard a guess at a dozen?"

"What's your game?" asked the girl, moving in front of her brother.

"No game," said Andry. "I'm just thinking that those aren't *your* nothings, and you should give them to *me*, so I can return them to their rightful owner."

"And what if we don't?" asked the girl, setting her hands on her hips and sticking her chin out.

"Well, I suppose I'll just have to *take* them, won't I?" said Andry.

While they'd been talking, each exchange closing the gap between them, Andry had been passing the pickle jar from hand to hand. She held it behind her back and took a step forward.

"You stop right there!" snapped the girl. "One wrong move, and I'll paste you!"

"Leave off, Fay," said her brother. "You can't fight with tourists."

"She's not a proper tourist," said the girl. "Look how she's dressed."

"Charming," said Andry with a chuckle. "But guess what."

"What?" said the girl.

"Think fast, bum-bag!" yelled Andry and threw the jar at her.

She could have aimed directly at her head and knocked her out, but she was throwing to distract, rather than to wound. The jar struck the girl in the chest, and she gave a shrill cry, her arms flailing as she simultaneously tried to catch the jar *and* bat it away.

Andry swiftly advanced on her brother, who took several, faltering steps backwards, the box still held to his chest. As she backed him up against one of the hedges, his face broke out in pure terror.

"If you hit me," he squeaked, "I'll scream."

"I'd be disappointed if you didn't," said Andry. She then stamped on his foot.

She didn't think her dad's 'Martin Watt original' was ever meant to be played out so literally, but it certainly worked.

The boy gave a peeling wail, dropped the box, and it hit the ground with a wet crunch. Andry snatched it up and sped off along the path, the box's sticky contents running down her arm.

When she was sure she wasn't being pursued, she slowed down and tried to catch her breath. She opened the box. Just as she'd guessed, it was full of eggs packed in straw. Three had broken, and she saw that Morgan's mum hadn't been exaggerating. They all looked to have been double-yolkers, much of which was now smeared across the front of her jumper.

She looked around, trying to find the church spire. Spotting it, she realised she'd come completely the wrong way, but it wasn't as though she could go back. Instead, she carried on in the same direction, hoping that she'd find a road or lane eventually.

She was now more eager than ever to find Morgan. Yes, she'd retrieved the eggs, but what was to stop the diabolical duo she'd just encountered from hot footing it back to where they'd seen Morgan, then adding injury to insult by giving him a kicking over the loss?

As she walked on, she picked the broken shells out of the box and flicked them into the bushes, trying to make the remaining eggs look more presentable. Morgan would have to come up with his own story of how some had been broken, as she was going to have a hard enough time thinking of an explanation if the case of the missing pickle was raised. She wasn't too troubled by the idea of the thieving siblings snitching on her. Why would they be so quick to admit that they'd had their backsides handed to them by a badly dressed tourist girl? Even if they did, Andry knew she could turn the tables on them if Morgan could be persuaded into her corner. She didn't know an awful lot about rural folk, but she assumed they treated thieves in a much harsher and more straightforward way than folks back in Leicester, and in Leicester, people with light fingers were dealt with very harshly indeed.

The path took her around another bend, and she finally spotted something church-like. The hawthorns changed to wide yew trees, their gnarled and twisted trunks almost alien looking, between which she saw a row of gravestones. There was no wall or fence, but a strange, covered entryway stood a few yards ahead of her. There must have been a border to the graveyard at some point in the past, but this was all that remained of it. She carried on towards it, thinking that, for some reason she couldn't quite explain, it would be improper to just make a B-line for the stones.

A gate hung open beneath the entryway, only further highlighting its uselessness, but what struck Andry was what good condition it was it. There was no graffiti, no cigarette ends, no discarded cans or bottles, these being hallmarks of the few churchyards she was familiar with back home. Instead, it appeared to be treated with a great deal of respect, the posts which held up the covering looking to have been recently coated with a dark wood stain, their faces carved with intricate, Celtic style knots.

She passed under it and wandered among the first few rows of stones. They were all very old, some not even legible, and stuck out from the ground at odd angles.

"Pretty spooky," she said, addressing the occupants of the graves, "but you're nowhere *near* the scariest thing I've seen so far. Sorry." She moved on to the next row. These were much easier to read. "Elizabeth Hines," she said, leaning forward to make out an inscription. "Aged 14. Damn. Sucked to be *you*, darling." She moved to the next stone. "Peter Bainbridge.

Ooh, *and* his wife. Hope you're not up to anything raunchy down there, you two. Okay. Who's next?"

"You shouldn't do that."

The sudden voice gave Andry such a shock that she almost dropped the egg box.

It was Morgan, leaning against the trunk of a yew tree, his hands in his pockets.

"*There* you are," said Andry, trying to fight back the jangle in her nerves. "I've been looking everywhere. Don't you know it's rude to sneak up on people?"

"I didn't sneak up," said Morgan, walking over to her. "You were just too busy messing around. Like I say, you shouldn't do that."

"Do what?" asked Andry,

"Make fun of the dead," said Morgan.

"I wasn't making fun," said Andry, walking through the stones towards him. "I'll bet no-one takes the time to talk to them anymore." She offered him the box. "I got your eggs back, by the way."

"You did?" said Morgan. "Gosh, thanks."

As he took them, Andry noticed that the knuckles on his right hand were grazed.

"Hang on," she said. "Look at me."

She placed a finger under his chin, forcing him to raise his head. A pallid yellow bruise ran along his left cheekbone, and his eyes were red and puffy.

"I didn't just *hand* them over," he said, brushing her away. "I tried taking your advice."

"What advice?" asked Andry.

"To not be such a pushover," said Morgan. "It didn't work, but at least I tried."

"I never told you to get yourself beaten up over a few eggs," said Andry.

"They didn't beat me up," said Morgan with a frown. "I gave as good as I got."

"When I had the pleasure of meeting the pair," said Andry, "they didn't look like they'd been *given* anything."

"Whatever," said Morgan. "I don't understand people like them. What do they want with stupid eggs anyway?"

"I'm guessing you don't have any money on you," said Andry.

"Of course I don't," said Morgan. "I've hardly *ever* got any money on me. Those two know that."

"Exactly," said Andry. "The eggs were all you had to take. *You* might not understand people like them, but *I* do. It's not about the eggs. It's about the fact that they *took* them from you."

"And I needed you to get them back for me," said Morgan with a tut. "A girl. A *tourist* girl. I'm sure that'll be the talk of the yard when school starts again."

"I don't think they'll be too chatty," said Andry. "If they are, just remind them that I gave *better* than I got."

"Did you beat *them* up?" asked Morgan with a gasp.

"I wouldn't call it that," said Andry, laughing and tipping him a wink. "I got the eggs back, though, didn't I? Seriously, mate, I can handle myself, but I'm not a yobbo, even if I *am* dressed like one."

"Including egg," said Morgan, pointing at the smear across her jumper. He opened the box. "Oh, no. Three missing."

"They didn't just *hand* them over," said Andry. "Also, I'm now down a jar of pickle, so that makes us even."

"Pickle?" said Morgan. "You went to Dave Lampard's place?"

"I did," said Andry. "I was looking for *you*. He seems like a nice enough chap. I don't see why everyone says he's mad."

"Mad people don't always *act* mad," said Morgan.

"From what he told me," said Andry, "he's the only person around here who acts normally. Well, apart from his big, rune mural thingy. Which reminds me, he says there's something strange going on at the lake-house. As in, a weak spot, where the …" She trailed off. "The 'You know what' get through."

"I had a feeling you'd come back to that," said Morgan.

"Do you think he's right?" asked Andry.

"If he *is*," said Morgan, "then we don't want to go there, do we?"

"Oh, we're still going," said Andry. "Now more than ever. Look at it like this. If there's a weak spot, what if we can think of a way to plug it up?"

"If there's a weak spot," said Morgan, rolling his eyes at her, "it would've been plugged up years ago. Remember who you're talking to."

"Yeah," said Andry. "Dave told me that it *was*. The people who used to live in the lake-house. He says there'd be whole winters without any trouble."

"That was ages ago," said Morgan. "Things have changed since then."

"Well, duh!" said Andry. "Haven't you thought about *why* they've changed? If there's something going on at the lake-house, or something that *isn't* going on anymore, something that could *help*, then we need to go and find out what it is, instead of shying away from the place like it's an entrance to Hell or whatever."

"And what if you're wrong?" asked Morgan. "What if we go there, and there's a whole bunch of 'You know what', all having moved in now the place is empty?"

"Then we run away," said Andry. "Honestly, one sniff of

something I don't like, and we're out of there. Does *that* make you feel any better?"

"No," said Morgan. "It makes me feel like an idiot for getting you interested in all of this to begin with."

"Fair enough," said Andry. "Only, how much of an idiot would you feel if me and my dad moved into the lake-house and got nailed by a bunch of 'You know what' on the first night? I bet you'd wish you'd gotten me interested *then*."

"I suppose so," said Morgan with a shrug.

"You *suppose* so?" said Andry. "I thought you were starting to like me."

"I am," said Morgan. "I mean, I *do*. It's just … look, you need to understand something. Like I told you, the lake-house is a Wyrd place, and that doesn't mean it *only* has something to do with those from the other side. There might be something else, something that could cause more problems than we solve."

"Well, I'm the Wyrd *girl*," said Andry. "Dennis asked me to pull a rune out of his bag, and I got it first time. Who better to check out a Wyrd place?"

"Pulling a rune out of a bag doesn't put you on the right side of the Wyrd," said Morgan. "If anything, you should've taken it as a warning."

"It seems to be working out for me so far," said Andry. "I'm finding clues wherever I turn, and that's not one of my usual talents."

"Yeah," said Morgan. "You're finding them a bit *too* easily."

"I put it down to luck," said Andry.

"Luck and the Wyrd go hand in hand," said Morgan, "until it decides to bite you. If you flip a coin twice, and get heads both times, it's the Wyrd that tells you, 'Flip it again. How could you possibly lose?'. If you stand on the edge of a cliff, it's the Wyrd that says, 'Jump. How do *you* know you can't fly?'"

"I think I know better than to listen to something like that," said Andry.

"You clearly don't," said Morgan. "If the Wyrd has its hold on you, you go deaf to everything else. You won't even listen to *me*, your *occasional* best friend."

"I'm perfectly fine," said Andry, stepping forward and setting her hands on his shoulders. "Look at my eyes. Do you see any Wyrdness in there?"

Morgan peered into her eyes and squinted, checking each one in turn.

"No," he said. "They're mucky green as ever."

"You're *meant* to say they're like shining emeralds," said Andry, letting go of his shoulders and rapping a knuckle on his forehead, "but at least you got the colour right. Been stealing glances, have you?"

"I noticed them," said Morgan, ruffling his fringe.

"God, you're such a charmer," said Andry with a tut. "Good thing I'm *not* sweet on you, like everyone else seems to think. I wouldn't stand a chance. You're about as romantic as a kick in the teeth."

"*Who* says you're sweet on me?" asked Morgan, appearing genuinely shocked.

"*My* dad, *your* dad," said Andry. "It's stupid. You stand a boy and girl next to each other, and everyone thinks they're an item."

"Don't you have a boyfriend back in Leicester?" asked Morgan.

"Do I heckers," said Andry with a laugh. "Friends who are boys, yes, but that's as far as it goes. If you met any of them, you'd see why. The closest I'd get to being wined and dined is a can of lager, a bag of chips and a sniff of glue."

"Glue?" asked Morgan.

"Something you should be glad you don't know about," said Andry. "Come on. Let's not hang around here. People might think we're queer."

"I'm in no rush," said Morgan, tucking the egg box under his arm. "I've got to explain where three of these have gone."

"Yeah," said Andry, "and why you look like you've been in a bare-knuckle boxing match. Just say you fell over. That seems believable."

"Doesn't explain how it got all over your jumper," said Morgan, nodding at the sticky smears. "You weren't wrong. Look how stiff it's gone. If you put that in your hair, it *would* stand on end for days."

"I'll dash up to my room and change as soon as we get back," said Andry.

"Okay," said Morgan. "Only, don't come back down in the shirt with the safety pin Queen."

"You mean, *this* one?" said Andry, tugging up the front of her jumper.

"Yeah," said Morgan. "Some of the older blokes would hit the roof if they saw that. Don't you have any normal clothes?"

"There's nothing normal about me," said Andry as they started towards the path. "Haven't you noticed that yet? Anyway, what *I'm* wearing is actually quite tame. You should see some of the people back home. Hair all sorts of colours, jackets bristling with badges and studs. Some of them look like they've just landed from space."

"And you want to be like them?" asked Morgan.

"Not really," said Andry. "I'm all for expressing yourself, but not when it has anything to do with a trend or fad. For some of the people back home, it's turned into just another kind of uniform, and you need to wear it to be accepted by them. What's rock and roll about *that*? Why call yourself a nonconformist if you have to conform to something in order to *be* one?"

"I wouldn't know," said Morgan. "To be honest, it sounds like a lot of hassle. This is all to do with music, is it?"

"In a way," said Andry. "Punk is more of an attitude than a style. Anything can be Punk if it's done the right way. Even the music you lot play here could be Punk if you put some oomph behind it."

"I don't *only* listen to the old music," said Morgan. "Do you like The Shadows? I think they're great."

"I'm gonna pretend I didn't hear that," said Andry.

"Oh, come on," said Morgan. "How can you say no to *this*?" He held out his right arm, as though he was holding the neck of a guitar, and tapped on the egg box with his other hand. He then began a vocalised version of what Andry, much to her chagrin, recognised as the main riff from 'Apache'. "Dee-da-ding-ding-dee-da-ding-ding-deee!"

"Stop it," she said, taking a swipe at the neck of his invisible instrument.

"Dee-da-doo-doo-dee-da-ding-ding-deee!"

"Pack it in!" she cried and clasped her hands to her ears, though she couldn't stop from laughing. "Argh! It's torture!"

"Dee-doo-dah-dee-doo-dah-dee-da-dee-deee!"

"Right!" she said. "That's it!" She reached behind Morgan and pinched him on the small of the back. "Bzzt! There, I just unplugged you."

"Ah, you're no fun," said Morgan.

"Ever thought of getting a real one?" asked Andry.

"A real what?" said Morgan.

"I real *guitar*," said Andry. "Put all of your dees and doos and dings to good use."

"I don't think I'd ever have the time," said Morgan. "Don't think my dad would approve, either."

"If we sort things out at the lake-house," said Andry, "you'll have plenty of time."

"You really think we can?" asked Morgan.

"Sure, we can," said Andry. "You and me? We're unstoppable."

They walked on in silence for a short while, but Morgan then turned to her.

"Could I …" he said. "Could I ask to hold your hand?"

"Why?" said Andry. "Worried you might get lost?"

"I'm only asking," said Morgan.

"Okay," said Andry. "Just so I've got it straight, you're asking if you can ask to hold my hand? That's a lot of asks."

"There's no need to be like that about it," said Morgan, his signature blush flaring up in his cheeks. Andry gave a sigh and dropped her shoulders.

"Switch around," she said, raising her right hand. "This one's got egg on it."

"Good point," said Morgan.

He put the box under his other arm, they swapped sides on the path, and he took hold of Andry's hand.

"Do it properly, then," she said.

"Like what?" asked Morgan.

"You link them together," said Andry, wriggling her fingers between his. "Are you holding it, or shaking on a business deal?"

"*I* don't know what I'm doing," Morgan protested. "I've never held a girl's hand before."

"Yeah," said Andry, "I can tell."

"I saw you come in under the gate," said Morgan, nodding back towards the churchyard. "Do you know what one of those is called?"

"A gate without a wall attached to it?" said Andry. "I'd call it pointless."

"It's called a lychgate," said Morgan, "like our place."

"You named your pub after the entrance to a graveyard?" asked Andry. "That's a bit of a self-low-blow."

"Long ago," said Morgan, "before they had, like, hospitals and morgues and stuff, when someone died, their body was kept under the lychgate until the funeral, and people would sometimes stand with it, to stop anyone from coming and pinching the body. It's said that the ghost of the last person buried in the graveyard stands watch at the gate until the next person comes along. Only, they don't bury people in that yard anymore, so I've always felt sorry for whoever was the last in."

"Probably Elizabeth Hines," said Andry. "She was only our age, the poor sod. Anyway, still not a great name for a pub. It's a good thing that we southern tourists *don't* know what it means. You'd never get any bookings."

"I think it's supposed to be symbolic," said Morgan. "A lychgate is a border between ground that's holy and ground that isn't. So, when you come into *our* place, you can leave your religious values at the door."

"That makes it sound even worse," said Andry. "Don't let my dad find out. He thinks the place is all quaint and cosy and *authentic*."

"It makes sense, though, right?" said Morgan. "I mean, if you're going to come to a share and eat the ... the 'You know what', then it's best to do it in a place where *Him* upstairs isn't watching."

"Hmm, very clever," said Andry, "but the people here don't strike me as church every Sunday bible thumpers, with their runes and all."

"You'd be surprised," said Morgan. "A lot of it gets mixed up. You do know Christmas used to be a pagan festival?"

"Hark at *you*, history boy," said Andry, swinging their joined hands. "You should do guided tours. You'd double your revenue." She stopped their hands mid-swing and held them up. "So, *I* might not be sweet on *you*, but I'm guessing this means *you're* sweet on *me*?"

"I think you're very pretty," said Morgan, looking down at his shoes.

"That's a new one," laughed Andry. She tilted her head and looked up at the sky. "A boy back home once called me 'Tasty', and I punched him in the throat. If he'd said 'Pretty', I might've let him get away with it."

"Will you let *me* get away with it?" asked Morgan, raising his eyes cautiously.

"I haven't punched you yet, have I?" said Andry.

"You really *are* a fire girl," said Morgan. "*And* a Wyrd girl. My dad was right when he said that fire and water don't mix, but fire and Wyrd? I'll bet even *he* doesn't know how well *they* mix."

"We'll just have to find out," said Andry. "From now on, if you want any more hand holding or calling me nice things, you'll do *exactly* as I say."

Chapter Six

WHEN THEY GOT back to the pub, they found that Andry's dad was up and about at last. He was sat alone in the barroom, sipping a cup of tea and going through a sheath of paperwork. He still looked a little green around the gills, but nowhere near as wretched as he'd seemed when Andry had left him.

"There you are," he said as they came in. "Thought I'd lost you for the day."

"Here *we* are," said Andry. "We brought eggs. Fancy an omelette?"

"Eurgh, God, no," said her dad, a shudder of revulsion running through him. He tapped his pen against his cup. "I'm just about keeping *this* down. Can I have a word?"

"Sure," said Andry, pulling up a chair. Morgan made to do the same, but Andry's dad shot him a look.

"Alone," he said. "No offence, lad. Father, daughter business."

"Go on," Andry said to Morgan. "Try and clean yourself up."

"You've got it pulled pretty tight," said her dad as he watched Morgan go.

"Got what?" asked Andry.

"The lead you're dragging *him* around by," said her dad. He took a sip from his tea and leaned forward on his elbows. "What've you been saying to Pat?"

"Why?" Andry replied, narrowing her eyes. "What's *he* been saying?"

"Look," said her dad, resting his head in his hand, "if you

don't like it here, just say, and we can leave. I'm willing to lose the deposit *and* the room fees if it stops you being miserable. Okay, I admit it was a bad idea to come this early. I should've waited until the sale had gone through and the property was at least partly refurbished."

"Is *that* what he said?" asked Andry. "That I told him I was miserable?"

"He didn't exactly use those words," said her dad, "but I think he was trying to spare my feelings. The same as *you* obviously are. The weather is awful, I get sick on the first full day, and I'm apparently being hit with phone calls and documents that I *need* to be back at the office to deal with. All in all, this has been a bit of a disaster." He gave a huff and ran a hand down his face. "Last time *I* try playing at travel agent."

"If you'll let me get a word in," said Andry, "I'm *not* miserable. I'm actually starting to warm to the place."

"You're starting to warm to *him*," said her dad, nodding over his shoulder. "That's not the same thing. You think this whirlwind romance will last, once he finds out who we really are?"

"Romance?" said Andry. "Is that what *Pat* told you?"

"I understand that you're not a little girl anymore," said her dad. "I can't follow you around with a stick and fight off any boy who comes near you. All I'm saying is we don't know how sour everyone here is going to turn when the truth comes out. From what Pat's telling me, the people who used to live at the property were very well liked, but they met a bad end, meaning it won't be so easy for us to slip into their spot, no matter *how* nice we are."

"*I* told *him* that," said Andry, trying her best to keep her voice down.

"Told him what?" asked her dad.

"That they met a bad end," said Andry. "He just said he'd heard something similar. He's not doing any real investigating. He's just twisting things. Seriously, Dad, the man's a snake. Wait until I tell you what he's planning."

"Calm yourself down," said her dad. "I *know* what he's planning, and I agree with him."

"You do?" said Andry.

"Yes," said her dad. "Why wouldn't I?"

"Wait," said Andry, realising that they couldn't be talking about the same thing, "what did he tell *you* he was planning?"

"We don't come back near the place until it's finished," said her dad. "Pat says he can put me in touch with these guys who are the best in the north-west at doing up old properties privately. They turned over a farmhouse near Rochdale a few years ago. Good work, I've seen it. They come with these portable huts and set up home on-site for the length of the job. The thing is, I need to keep my hand out. You don't muddy the waters between private and commercial, because it's a minefield. I'll still be paying, but everything gets done through Pat. It means I won't be able to turn the whole ordeal into a tax write-off, but the last thing I need is the Inland Revenue up my backside."

As she listened to this, Andry felt a fresh horror begin to creep over her.

"You can't do that," she said. "Workmen from the city, living at the lake-house all the time? You *can't* do that."

"I'm not paying local contractors," said her dad with a shake of his head. "I want people who I can trust. I don't care what the four men and a dog sat in a pub which this place calls a council have to say about it. When the boots hit the mud, I want to know that the feet in them are working for *me*."

"Pat wants the lake-house for himself," said Andry, deciding there was nothing else for it but to play her trump card. "He said you'll lose interest and sign it over to him. If you let him take charge, he'll steal it from you without you even noticing."

They locked eyes, hers pleading, his bewildered. Just when she thought she'd finally hit the right nail, he leaned back and laughed.

"Is *that* what this is about?" he said. "You think he's doing the dirty behind my back?" He rasped his lips. "Fat chance. If Pat was going to try and cheat me, he'd have done it long ago. God knows I've dangled enough bones in front of him, testing his loyalty, but he never once took a bite. *He* wants all of this out of the way as soon as possible, so we can focus on the shopping centre next year. Pat is interested in cold, hard cash, not troublesome holiday homes."

"He *said* you wouldn't believe me," said Andry. "He says you trust *him* more."

"It sounds like you've just gotten your wires crossed," said her dad. "I know you don't like him. To be honest, I don't think he likes *you*, either. It's nothing personal, but I once heard him refer to children as 'Sexually transmitted parasites'. If you want me to have a word with him about trying to confuse you, then I will. Only, I promise, there's nothing dodgy going on."

"What if said I was lying just now?" asked Andry. "What if I told you that, yes, I *am* miserable, I hate it here, we should leave right this minute, and I never want to come back, so you shouldn't bother buying the lake-house at all?"

"You'd turn down becoming the sole inheritor of a six-figure property," asked her dad, now setting both elbows on the table and steepling his fingers "*plus* the money it makes through rentals in the meantime, money that could make university *very* comfortable for you?"

"Yes," said Andry, not missing a beat. "It isn't worth the trouble."

"*What* trouble?" said her dad, letting his arms fall to his sides, totally exasperated. "So, the locals don't like us. Who cares? Don't let yourself get caught up in all this backwards, folklore rubbish. They probably think the property is cursed or something, like you *joked* about before, but I'm willing to risk a curse to secure my daughter's future, whether *she* likes it or not."

"Then buy it and leave it empty," said Andry. "Don't get Pat involved. Don't bring in workmen. Just leave it there, like a nest-egg, and I'll deal with it when I have to."

Her dad gave a long sigh and pinched the bridge of his nose.

"You don't understand what's at stake," he said, not looking at her. "Word about this will have, undoubtedly, already started to circulate back home. I'll admit that I was maybe a bit too loose lipped about it myself, because I *assumed* it'd be straight forward. The contract on the shopping centre, as well as a number of other contracts, is not secure. I have *competitors*, Andry. People who would love nothing more than to whisper the wrong things into the right ears and tell them Martin Watt has lost his edge. He let a string of successes go to his head, thought he was bombproof, but then couldn't even break ground on a *vanity* project." He gave a high laugh and slapped his leg before changing his voice to a shrill, mocking tone. "Have you heard? He got spooked by the locals and doesn't even *visit* the place anymore. He says it's for his daughter to inherit, but what's she going to do with a crumbling wreck that she can't renovate? Wow! Father of the year!" He leaned in towards Andry, making eye contact again. "Do you really want to trust *him* with your business?" He shook his head. "The sale and works go ahead as planned. Even if you never set foot in the place, I can make sure it's doing something for you behind the scenes. Then, when I die, you can do what you want. It's not like I'll care at *that* point."

"What do mean, behind the scenes?" asked Andry.

"Like I told you," said her dad, "rentals, money under the table. I've got plenty of friends who'd like to spend a bit of time here. If I can fill it for even ten weeks a year, at a hundred pounds a week, that's a grand a year to help you while you're at school. After that, anything else it earns can go into a private account that *I* will decide when you can have access to."

"You mean, *Pat* will decide," said Andry. "I'm sure he'll be cosigning everything, right?"

"Look, *enough* of this," her dad snapped. "If you want, we can stay for the rest of the time we have booked. You can say your goodbyes to Mister short, blonde and stupid, then that can be an end to it. But this Miss Marple stuff has to stop. Pat signs whatever I *tell* him to. He might dance a bit off kilter, but it's always to *my* tune. You talk about trust. Who am I supposed to trust more? The man who trusts *me* enough to follow me all the way up from Leicester and help to establish a business that's going to have *you* set up for life, or my teenage daughter, who screams conspiracy after a bit of teasing?"

"Fine," said Andry, shoving her seat back and getting up. "I'm glad I know where I stand." She slammed the chair against the table and headed towards the front entrance.

"Oi!" her dad called after her. "Don't you storm off from me! You're not your mother! It doesn't suit you!"

"Get stuffed!" Andry shot back.

"Where are you going?" her dad persisted, though he made no effort to follow her.

"I don't know," said Andry, struggling with the door handle in her anger. "Just away. Away from *here*. I'm sick of how *authentic* it is!"

She crossed the carpark at a jog, more to run out her pent-up frustration than to cover any distance.

She carried on for what felt like a long time, but she didn't get very far before her legs started aching. Her Doc Martens were sturdy, but they weren't the best choice of running shoes. She slowed to a walk and followed the drystone wall at the side of the road, snatching out a hand every now and then to decapitate a tall weed or yank a fistful of leaves from a bush, growling and spitting swearwords.

Once she'd blown off some steam, she looked around to try and figure out where she was. She'd already passed the stile that she and Morgan had used to cross the fields, but she hadn't yet joined the lane which led towards the lake. She could make out the start of the woods from here, and she decided to head towards them, thinking that she could cut through and come up on the standing stone from the side. Something Morgan had said about it being a safe place came into her mind, and she felt she could do with some safety right now. If Morgan came looking for *her* this time, maybe he'd have the same idea.

She crossed the road and started up the lane towards the woods. As she trudged on, she saw that there were fresh tyre tracks in the dirt, probably no more than a few hours old, the churned-up ground still wet. She stopped to inspect them but couldn't tell if they were leading to or away from the woods. She carried on, keeping a close eye on the path ahead of her, but also taking the occasional look behind. She didn't fancy running into anyone out here on her own. Dennis had given the impression that he made regular patrols of the area, and she, of course, knew that Morgan's dad did. If anyone came across her, they'd probably insist on taking her back to the pub, or at least warn her against going any further by herself, and she wasn't in the mood for either.

She eventually came to a gate similar to the one where Morgan had taken her to the stone, so she knew she was on the right track. This one, however, wasn't chained. It was also as far along the lane as she could go, the track coming to a stop in front of it. The tyre marks also came to an end here, and there was clear evidence of the vehicle having performed a turn just before the gate. Someone must have been here quite recently, but she couldn't think why they'd come all the way up the lane, only to turn back.

She slipped between the gatepost and the nearest tree trunk, then looked around on the other side for any footprints. Sure enough, there were prints and disturbed leaves, all of which appeared to be as fresh as the tyre tracks. Unfortunately, she couldn't tell which way the person had then gone, as there were no more visible prints once the bracken started.

There were three trails leading away from the gate. One looked more well-trodden than the others, so she chose to follow it.

She hadn't been going for more than a few minutes when she heard something up ahead of her, a rustling and the snapping of branches. She froze, then looked left and right, thinking she could make a break for it into the trees if anyone appeared. No-one did, but she stayed perfectly still, listening for any further sound. It came again, a crunching of leaves, and then what she thought was a voice. Panic shot through her as she recalled the awful, strangled voice of the snared 'You know what', its horrid combination of the human and the bestial.

She was just about to hightail it back to the gate, when the sound came once more. It wasn't a voice, as in it wasn't speech, but it was definitely the sound of something alive and was far too loud and guttural to be a bird. Only, this time, it was accompanied by something which she recognised, a dull, metallic clatter.

"Oh, you're *kidding* me," she said to herself as she started walking.

The trees thinned, and she came upon the stone. Standing in front of it, tied to a stake in the ground, was a goat. It turned to look at her as she approached it, the small tin bell around its neck clinking as it jerked against the rope.

"Hello, you," she said to it. "Now, there's no *way* you're the same goat as before, right? That'd be a bit *too* Wyrd."

The goat bleated at her and tried to back away, but the rope didn't give it more than a few feet. She came further forward, shushing and clicking her tongue, in an attempt to soothe the poor thing. Once she was close enough, she carefully reached out and stroked it on the head, running her fingers down its silky ears and across its nose.

"Hello!" she called out, looking around in all directions. "Whose goat is this?"

There was no reply, and the goat bleated again.

"Well, you didn't stake *yourself* to the ground, did you?" she said to it. She then remembered the tyre tracks at the gate, how they'd turned and headed back. "Why have they just left you here?" She dropped to one knee and peered directly into the goat's eye. "I get it. I think you're supposed to be a sacrifice, but what you *really* are is bait for the … well, the 'You know what'. They don't want them going into town and raiding henhouses, but this is where they lure them to on purpose, so they can make their magic stew. Safe place, my backside." She moved to the stake and began tugging at the knot. "Don't you worry, though. I'll get you out of here. If anyone asks, just tell them you did it on your own."

Once she had the knot undone, she expected the goat to bolt right away, but it just stood there and stared at her. She was forced to clap her hands and yell at it before it finally ambled off into the trees, the clinking of its bell fading as it went.

She turned and looked at the stone. The grass around the base had been trodden flat, but it was out of range for the goat to have done it. She walked up to the stone and looked at the carvings upon it. She'd had no idea what to make of them when Morgan had first shown them to her, but she now recognised a few. She dropped to her haunches and placed a hand to the stone, tracing a finger across the carvings. Some were the right way up, while others were inverted. She slowly edged around the stone, keeping a finger to the marks, and found that they ran all the way around the base, with no noticeable breaks. If they were meant to spell out words, then it was a sentence that went on and on, around and around, without a beginning or an end.

"So," she said, setting her hands on her knees, "where does *my* one fit into all this?"

She considered the possibility that the Wyrd rune was maybe meant to be silent, like the K in 'Knife', but something told her it wouldn't be that simple. What made more sense was the idea that the Wyrd ran through *all* of the other runes simultaneously, its presence enforced by its absence, invisible but always there.

She gave a chuckle and rose to her feet, thinking that her mum would be proud of her. She'd tried numerous times to get Andry involved in her more 'Alternative' interests, but she'd inherited far too much of her dad's scepticism. Tarot cards and palm-reading were entertaining enough, but Andry was always able to see through the veneer of their pageantry, especially given the fact that those who practiced these arts used the old get out clause of 'It only works if you believe in it', which covered their backs once they'd taken your money but couldn't scry or divine a single thing about you, hence why they asked for the cash first.

She couldn't remember her mum or any of her friends mentioning the runes, but her dad had said he'd seen them before, so one of her mum's motley crew might know something. She just hoped it didn't turn out to be Malcolm the Medium. She hated that guy. He refused to put anything on his body which wasn't 'Natural', and thus stunk out any room he was in. He claimed to be followed at all times by the spirit of a Druid and always insisted that a chair be set out for his unseen companion wherever he went. Andry had done a number on him when he'd once come to visit her mum for the weekend. He'd boasted about travelling first-class on the train, saying his psychic evenings in Leeds were earning him enough money to get around in style. He'd even shown them the fancy ticket. When Andry asked why he'd been so cruel as to not also buy a first-class seat for the noble Gwenc'hlan, he'd gotten very flustered and told her to mind her own business.

She couldn't say if she believed in the runes or not, but whoever had made the carvings on the stone certainly did, not to mention the locals she'd encountered, the belief being so strong that it had stood the test of ages and survived the encroachment of newer, more fashionable religions and practices. She was no historian, but she was pretty sure that messing around with runes was the kind of thing that got you burned at the stake when followers of the new, trendy religions found out.

Her mum had often said that she'd make a very good witch, if she only applied herself, but Andry wasn't having any of it. For starters, she didn't like the clothes. Her mum's more esoteric friends dressed both themselves *and* their kids in awful garments, usually made of hemp or hand spun wool, which looked as if they were specifically designed to be as uncomfortable as possible, though they cost a fortune and were made by companies just as soulless and profit orientated as Doc Martens or Levis. Like she'd told Morgan, she wasn't a fan of uniforms. Still, she wondered what her mum would think when she returned to Leicester and declared herself as the Wyrd fire girl. She'd probably be very pleased.

She walked around the stone one more time, then squared up to it.

"I suppose you'll want something in return for me letting the goat go," she said. "Can't leave the poor stone wanting." She patted her pockets, looking for anything which might make suitable as a sacrifice, but they were empty. She then remembered the pendant around her neck. She unhooked it and held it out, swinging it back and forth. "You can have this if you make sure things go well for me and Morgan." She approached the stone and knelt back down before it, pulling some of the grass aside. "I don't know if it's the real deal. The shopkeeper probably buys them in bulk and just *says* they're from the lake, but it's all I've got." She pushed the pendant down into the soil, covering the divot with fallen leaves. She stood up and pointed at the stone. "If things *don't* go well, I'll come and have it back. I don't care if it's 'Meant to be' or not. That thing cost three quid, so I want your help."

She nodded and folded her arms, but she then frowned to herself. She was about to say, 'Why am I talking to a stone?', but she remembered that she'd also been talking to a goat not long ago.

She walked towards the path, stopping to pull up the stake and throw it into the bushes. She'd let whoever left the goat there think it *had* broken free on its own. Even though she was far from a vegetarian, much to her mum's protest, she assumed that the 'You know what' wouldn't be the most ethical sorts when it came to what they ate, or *how* they ate it.

She didn't see the goat again as she made her way back down the lane. She kept an ear open for the clinking of its bell, but there was nothing. She just had to hope that it'd go back to its herd and blend in unnoticed. No doubt another would be brought to the stone in its place, either tomorrow or whenever, but there was little she could do about that.

She took a rest about halfway along the lane and looked around. She could see part of the lake from this direction, but there was no sign of the lake-house, not even the highest part of its roof. It crossed her mind to just go straight to it. During daylight, she'd be able to get a better idea of what she and Morgan would be facing once night fell. If there was a low point in the wall, or a fence which could be gotten under, it'd be best to know about it before they attempted to get in. However, the only way she knew of to approach the lake-house was via the road, and she didn't want to be spotted snooping around. She was pretty sure that Dennis was already onto her, so having his Range Rover pull up as she was scoping out the lake-house's defences wouldn't look good at all.

She also wasn't looking forward to having to return to the pub and face the music with her dad. She knew from experience that he could hold a grudge for a long time whenever she dared to get lippy with him, his initial fury quickly subsiding into a seething, drawn out ordeal of passive aggression, barbed with sarcasm and mockery, which was much more punishing than anything regular parents dealt out.

She'd gotten her ears pierced at thirteen, and he'd hit the roof to begin with, telling her that she was grounded for the whole of her stay with him. When he'd realised that this essentially made her stay pointless, he'd instead spent the next two days shooting jibes and off-colour remarks at her, saying if she wanted to look like an 'Eastern hooker', then that was *her* choice. She'd eventually taken the studs out from her ears, dropped them down the sink, and the subject was never raised again.

She could only imagine what he had in store for her this time. It would probably centre around Morgan. The poor boy would disintegrate with shame if her dad turned his razor-tongued wit on him. What made matters worse was that she could practically hear Pat laughing all the way from Manchester. She'd played right into his hands. It wasn't that she was stuck between him and her dad. It was more a case of him and her dad were now stuck together in a place where she couldn't reach, and she'd only be shot down if she tried.

It was the same as with the pierced ears. No matter what she said, she'd just be ignored or brushed off or condescended to, until she finally agreed to drop the entire thing down the sink, even if the plughole was spitting out blood.

She balled her hands into fists and thumped them onto her thighs as she started walking again. She wouldn't allow herself to be so easily deterred. She *couldn't* allow it. Like her dad had said, she didn't ever have to set foot in the lake-house if she didn't want to, but it wasn't just about her. She knew she'd never be able to live with the thought of a workman, a rental guest, or even, God forbid, her dad himself being awoken in the night by the sound of one of those dreadful, croaking voices, nothing being found the next day, apart from what would fit into a pint glass. If the locals put goats out as sacrifices to the 'You know what', then that wasn't her problem, but there was no way she was going to allow a string of fresh, *human* sacrifices to be dropped into their clutches, like some vile takeaway delivery service. If there was anything, anything at all that she and Morgan could do to make the lake-house safer, then they had to do it, and they had to do it tonight.

She spent the walk back to the pub rehearsing what she was going to say to her dad. She had no skill at apologising. Even when she meant it, it always came out sounding forced or contrived. She decided that the best course of action wasn't to say that she was sorry, but that, upon reflection. her dad's explanation of the matter had won her over for now, and she was willing to concede to him. She knew that a confession of 'I was wrong' wouldn't have the same impact as a declaration of '*You* were right'.

When she reached the pub, she saw that a few vehicles had arrived, Morgan's dad's Range Rover among them. As she walked across the carpark, she spotted the man himself. He was standing outside the sliding side door of the shed, and he raised his chin when he saw her.

"I was hoping I'd run into you," he called to her, beckoning her over with a flick of his fingers. He was wearing a leather apron, like the one his wife wore behind the bar, and his sleeves were rolled up to the elbows. As Andry approached, he cupped a hand to his mouth, drawing on a cigarette held between his knuckles.

"You *smoke*?" she asked.

"Sometimes," he said, hissing the smoke out through his teeth and looking at the glowing ember at the end of the cigarette. "It helps to clear the old lungs when you've been breathing in something horrible."

"Muck and blood and stink," said Andry.

"You bet," he said. "Look, the Squire told me what you did. Morgan, I mean."

"He did?" asked Andry, trying to supress a flinch of shock.

"Aye," said Morgan's dad. "He told me everything."

"He *did*?" Andry repeated.

Morgan's dad took another drag and flicked the cigarette away.

"I try," he said. "I really do. I sometimes think he'd do better if he was somewhere else. Somewhere he could excel at whatever it is he's meant to excel at. The bigger landowners around here, they send their kids off to private boarding schools, so they can see what life's like *away* from here. I can't do that, though. I can't afford it, for one thing. Also, I need him here, by my side."

Andry listened and nodded, but she had no idea what he was talking about. If Morgan *had* told him everything, then he was taking it surprisingly well.

"What exactly did he say to you?" she asked.

"He got jumped by that nasty pair of creatures who Ned Stewart calls children," he said. "The *lad*, I can understand, but that *girl's* a terror to match. Morgan says he got knocked about because he was trying to stick up for himself." He pointed at Andry. "Just like *you* told him to."

"Oh," said Andry, feeling a great weight drop from her. "I *might* have said something like that to him. He says he gave as good as he got, and he only lost three eggs."

"From what *I* hear," said Morgan's dad, "he lost the lot, but you got them back."

"I couldn't leave him all beaten up and eggless," said Andry with a shrug.

"I don't know where I stand on the Squire being given fighting tips by a girl," said Morgan's dad, taking a pack of cigarettes from the bib of the apron and tapping a fresh one out, "but I suppose it has to come from somewhere, and you're not like any girl I've met before. You saw how he wanted to impress you by shooting the gun. He's clearly taken a shine to you. If you can give him some useful, *southern* advice," he winked at her, "and he's willing to listen, then I'm all for it." He took a chunky, brass Zippo lighter from his back pocket and sparked the cigarette. "Not a word to his mother, mind. She can't stand the idea of him scrapping. It's like she thinks he's made of glass."

"How did he explain the broken eggs and broken face to her?" asked Andry.

"He told her he fell over," said Morgan's dad, inhaling deeply on the cigarette and shaking his head, "and she believed him. That's not surprising, though. He does it all the time."

"Why do you think he told you the truth?" asked Andry.

"Beats me," said Morgan's dad. "I suppose he's trying to get me to like you."

"*Don't* you like me?" asked Andry with a grin.

"I'm getting there," said Morgan's dad. "Besides, I've been talking with your fatha', and he says we might be seeing a lot more of you in the future, so I guess we should be on good terms."

Andry thought about correcting this and saying that what her dad had meant was they might be seeing a lot more of *him* in the future, but she decided against it.

"I can keep an eye out for Morgan whenever I'm here," she said instead, liking how noncommittal this sounded. "It's what he gets up to when I'm *not* here that worries me. I wouldn't like to come for a visit and find him in a full-body cast."

"No," said Morgan's dad with a short laugh. "Confidence is good, but don't go getting him to think that he's John Wayne or anything."

"You're right," said Andry. "The position of local cowboy is already taken."

"Cowboy?" asked Morgan's dad.

"Dirty Harry," said Andry. "Well, I mean, he's sometimes a cowboy, too."

"That's stuck, has it?" asked Morgan's dad, screwing his face up into the most Eastwood looking grimace that she'd seen him perform so far. "Cheeky bleeders. I've not even *seen* that film."

"We got it on tape earlier this year," said Andry, "so *I've* seen it, and I'm afraid they're not wrong. It's that thing you do with your eye. You should take it as a compliment."

"Maybe so," said Morgan's dad. "I can think of a few people around here who I wouldn't mind having a shootout with." He wriggled his fingers next to his hip, as though he were reaching for a holstered pistol, causing Andry to laugh.

"See?" she said. "At least you can be funny with it."

"Who says I'm joking?" said Morgan's dad. He dropped his cigarette and crushed it with the toe of his boot. "Right. I've got things to finish up. It's a share night again. You and your fatha' know the score."

"*Yes*," said Andry with a feigned sigh. "We don't get any of the special stuff. Not so special if you have it two nights in a row, though."

"It's peculiar," said Morgan's dad, "but not unheard of, especially this time of year. Wait until you come in the summer, and everyone's gagging for it."

"No eels in the summer?" asked Andry.

"Nope," said Morgan's dad. "They all disappear."

"Where's the Squire now?" asked Andry.

"Inside," said Morgan's dad, nodding towards the pub, "nursing his wounds, I'd imagine. Do me a favour. Don't tell him we had this chat. It might not seem like it, but his pride is easier to hurt than his body."

"Sure," said Andry. "After all, we wouldn't want him knowing that you *worry* about him."

"My point exactly," said Morgan's dad, stepping onto the gravel path and heading for the side entrance of the shed.

Andry started towards the door of the pub, but she hung back for a moment and watched Morgan's dad go into the shed. She couldn't be sure from this distance, but he appeared to take deep breath before entering.

Andry assumed that he must've gone back for the body of the creature she'd seen him kill, which explained the consecutive share nights. Either that, or he'd come across another between then and now. Also, if the captive goat was anything to go by, he was expecting a *third* night in a row.

She headed inside and looked around the barroom. Her dad wasn't there, nor did she recognise any of the patrons. No Dennis, no Bernie, no Ivor, not even any of those who she'd seen singing the night before. For such a small town, fresh faces seemed to turn up quite regularly.

She guessed that her dad was up in his room, but she didn't feel like facing him just yet. Instead, she went straight to Morgan's room. She knocked on the door, and he called for her to come in.

She found him lying on his bed, a wet, folded towel pressed to his face.

"You cry-baby," she sniggered as she shut the door behind her. "Anyone would think you'd done ten rounds with Muhammed Ali."

"It was my mum's idea," said Morgan, sitting up and tossing the towel aside. "It's not working, though. It hurts like Hell, *and* my hand." He displayed his grazed knuckles to her, the scuffed skin now sticky with forming scabs.

"They're your battle scars," said Andry, sitting down on the foot of the bed. "The football hoolies back home, they say you're not one of them, unless your knuckles are permanently smashed up."

"Delightful," said Morgan. "I just get the feeling that, when you try to fight someone, you're not supposed to hurt *yourself* more than *them*."

"Did you really take a swing at one of them?" asked Andry.

"Yeah," said Morgan. "Only, I … well," he showed her his hand again, "I missed."

"I bet you didn't go for the girl," said Andry. "You told me before, you're better than that."

"I went for her brother," said Morgan, "but he dodged me, I fell over, and *she* put the boot in on me when I was down."

"The dirty sods!" said Andry. "Two on one, and kicking a guy when he's down? I wish I'd given her a proper seeing to."

"That reminds me," said Morgan, lowering his voice. "I've been thinking about weapons."

"Yeah?" said Andry. "What've you come up with?"

"We shouldn't take knives," said Morgan. "It's not like we haven't got plenty of them, but they're the kind of thing you need to be good with. One wrong slip with a knife, and it's *you* getting cut."

"What else, then?" asked Andry. "No guns, no knives. We can't just pull scary faces."

"Fire pokers," said Morgan.

"Come again?" said Andry.

"Fire pokers," Morgan repeated, jabbing his unmaimed hand at her.

"You're kidding, right?" said Andry. "I thought you said you'd been thinking."

"Have you ever been *hit* with a fire poker?" asked Morgan.

"No," said Andry. "Have *you*?"

"No," said Morgan, "and I wouldn't *want* to be. A three-foot rod of metal? The big ones in the barroom have barbs on the end, too."

The only fire pokers Andry had ever encountered were the small, household sets, usually complete with a brush and a toasting fork, which were liable to break if you tried using one as a weapon. She hadn't looked at those by the fireplace in the barroom, but if they were as fearsome as Morgan was describing, they might do the trick.

"You're sounding pretty up for it," she said. "I've not given you a taste for this violence lark, have I?"

"I'm up for making sure we can *defend* ourselves," said Morgan. "If I can't talk you out of it, and I can't let you go alone, then I want to know that we're coming back in one piece."

"Have you done any thinking about how we'll get in?" asked Andry. "There's a point where the wall meets the shore. I bet we can slip in there. I was going to take a closer look earlier, but I didn't want to be seen."

"We shouldn't go near the water," said Morgan with a firm shake of his head.

"It can't be that deep," said Andry. "Have you got a spare pair of wellies I can borrow?"

"We *shouldn't* go near the water," Morgan repeated. "It doesn't matter how deep it is. They can hear a splash from a mile away, and they can tell if it's a person making it."

"Ladders it is, then," said Andry, slapping her thighs. "I hope you've got one laying around."

"We're not taking a ladder," said Morgan. "If we get caught, we might be able to explain the pokers. If we get caught with a *ladder*, it'll be obvious what we were up to."

"What happens if we get caught?" asked Andry. "In any case, I mean."

"With just the pokers," said Morgan, "I reckon I could talk us out of it. I'll say you ran off, I went after you, taking the pokers for protection. If we get caught with a ladder, which takes *two* people to carry, there'll be no talking our way out of *that*. As for what'll actually happen, I dread to think, so let's not think about it."

"You're not making this very easy," said Andry. "No guns, no knives, no water, no ladders. I'd say we should tunnel under the wall, but you'll probably say no shovels."

"The wall is lowest on the east side," said Morgan. "I've not been there in a while, but when I last saw it, it was covered in ivy. We can climb over it."

"On *both* sides?" asked Andry. "Remember, we've got to get out again."

"*Now* who's not making it easy?" said Morgan with a smirk. "I can get you in. I didn't say I could get you out."

"You better do," said Andry, "because you're coming with me every step of the way."

"Yeah," said Morgan, glancing away, "I know."

"I'll make it worth your while," said Andry. "As long as we *do* come out in one piece, I'll let you hold my hand again for the whole walk back."

"I'll want something a bit better than *that*," said Morgan with a huff.

"You cheeky git!" laughed Andry and slapped him on the arm. "Try anything more than hand holding, and I'll black your other eye for you."

"I didn't mean anything like that," said Morgan, his blush setting in with full force, even the bruised part of his face flushing.

"What *did* you mean, then?" Andry teased.

"Well," said Morgan, "*money* would be nice."

"Sorry," said Andry. "My dad told me not to tip you." She pointed at him. "What *you're* getting out of this is the knowledge that you've helped to protect people. Isn't that what you're supposed to do, being the gamekeeper in training? If we don't do something, my dad will have workmen here before the end of the year. They're going to set up a camp on the grounds of the lake-house."

"Oh," said Morgan, the colour draining back out of his face. "That's *really* bad."

"You're darn tootin', it is," said Andry. "So, if there's anything inside the lake-house that helps with stopping these things from coming, we need to find out what."

"What do you think it could be?" asked Morgan.

"*I* dunno," said Andry. "You tell *me*. You're meant to be the expert."

"I only know as much as anyone else," said Morgan. "*Less*, really. We don't talk about it a lot, especially not my parents. Whenever I ask questions, they go all quiet, as though I've used a bad word. My dad talks to the other grown-ups about them like they're just another pest, like foxes taking hens, or crows pecking up the sown fields, but I've always felt that there's something else going on."

"And you never wanted to find out?" asked Andry.

"I never *had* to," said Morgan. "When I was younger, my dad would catch maybe one or two a year. Sometimes none at all. I didn't even *see* one until I was nine. These last few years, though, there've been *loads* more. People with animals are sick of it, but those without any almost seem *happy*, because it means there're more shares."

"They only see the end product," said Andry with a nod. "Your dad told me people gag for it during the summer. So, it's, like, addictive?" She was thinking of what Dave had told her, about the stew taking a hold upon people.

"Maybe," said Morgan. "People *do* seem to get overly upset when there's none left. You've seen how quickly it spoils, so you've got to get it while you can. When did my dad tell you that?"

"We spoke just now," said Andry, nodding at the window. "He's in the shed. I reckon he's dealing with the one from this morning

"Strange," said Morgan, cocking his head in thought.

"Not really," said Andry, "if they go off *that* quick."

"Not that," said Morgan. "Him talking to you. He usually steers well clear of the guests. My mum says he intimidates them."

"I'm different, though, aren't I?" said Andry. "He says he wants us to be friends. Me and you, I mean."

"Gosh," said Morgan. "That's never happened before."

"From what you tell me," said Andry, "it sounds like you've never had any guests who were worth being friends *with*."

"Good point," said Morgan. "The guests our age, they look at me like I'm something they've stepped in."

"Aww, you poor soul," said Andry, scooting closer and bumping him with her elbow. "Grief from the local kids, grief from the guest kids. If this all turns out right, maybe you can come and visit me in Leicester. You can meet some of the kids there, and *they'll* give you grief, too."

"I don't think your dad would like that," said Morgan with a slight smile.

"Ah, you forget," said Andry. "My dad lives in Manchester. It's my mum in Leicester, and she'd think the world of you. You'd just have to spit out a few rustic sounding phrases, and she'll drop to her knees in front of you, calling you a 'Genuine son of the soil' or whatever. Not to mention if you got the runes out for her. She'd *eat* that up."

"You think so?" asked Morgan.

"Yeah," said Andry, starting to warm to the idea. She'd meant it as a joke at first, but she could see it working. "I always have to put up with her oddball friends, with their supposed magic powers. In fact, *they'd* probably love you as well. You could charge them a tenner a time for rune readings, give them any old gibberish, and they'll call you an oracle. What a blast it'd be!"

"That depends, though, doesn't it?" said Morgan. "On whether things here turn out right."

"They will," said Andry. "I'm telling you. I can feel it. We're gonna do something very special and *very* Wyrd."

"You've grown quite attached to that word," said Morgan. "You shouldn't throw it around so freely."

"I think I've figured it out," said Andry. "I went back to the old stone and looked at the carvings. Maybe the Wyrd isn't something that jumps out of nowhere to mess things up. Instead, it's everywhere, in everything, all the time. It's what holds everything together, and if you get a sneaky look at it, then you have a better idea of what's coming next."

"Wow," said Morgan. "And you think your mum's oddball friends would call *me* an oracle."

"It makes sense, doesn't it?" asked Andry. "Something here has been … you know, *disrupted*. You told me about things being 'Meant to be'. What if all of *this* is 'Meant to be'? What if someone else had wanted to buy the lakehouse? Someone who *wouldn't* go with you to the stone or listen to your stories, and who just looked at you like you're something they've stepped in. Someone who your dad *wouldn't* want you to be friends with. Don't you think this is all a bit …" She thought for the right word. "*Convenient*?"

"I took you to the stone because you dragged me out of my room," said Morgan, "and I told you stories because you chucked me on the ground."

"Exactly," said Andry. "If things had gone even an inch any other way, we wouldn't be where we are now, and me and my dad would end up on the monster menu without knowing it. Seriously, mate, what's happening here is happening for a reason. We're *meant* to do this together."

"Do you really believe that?" asked Morgan looking at her sidelong. "Or are you just getting carried away?"

"I believe it enough to do *this*," said Andry.

She grabbed Morgan by the front of his shirt, yanked him towards her, and planted a kiss firmly on his lips. There was no passion to it, she was just trying to get him enthused, but she let it go on for just a little longer than was strictly necessary to make her point. When she pulled away, Morgan had turned so red that it looked as though his face was going to burst into flames.

"Okay," he said.

"*Okay*?" said Andry. "Is that all?"

"Well, no," said Morgan. "It's just, for a second, I thought you were going to nut me."

"Maybe I *should* have," said Andry. "It might've gotten a better response. Didn't the Earth move? Didn't the heavens shake?"

"I don't think so," said Morgan. "Do it again."

"Not a chance," said Andry, letting go of his shirt and pushing him.

"Was I *that* bad?" asked Morgan, a look of utter dejection passing across his burning face. "Give me a break. I've never kissed a girl before."

"No, you weren't *bad*," chuckled Andry. "You're just not getting any more until the job's done. You should think yourself lucky. When I had *my* first kiss, our teeth cracked together, *and* he grabbed my bum."

"I can't imagine that went down very well," said Morgan, smiling again at last. "So, does this mean you *are* sweet on me after all?"

"It was only a kiss," said Andry, poking her tongue out at him. "Don't be expecting a marriage proposal any time

206

soon. I just wanted to get some energy into you."

"Okay," said Morgan. "When are we going to sneak out? When everyone's gone to bed, like last night?"

"No," said Andry. "We'll wait for the share to start. That way, everyone will be busy, and they won't notice us missing. The more people there are in here, the less there are for us to bump into while we're out. How much does your mum rely on you to help during a share?"

"She doesn't need me every time," said Morgan. "I can say I'm turning in early," he tapped gingerly at his bruised eye, "because of my battle wounds. What about your dad?"

"Leave that to me," said Andry, standing up. "I'll make sure he's in no state to realise I'm gone."

"You're not going to let him eat the broth again, are you?" asked Morgan. "Honestly, once is bad enough. Two times might do him some real damage."

"That *would* work," said Andry, "but no. There're other ways to put him out of the picture."

"Like what?" asked Morgan.

"Like getting him rollocking drunk," said Andry. "We're in a pub, on a Saturday night. It won't seem unusual."

"Fair enough," said Morgan with a shrug. "We should wait until the music starts. That's when people will be most distracted."

"Good idea," said Andry, starting towards the door. "You hang around in here, and we'll go out the same way as we did before."

"Just one more thing," said Morgan, standing up and following her a few steps.

"What?" asked Andry.

"Even if everything *doesn't* turn out alright," said Morgan. "I mean, if something bad happens at the lake-house, and we manage to get out, you and your dad might have to leave in a big hurry. If that happens, I hope there's still some way that we can be friends. I don't know if I *am* sweet on you, and I'm pretty sure that you're not sweet on *me*, but I wouldn't want us to never hear from each other again."

Andry let go of the door handle and turned to face him, setting both hands on his shoulders.

"Don't think like that," she said. "I need you next to me, in full, poker swinging fury. I don't want your mind all jumbled with worries about us never seeing each other again. I'll make sure we stay friends, no matter what. Yeah, we're not Romeo and Juliet, but some things are more important than just being star-crossed lovers."

"I hope we're *not* Romeo and Juliet," said Morgan. "They both die at the end."

"That's the spirit," laughed Andry. "Now, lay back down and pretend to be concussed."

Chapter Seven

ANDRY KNEW THE time had come for her to talk to her dad, but she wasn't sure which approach to take. Floods of tears would be most effective, but only if he didn't see right through them. Like she'd told Morgan, she could, indeed, turn them on and off like a tap, it'd gotten her out of scrapes before, but her dad's suspicions would still be on high alert, and something so dramatic might be seen as a little too much.

Instead, she decided that a subdued brooding would do the trick. It'd be enough to win him over, but not so out of character that he'd question its authenticity.

She climbed the stairs to his room and found the door already open. He was sitting on the bed, and Andry was glad to see a half-empty pint on the dresser, alongside a fully empty one. Her plan had begun before she'd even thought of it.

"There you are," he said, not looking up at her as she came in.

"Here I am," said Andry, putting on her best 'I'm not happy about this' voice.

"Finished with your hissy fit, are you?" asked her dad.

"Yes," said Andry, closing the door.

"I want you to apologise to Pat," said her dad, pointing at the phone.

Andry almost blew everything right away by yelling, 'No, I will not!', but she managed to contain herself.

"I'll call him from my room later," she said.

"No," said her dad. "You'll call him now. I want to hear you say it."

"Does he always answer calls on a weekend?" asked Andry. "Doesn't he have a life?"

"Andry!" growled her dad, fixing her with a glare. "I'm *not* asking."

"Fine," said Andry, stomping over to the table and snatching up the phone. "Give me the number."

Her dad passed her another business card, and she dialled. Unlike the phone in her room, this one was a rotary kind, meaning each digit took a painfully long time to enter.

It was answered halfway through the second ring, and Pat's voice slithered into her ear.

"Hello?" he said, but she could tell by his tone that he already knew it was her.

"Hi," she said. "Listen, my dad wanted …" She trailed off when she saw the look her dad was giving her. "I mean, *I* wanted to say I'm sorry for getting mouthy with you earlier. I'm thinking that I maybe didn't understand what you were telling me."

"Oh, there's no need to be sorry," said Pat. "These are complicated matters. No-one expects you to be knowledgeable of such things."

"Well, okay, then," said Andry, her fingers clenching around the handset. "I'm happy we've got that settled."

"Is your dad with you?" asked Pat.

"Yes," said Andry, not wanting her dad to know that he was being talked about.

"Is he in the room with you?" asked Pat.

"Yes," said Andry, turning to face away from her dad, but she could almost feel his eyes on her.

"What does his face look like?" Pat continued.

"The same as always," said Andry. "What's your point?"

"He's not smiling?" asked Pat.

"No," said Andry.

"Strange," said Pat. "I would've thought he'd be grinning from ear to ear. Damn, Audrey, you must've *seriously* ticked him off."

"What's this got to do with anything?" asked Andry. "What're you up to?"

Her dad gave a cough, and she turned back around. The look on his face had changed. It was still stern, but there was a slight hint that the ice was beginning to thaw.

"What I'm *up* to," said Pat, "is putting the finishing touches to the purchase agreement on the lake property. I've got the document in front of me as we speak. All that needs to happen is I send it to the current owners, they sign a carbon, send it back to me, and we're done."

"Just like that?" asked Andry.

"Just like that," said Pat. "Your dad called me after you'd made your dramatic exit. He said he wanted to go full speed ahead. He's made an offer of one-ninety, and it's been accepted. Not *too* much more, I suppose, but don't be expecting him to pay out for linen sheets in your dorm room at Rossall."

"On a Saturday?" asked Andry, still not quite able to believe that these sorts of things got done so quickly on a weekend.

"Business doesn't take days off," said Pat, "especially when it's to do with *this* amount of money."

The line went quiet for a moment, and Andry looked at her dad. The smile which Pat had been speaking of was starting to appear.

"I guess not," she said.

"So?" said Pat. "What do you say?"

"I don't know *what* to say," said Andry.

"You say, 'Thank you,'" said Pat. "You say, 'Thank you for sorting all of this out on a Saturday, Pat. You're such a helpful fellow. Gosh, golly, my dad must be pleased'. And then *I* say, 'You're very welcome, Audrey. Now, I hope there'll be no more talk of dirty dealing or backstabbing'. There *won't* be, will there?"

"No," said Andry, fighting back the urge to add, 'For now'.

"Good," said Pat. "Okay. Got to go. Busy, busy, busy."

There was a click, and the line went to a dial tone.

"He hung up on me," Andry said to her dad.

"He's got things to do," he said. "The offer has been accepted, but the paperwork will have to go through at least one more draft before we send it. I want all loose ends tied off."

"A hundred and ninety?" said Andry, setting the phone down. "I thought you said one-seven-five was as high as you'd go."

"I see," said her dad. "You put your haggle hat on *now*."

"Why, though?" asked Andry.

"I needed to get it done," he said. "No pre-surveying, no dickering about. I just wanted it bought, to show you I'm serious."

"About what?" asked Andry.

"There's a *second* stage of the plan," said her dad with a sigh. "The idea was I bring you here, you fall in love with the place, and then the renovations and refurbishments could be done with you as my sole consultant. I could send you catalogues and samples, photos of the progress. It could be an ongoing project, a way to shorten the distance between us, which seems to have gotten pretty bloody wide recently, and I'm not just talking about drivetime."

"Why didn't you mention this before?" asked Andry.

"It was *meant* to be a surprise," said her dad with a tut. "Little did I know it'd backfire like this. If you're not interested,

I can do it all on my own. I should've seen it coming that lakeside holiday houses weren't your thing, just because *I've* got childhood ties to them. You're *not* me, you're never *going* to be me. It's just that, now me and your mum have separated, I don't want our relationship to become like …"

"Like a business?" Andry finished for him, remembering what Morgan had said.

"Exactly," said her dad. "Meeting each other at set times every year, all formal and regimented." He gave a short, sarcastic laugh. "And what's the best I can come up with? I offer to take you on as a decorating consultant. I mean, damn, *they're* lower than plasterers."

"What if I told you," said Andry, shifting her weight from one leg to the other, "that everything's going to be okay?"

"I don't see how," said her dad. "Fifteen grand over my lowest offer, and I've got the get the place up and running as soon as possible. I might *have* to turn it into a commercial property, and that's a tin of worms that I'm *not* ready to open."

"You need to learn to stop being so hot and cold," said Andry, sitting down next to him on the bed. "I can't read your mind, and these mood swings don't help."

"*Me,* hot and cold?" said her dad. "You told me to get stuffed not long ago. Now you're telling me everything will be okay?"

"If you don't want our relationship to be like a business," said Andry, "then you need to stop acting like you're my boss. I'm not an employee, I'm not a client, and I'm certainly not a consultant. If you can just be my dad every now and then, things will be much easier. No more demands to attend Rossall, no more talk of secret bank accounts and stuff like that."

"Rossall, I can understand," said her dad with a huff, "but you'll change your tune when the *secret* bank account starts filling up."

"There," said Andry, elbowing him in the ribs. "*That*. Stop doing *that*. Pat might have a mind that runs on money, but how you were talking just a moment ago, it sounded like you wanted this to be a passion project, something that means *more* than money."

"Are you saying you're up for it?" asked her dad, a glimmer of hope passing across his face.

"I'm thinking …" said Andry, furrowing her brow and twisting her lips. "Black! The whole place, black! Walls, carpets, curtains, everything. We could call it 'Shadow Hall.'"

"Hmm, yeah," said her dad. "Maybe I won't have you as my *sole* consultant."

"Why did you want Pat to tell me about the sale?" asked Andry.

"If you heard it from him," said her dad, "you'd know it was legit. Anyway, I *did* want you to apologise to him. I know he's not always the easiest person to deal with, but he's a good and *loyal* business partner, who I might go as far as to call a friend, as long as he doesn't hear me say it. The last thing I need is him thinking that you're trying to sow mischief. It's just the kind of feather he needs in his cap to use as an excuse to become difficult."

"How so?" asked Andry.

"When someone thinks you don't trust them," said her dad, "they're more likely to do untrustworthy things. If Pat isn't sure that he has my full support, I can't guarantee that he'll always lend me *his*. Believe it or not, buying the lake property was as much a test of *his* mettle as it was *mine*. If this all went wrong, he might've found himself looking for a new boss, and who's going to want to take on the disgraced Martin Watt's leftover guy?"

"Seems like a big risk," said Andry, "for *both* of you, especially if there's nothing in it for Pat."

She wondered if this was the reason for Pat's underhanded scheme, and why he'd been so cocky about it with her. It wasn't that he was looking to snatch the lake-house right from under her dad's nose, but was, instead, laying the groundwork for him to 'Acquire' it, should their business relationship come to an end in the future. This actually made a lot more sense, and she wished she'd thought of it sooner. The way for her to keep Pat's mitts off of the lake-house wasn't to say that she had no interest in it. What she had to do was stick to the place like glue, to keep it in her dad's mind, so that it didn't become just another asset to be shifted around with the stroke of a pen.

"It's all about risk in this game," said her dad. "Everyone laughed at me, Pat included, when I bought those canal-side warehouses in Nottingham. No-one else would touch them, but what are they now? High-end office suites, and they bagged us our first million when they sold. Gross, of course. Hardly any of it ended up in *my* pocket, but I made the point that I was someone who could take a risk and have it pay off. After that, the offers to develop properties for other people came rolling in."

"Which is why your competitors at home are keeping an eye on what you do here," said Andry with a nod. "They want to see if this is one risk too many."

"Imagine their faces," said her dad with a grin, "when I go back and spread the word around that I got the place for sixty thousand below asking price. No-one knows what I originally offered, so I can still make it look like a steal."

"And there's really *nothing* in it for Pat?" asked Andry.

"Oh, I'll slip him a bonus of some sort," said her dad. "A few grand should keep him happy. It should also keep him off my back when he finds out how much it's going to cost to refurbish the place. I'm guessing you don't want just matt black from B&Q. You'll be after fancy stuff, with metallic flakes in it."

"Ooh, that *would* be nice," said Andry, "but I'm sick of business talk." She stood, grabbing both of her dad's hand and hauling him up with her. "I think we should celebrate."

"Celebrate?" said her dad. "This is a nice enough place, but it's hardly a party venue."

"*You* didn't see what it was like after you went to bed last night," said Andry. "They played music and sang. It was great."

"Wasn't that a one off?" asked her dad.

"Nope," said Andry. "They're doing it again tonight. Only, *don't* have any more of the weird stew. I'm sure it's what made you sick."

"I still reckon it was the beer," said her dad.

"You've gotten through *those* without a problem," said Andry, nodding at the pint glasses on the dresser.

"Ah, touché," said her dad. "Okay, we'll celebrate. Just don't let anyone catch on as to *why* we're celebrating. If they ask, we'll say it's my birthday."

"Is Mister short, blonde and stupid invited?" asked Andry.

"Yeah, alright," said her dad, after feigning deliberation. "I suppose he should be on the guestlist. By the looks of it, I might end up with him as a bloody son-in-law one day."

They made as merry as they could while they were by themselves, but it wasn't until people started showing up for the share that things really took off.

They kept coming up to their table, nodding and tugging their caps to Andry's dad, and saying things like, "Thank you, Sir," and "Many happy returns, Sir."

"What's with them all?" asked Andry, after this had happened for the fifth time. "Why are they so nice? And what're they thanking you for?"

"I stuck twenty quid behind the bar," said her dad. "It's not cigarettes in gold foil packets, but I figured it might win us a few fans." He took a sip from his own drink, his third so far, not including the two in his room. "Where's your paramour? I thought you wanted him here."

"He's in his room," said Andry. "He took a fall earlier, so he's resting up."

"Well, you can go and ask if the poor sod wants to join us," said her dad. "We can say it's a special occasion, so his mum won't have him scurrying around collecting glasses, seeing as he's wounded."

"I'll go and find him," said Andry. As she got up from the table, she pointed to the other side of the barroom. "Don't just sit here. Go over by the fireplace. You'll want a good seat for when the songs start."

As she headed for Morgan's room, she looked back at her dad. He'd gotten up to switch seats, but there was a noticeable sway to his stance, and he was forced to steady himself against the back of his chair.

She slipped into Morgan's room and found him with his coat and wellies already on.

"Are you ready?" he asked.

"I'm getting there," she said. "I've told my dad you're hurt, so it won't seem odd if I come in here again."

"What if he comes looking?" asked Morgan.

"He won't," said Andry. "A few more drinks by the warm fireplace, and he'll have to be *dragged* up."

"I hid the pokers outside," said Morgan. "I grabbed them when my mum wasn't watching and put them by the door."

"Nice one," said Andry. "What if we need to ditch them? Will anyone notice they're gone?"

"Only when the fireplace gets cleaned tomorrow morning," said Morgan, "and that's usually *my* job. If I'm the one to say they've gone missing, my parents will think it was one of the sharers who took them."

"That's *if* we make it back," said Andry,

"Hey," said Morgan, frowning at her. "You said not to think like that."

"Sorry," said Andry, "I can't help it. I mean, all of *this* is just to get us out the door. We've not really planned for what might come next."

"Don't go having second thoughts now," said Morgan. "It'll spread to *me*, and I won't want to go."

"I'll shut up, then," said Andry. "The next time I come knocking, it'll be time to move."

She went back to the barroom and noticed that the strange smelling steam had made its appearance, along with half a dozen or so more people. Seats were being claimed, the fiddle was being tuned, and she had to push through the throng to reach her dad. She saw that 'One too many' Terry was with him.

"Nah, you're not a day over thirty-five," he said to her dad. "I refuse to believe it."

All of his previous menace seemed to have vanished, but Andry supposed that the offer of a free drink or two was the likely cause.

"What about *her*?" asked her dad, pointing at Andry as

she joined them. "She's nearly sixteen. Do the maths. I came straight out of university, and straight into business. I didn't have *time* to be siring any kids until I was in my thirties."

"Must be something in that city water," said Terry. "Keeps you looking youthful."

"Yeah," said her dad. "*Lead*, most probably. We city folk don't have to worry about nuclear bombs, because we're full from head to toe with lead. Radiation wouldn't touch us."

"He moisturises," said Andry, taking a seat next to her dad.

"He what?" said Terry.

"Moisturises," Andry repeated. "Twice a day. *That's* how he stays looking so young."

"Really?" Terry asked her dad. "You slather yourself up like a woman?"

"Mate, the birds *love* it," her dad retorted. "We're not talking about any little pots of perfumed poofy stuff. It's a big tub, costs about a quid and lasts ages. It works on your hands, too."

"Oh, aye," said Terry with a snigger. "Shuffling through stacks of paper must make your hands as rough as owt."

"I'll have that pint back off you in a minute," said her dad, wagging a finger at Terry and grinning. "I'm telling you, pal, men taking care of themselves is the future. Just you wait and see."

"He's right," said Andry, linking an arm through his. "A man being in touch with his feminine side only makes his masculine side *more* masculine. We girls don't care if he moisturises, or if he dyes his hair. We care that he makes the effort."

"My hair is *not* dyed!" said her dad as Terry broke into further chuckles. "Anyway, if we're talking about masculine, where's your countryside Samson?"

"He's still feeling bad," said Andry. "I said I'd go and keep him company a bit later."

"I'll leave you be," said Terry. "I want to be up front for the share. Happy birthday to you, and thanks again for the ale."

"This is going well," said Andry. "If we'd known that all it would take was a few free pints, we could've done it yesterday."

"No, that would've seemed suspicious," said her dad. "One foot through the door and throwing money around? They'd have taken it, but they wouldn't have been *this* pleasant about it. Besides, I've not won them *all* over." He nudged her with his knee and nodded to the other side of the room. "*He* hasn't thanked me yet."

Andry saw that he was nodding towards Dennis, who was sat in the same place as the previous night, puffing on his pipe.

"He probably thinks your bad luck," said Andry, "because you pulled the dodgy rune."

"Runes, spoons, balloons," said her dad with a tut. "If he wants to be a grump because I don't believe in his rubbish, then let him. I'll bet he didn't pay for that pint he's drinking, though."

The man with the dog on a rope walked by them and pointed at her dad's empty glass while raising his own.

"Another, Marty?" he asked.

"Why not," her dad replied. "Actually, make it two. I don't feel like getting up again."

"He just called you Marty," said Andry, watching the man waltz eagerly towards the bar, the dog following with less enthusiasm. "Who calls you Marty?"

"Apparently, *he* does," said her dad. "Good sign, eh? Get yourself a nickname, and you're sorted."

"You've not been handing out cards, have you?" asked Andry, frowning at him. "One pint, one card, call me if you change your mind?"

"Of course not," said her dad. "By the time word gets out that it's me who's bought the lake place, and this lot put two and two together, we won't be back until the labourers break ground. It should work in our favour. 'Marty Watt?', they'll say. 'Why, *he's* the guy who got all the drinks in that night. Jolly nice fella.'"

A ripple of excitement passed through the crowd, signalling that the share had begun. Morgan's dad appeared behind the bar and gave almost the exact same speech as he had the previous night. A line then formed, and everyone received their bowls.

"There's more this time," said Andry as a sharer passed by them, his bowl cupped in both hands to stop the contents from spilling.

"Must've been a good day for eels," said her dad, sniffing the air. "I don't understand how something can smell so good but make you feel so bad."

"Remember how that paella in Tenerife made *me* feel bad?" said Andry. "It must be like that. Only the natives can stomach it."

"We'll be semi-native at some point," said her dad, "then we can find out what it *really* is."

Andry had to fight back the urge to say something witty, like 'If I told you, you'd puke on the spot'.

"It must be special, rare eels," she said instead. "*Electric* eels, maybe. I can't imagine eating one of *them* would be very nice the first few times."

The man with the dog reappeared, carrying three pints on a tray, along with his brimming bowl.

"Will you give us a song?" he asked Andry's dad, nodding at the fiddle player, who looked to be about ready. "It's usually only those who partake of the share who sing. Seeing as it's your birthday, though."

"Oh, you do *not* want to hear me sing," said Andry's dad, taking two of the pints and shaking his head. "I've got a voice like hitting two cats together."

"Ah, we're hardly a church choir," said the dog man. "See how you feel once we start. We don't hear many southern songs. It'd make a nice change."

"Yeah, we'll see," said Andry's dad.

The fiddle struck up, and the first singer stepped forward. He sang a very upbeat jig about bringing in the harvest. Andry kept sneaking glances at her dad. His face remained stoney, but she saw that his foot began tapping against the leg of the table by the third verse.

"What do you think?" she asked as they applauded the end of the song. "Not bad, eh?"

"Pretty good," said her dad, draining the first of his pints. "The lyrics were a tad cheeky."

"They're all a bit samey," said Andry. "I don't see why everyone gets so excited about harvesting. It sounds like a lot of hard work."

"That's one way of putting it," said her dad with a snort.

"What do you mean?" asked Andry.

"You understand it was about sex, right?" said her dad.

"It wasn't," said Andry.

"It *was*," said her dad with a nod. "A seed laid down in fertile soil by labour's loving hand?"

"Crops," said Andry.

"Sex," said her dad. "*All* these old pastoral songs are about sex."

"Apart from the ones about drinking," said Andry.

"Well, yeah," said her dad. "That usually comes first. Keep it in mind if him in his room ever starts singing you any songs."

"I doubt it," said Andry. "He likes The Shadows."

"Really?" asked her dad. "Well, I guess there's hope for him yet."

The performances continued, and even though Andry was now looking for an excuse to slip away, she kept an ear open to the songs and found that many of them did, indeed, contain lines which could be taken as double entrendres. Maybe these country folk were more Punk than she'd thought.

Her dad quickly progressed from foot tapping to thigh slapping to clapping his hands above his head. She was glad that he was getting into the swing of things and knew it was time to act.

When Dennis finally got up to sing, she spoke into her dad's ear as a hush fell over the room.

"Check *this* out," she said. "I'll be right back."

She headed for Morgan's room, stopping on the way to speak to the dog man.

"My dad says same again," she told him. "I think that means for both of you."

"If he's footing the bill," grinned the dog man, "I'll play waiter all night."

This time, instead of taking the dog with him, he raised a leg of his chair and slipped the looped end of the rope under it. The dog watched him go, took a wary look at Andry, then hopped its front legs up onto the table and began lapping at the dregs in its master's bowl.

Andry was about to tell it that this might not be good idea, but she decided she'd had enough of talking to animals and stones.

When she reached Morgan's door, she stood with her back to it, making sure no-one could see her, and knocked. It opened a crack, and Morgan peered out.

"Is this it?" he asked.

"Yes," said Andry. "Quick, while everyone's distracted."

They went to the side door and stepped outside. Morgan took a stone from the path and set it in the gap, closing it slowly.

"Not as good as before," he said, "but we can't risk someone noticing that it isn't shut. I left my bedroom window open, just in case, but it'd be a tight squeeze."

"You're calling me fat again," said Andry.

"No," said Morgan with a tut. "The ground floor windows open from the top," he held his hands out, about two feet apart, "by *that* much."

"What if we get back," asked Andry, "and this door *is* shut? The front ones, too."

"Then we find out how not fat you really are," said Morgan, "and we hope that whoever catches us thinks they've nabbed us on the way *out*, not on the way back *in*."

"At least you've thought ahead," said Andry. "You're good at this. You should sneak around more often."

"After tonight," said Morgan, "I'm never sneaking anywhere again. You're a bad influence."

"Yep," said Andry. "It's another one of my talents."

As they headed across the carpark, Andry saw that it wasn't yet fully dark. The sun was still hovering on the horizon, but thick clouds had rolled in, meaning it wouldn't be long before the night took hold, and it'd be a black one at that.

Morgan guided her to a bush by the roadside, pulling aside the lower branches to reveal the stashed pokers. He'd put the torch from the shed there, too, which he slipped into his pocket.

"We don't use it unless we absolutely have to," he said. "I hope you've got good night vision."

"All the more reason to hold hands, eh?" said Andry.

She picked up one of the pokers and gave it swing through the air. Morgan hadn't been kidding. She definitely wouldn't want to be on the receiving end of a blow from one. The rod was thick and heavy, tempered by years of use, the barb at the end long and savage, more like a shorter version of a whaler's blubber hook than a poker.

"Think you can handle it?" asked Morgan, picking up the other one.

"It doesn't really matter," said Andry. "If I saw someone holding *this*," she shook the poker at him, "I'd run off without throwing a punch."

"That's the idea," said Morgan. "I'm just hoping we don't have to test it"

They set off along the road until they reached the first drystone wall, clambering over it to use as cover.

"What's the best way to go?" asked Andry when they got to the corner of the first field.

"We follow the road around where it bends," said Morgan. "There's about a hundred yards where we'll be out in the open, but it's the quickest way to the lake-house."

"It felt like no time at all in the car," said Andry.

"You keep a *look* out for cars," said Morgan. "If one catches us on that open stretch of road, the show's over."

They hopped over the wall, crossed a lane, and went into a row of trees along the side of the road. This kept them out of sight for most of the bend, but the trees eventually ceased. Just as Morgan had warned, the tightest part of the bend, and the straight which led towards the lake, offered no cover at all.

"We're just gonna have to make a dash for it," said Andry. "I don't hear any cars. I don't see any lights. There's no-one coming."

"Okay," said Morgan. "Only, don't stop when we reach the lake-house. Keep going. It's the far wall that we need."

They came out from the treeline and hit the road at a jog. It didn't take long before Andry was cursing her boots again, they really *were* terrible for running, and Morgan didn't seem to be having a better time in his wellies. The slaps of their feet on the surface of the road seemed uncannily loud as they headed around the bend. It sounded as though a whole troupe of people were on the march.

When the road straightened again, Andry saw the upper part of the lake-house coming into view. She could just about make out the highest part of the roof, as well as a glimmer off to the right, where the last rays of the sun struck the conservatory.

When she reached the wall, she darted towards it, running alongside it to keep her bearings. She passed the gates but didn't stop for a better look at the darkened house, instead carrying on, just as Morgan had instructed.

She tried a few times to look over her shoulder, to see if he was still following, but this was difficult to do at such a pace and while trying not to drop the poker.

The wall abruptly ended, and it took her a few more strides to slow down and turn back around. Morgan was, of course, still following, and he went sideways at the apex of the wall.

"Come back!" he said, trying to shout and whisper at the same time. "You've gone too far!"

She'd steadied herself by now and went to join him, both

of them stooping down and pressing themselves against the wall, the dense tendrils of ivy cracking and rustling as they leaned into them.

"Keep your hair on," she said. "We've made it."

Morgan was breathing heavily and sniffing from the ordeal of the run.

"I … I almost …" he panted. "I almost dropped the poker."

"Me, too," said Andry. "You didn't, though. Good on you."

"Let's just … just sit here and listen for moment," said Morgan, his breath slowing a little.

They went quiet and listened hard. There was a slight breeze blowing through the ivy fronds, and Andry was sure she could make out a faint lapping of the water on the lakeshore. It could almost have been serene if they'd been there for any other reason.

"I don't hear anything," she said. "Come on. We've got to move."

She stood up, grabbing Morgan by the arm and dragging him to his feet.

"Who first?" he asked, looking up at the thick wall of ivy.

"Here," said Andry, giving him her poker raising a foot. "Give me a leg up."

"What about me?" asked Morgan, leaning the pokers against the wall before lacing his fingers together.

"I'll get on the top," said Andry, setting her boot into his hands, "then I'll reach down for you."

"Crikey," said Morgan through gritted teeth as he heaved her up. "I thought you said you weren't fat."

"Not the best time to be cracking jokes, mate," said Andry, grabbing hold of the ivy.

The plants were thick and strong but climbing them was nowhere near as easy as she'd imagined. The density of the leaves forced her to keep her head down, and the stems gave off powdery flakes when clutched, which got into her eyes and mouth. She managed to find occasional footholds in the bricks, helping her to drag herself up through the foliage.

When she reached the top, she leaned over it on her belly and turned back around, her legs dangling behind her.

"Are you there?" asked Morgan when the leaves stopped shaking.

"Yeah," said Andry. "Pass me one of the pokers, then I'll use the other to help you."

Morgan took the pokers from the wall and stood on his tiptoes, thrusting one up, handle first, towards Andry. She seized it and set it down on top of the wall beside her. When she had a grip on the handle of the next one, she pulled as hard as she could, hearing Morgan coughing and spluttering as he was hauled through the leaves. When she saw the top of his head emerge, she reached down with her other hand and took hold of the collar of his coat. He let go of the poker and grabbed her forearm. Between them, they got him up on the wall next to her, where he sat with one leg hanging at either side.

"That's stage two, then," he said. Andry couldn't quite make out his face, but she could tell from his voice that he was smiling. "We're doing okay so far."

"The ivy isn't as thick on this side," said Andry, shifting around on the wall to face the house. "We can slide down it, to save us from jumping, but this might not be our exit route."

"If we have to come out in a hurry," said Morgan, "I'll be scared enough to jump over in one bound."

"We'll see," said Andry. "If there's nothing in there, we can take all the time we want."

She picked up one of the pokers, turned over, and carefully started to lower herself down the other face of the wall. The ivy was, indeed, much thinner, and she slid the last third of the way, her knees scraping against the bricks. Luckily, her boots made up for their lack of running ease, and she landed without stumbling.

Morgan came after her, but he began slipping before he was even halfway down, and she hopped forward to try and break his fall. He must have struck his chin on a jutting brick, as she heard his teeth crack together with an awful snap before he collapsed backwards and she grabbed him under the armpits.

"Ah, ya bleeder!" he groaned, clasping a hand to his mouth.

"Why did you let go?" Andry hissed, yanking him to his feet.

"I didn't let go," said Morgan, looking around for his dropped poker. "I didn't have anything to let go *of*."

"Are you alright?" asked Andry.

"I don't know," said Morgan, sounding a bit dazed.

"Come here," said Andry. She took hold of his chin and stuck a finger into his mouth, quickly probing around inside. "Yeah, they're all there. You're fine."

Morgan gagged and slapped her hand away.

"I was better without a gobful of ivy muck," he said, coughing and spitting.

"Find the poker," said Andry, tightening her grip around her own, "then follow me. The conservatory is where we'll get in."

Once they'd readied themselves, they headed across the lawn towards the front of the house. The grass was tall and dense with weeds after years of no maintenance, so walking through it caused more noise than they were comfortable with. To make matters worse, the paths at the front and sides of the house were covered with flint gravel, which crunched like crisp packets as they trod on it.

It occurred to Andry that all this sneaking could be for nothing. They hadn't heard or seen a single car as they'd made their way here, none had passed while they were dealing with the wall, and there didn't seem to be anyone waiting for them now that they were in the grounds of the house. Still, she had to remind herself that it wasn't just other people that they had to worry about. For all she knew, every one of the house's darkened windows could be hiding a 'You know what', and them stomping up to the place without a care would sound the alarm and bring on all sorts of trouble. With this in mind, she stepped very lightly across the stones of the path.

When they reached the conservatory, she dropped to her haunches and began slowly inching around it, scanning each pane.

"Why here?" whispered Morgan, hunkering down next to her.

"Because," Andry replied, keeping her own voice low, "if we're *really* lucky." She carried on sideways, running her hand across the plastic divider between the glass. "Bingo."

The fourth pane along was broken. Most of the glass was still intact, but there was a hole in the bottom corner, just large enough for her to fit her hand through.

"I don't get it," said Morgan. "That bit doesn't open."

"It doesn't need to," said Andry. "Take your coat off."

Morgan did so, and Andry took it from him, turning one of the sleeves inside out and scrunching it up. She threaded the end through the hole in the glass, let it expand, and then pressed the rest of it against the pane. She spun her poker around, levelling the handle at the edge of the hole.

"Wait," said Morgan, grabbing her shoulder. "You can't *break* it."

"I can," said Andry. "I own the place now. I can break whatever I like."

"The noise, though," said Morgan.

"There won't be any," said Andry. "I once saw a guy bust into a shop this way. A little hole makes the rest come out easy."

Before Morgan could protest again, she struck the poker handle against the coat. The result wasn't completely silent, but the glass was weakened enough for a large chunk of the pane break away with a single, sharp crack. She kept hold of it with the coat and slid it out, setting it down carefully. In this way, she was able to get the entire pane out with only two more strikes, giving them enough room to squeeze through.

"You're really clever," said Morgan, the smile clear in his voice again. "I'd have never been able to do that."

"Street smarts, I suppose," said Andry. She hadn't been lying when she'd said she'd seen someone break into a shop using this method, but she didn't want to burst Morgan's bubble by admitting that she'd seen it on the telly and hadn't been entirely sure that it'd work.

She flipped his coat the right way around and used it to pat at the edges of the window frame, checking for any stray shards. When she was satisfied, she laid down on her front and began crawling through.

"Maybe I should wait here," said Morgan, pulling his coat back on, "in case anyone comes."

"So they can *see* you waiting here?" said Andry. "Get shifting. I'm not going in alone."

After a bit of hesitation, Morgan followed her, sliding his poker through the gap before pulling his coat collar up over his neck and inching his way forward, obviously still worried about glass shards.

"Shall we go upstairs first?" he asked when he was through.

"No," said Andry. "We don't know the layout of the place. Going upstairs could trap us."

"*You* own it now," said Morgan standing up and shaking himself off. "Weren't you shown a floorplan or something?"

"That *would've* come in handy," said Andry, looking around for a door leading into the main building. "Pass me the torch."

"Not in here," said Morgan, placing a hand over his pocket. "A room made of windows? It'll shine like a lighthouse."

"Fine," said Andry. "You keep an eye on the rear."

She found the door, which, to her relief and slight astonishment, wasn't locked. It led into what she guessed was the kitchen. There were no appliances, nor any pots or utensils hanging anywhere, and she figured that the place must've been thoroughly emptied upon the death of the previous owners. There was a counter in the centre of the room, and she made towards it, finding a double basin sink in the middle, definitely the kitchen.

"Okay," she muttered to herself. "Kitchen, conservatory, out."

"What?" whispered Morgan as he came up behind her.

"I'm making a floorplan as we go along," said Andry. She stepped away from the counter and towards the darkened doorway on the other side of the room. She peered around it, looking both ways. On the right was the front door, and the left led to the bottom of a set of stairs. "Bottom of the stairs, hallway, right, kitchen, conservatory, out."

"Are you going to do that in every room?" asked Morgan. "Can't you do it in your head?"

"Just keep close by me," said Andry. "Remember what you said about leaving in a hurry? It'll help if we're not running through random doors like the Mystery Gang."

She stepped into the hall. Thinking that the stairs were still a bad idea until they'd checked the ground floor, she went by them and found another doorway, this one leading into a large, open room.

"It looks smaller on the outside," said Morgan. "Do you even know how many rooms there are?"

"Five beds, two and a half baths is all I was told," said Andry. She snapped her fingers. "It's definitely torch time."

Morgan brought out the torch and flicked it on. The space was some sort of lounge or drawing room. A large fireplace was built into the internal wall, and they could see marks on the carpet, where furniture had once stood.

"Gosh, they didn't leave a stick," said Morgan, passing the light over the floor.

"Doesn't matter," said Andry. "I'd have thrown it all out anyway." She rubbed her foot at one of the indentations on the carpet. "*This'll* be the first thing to go."

Further exploration revealed three more rooms and a hallway which went right along the rear of the building, taking them through a pantry, a small washroom, and back to the stairs. During their search, they didn't see or hear anything out of place. There wasn't even anywhere for anyone to hide. As Morgan had said, the whole place was as bare as though it'd just been built.

By now, Andry's mental floorplan was getting rather mixed up, and she kept trying to run it through her head in the right order. She decided that, as long as she knew where the stairs were, there wouldn't be too much of a problem, trusting that she and Morgan didn't get separated.

They turned off the torch as they climbed to the next floor, not wanting to announce their arrival to anything that might be waiting up there. They needn't have worried, however, as all that greeted them was a long hall with several doors, much like the ones back at the pub. They checked each room in turn, opening the doors, pokers raised, and briefly shining the torch into them. Every single one was completely empty. The only fright they got was when they opened one of the doors, only to be startled by what appeared to be two figures looking back at them. Morgan had about jumped out of his skin and began waving his poker side to side, but all it turned out to be was a mirror fixed to the opposite wall.

"There's no-one here," said Andry, when they'd finished checking the bathroom at the end of the hall. "We're good."

"So, what now?" asked Morgan.

"Now we're sure we're alone," said Andry, "we can have a *proper* look around."

"I thought we just *did*," said Morgan. "Shouldn't we get out of here?"

"We haven't found anything yet," said Andry.

"There's nothing to find," said Morgan, frustration mixing with the nerves in his voice. "We searched every room."

"There has to be something that we won't see at first glance," said Andry. "If the 'You know what' *are* interested in this place, then there must be a reason why. They're clearly not holding up in any of these rooms. So, what's the deal?"

"I don't think they *have* a deal," said Morgan. "Who knows why they do what they do."

"Do I have to remind you what happens if we don't figure this out?" snapped Andry. "Give me the torch. I'll make another pass up here, and you stand watch by the stairs. *Don't* go back down them. Empty or not, we shouldn't split up."

"I have to stand there in the dark?" Morgan whined. "On my own?"

"Oh, give over," said Andry, snatching the torch from him. "I'm only going back up the hall. I'll hear you if you shriek."

She returned to the bathroom and began a more thorough inspection. She ran the beam of the torch across every wall, ceiling and floor, checking in the corners and behind the doors, but there was nothing. To make matters worse, the torch started blinking on and off. She stepped back into the hall, shaking the torch.

"What's wrong?" she heard Morgan ask from the top of the stairs.

"Bloody batteries are dying," she said. "Did you bring any spares?"

"No," said Morgan. "They *should* be alright. That torch hardly ever gets used."

"Typical," Andry tutted to herself as the torch blinked off. She shook it again, then turned it over, to see how to open it. It flickered back on, the light shining right into her eyes. She flinched, and as she jerked her head back, she spotted something on the hallway ceiling.

"Hey!" she called to Morgan. "I think there's a hatch here!"

Sure enough, as she held the torch up at arm's length, she saw there was a small door built into the ceiling.

"Oh, yeah," said Morgan, looking up at it as he came to join her. "How did we miss that?"

"This is why we needed a *proper* look," said Andry. "If we open it, I'll bet you anything a set of steps folds out."

"We *can't* open it," said Morgan. "It's all the way up there."

"I think we're supposed to have a hook on a pole," said Andry, running the beam of the torch around the edges of the hatch. "See? There's the ring." She handed the torch to Morgan. "Which of the pokers is longest?"

"They're about the same," said Morgan, "but they'll never reach that high."

"Give me a leg up again," said Andry, grabbing his shoulder with one hand, gripping her poker with the other, and raising a boot. "One big shove, and I'll try and snag it."

They tried this twice, but it didn't work. Morgan wasn't able to give a hefty enough pull to propel her within reaching distance of the hatch.

"You're useless," she said, preparing herself for a third attempt.

"Well, pardon *me* for not being able to fling you around like an acrobat," said Morgan. "Let's switch places. I'm lighter."

"Now, that's *definitely* calling me fat," said Andry.

"Not the best time to be cracking jokes, *mate*," said Morgan with a sneer as he tugged his coat off.

It turned out that Morgan *was* lighter than Andry, or that she was simply stronger than him, as she was able to keep him held up for a good few seconds before her arms gave out and she had to drop him, but he still wasn't able to secure the barb of the poker onto the hatch ring, not even after four tries.

"This is stupid," she said. "We can't keep playing at hook-a-duck. Why did they have to take *all* the furniture?"

"Just one more go," said Morgan, the eagerness in his voice so bright that it almost *was* as though they were playing a fairground game. "I almost had it."

"Alright," said Andry. "One more, but then we'll have to leave it."

They got back into position, Morgan steadying his foot into Andry's clasped hands. She gave it everything she had, launching him up towards the hatch, and then wrapping her arms around his calves, teetering from side to side as she clutched them to her chest.

"Come on, *come on*," said Morgan, the tip of his poker scratching against the wood of the hatch. He twisted in Andry's grip, so that she received a less than decent look at his backside. She jerked her head around and gritted her teeth. Lighter or not, him wriggling like this wasn't making things any easier.

She was just about to drop him, and tell him she wasn't a highchair, when something caught her eye. They were by the door to the room where they'd had their shocking run-in with the mirror. She could see herself in it, slightly distorted and lit from beneath by the torch, which she'd set on the floor to better illuminate the hatch. However, she now saw that there was another light source. A pale, shimmering haze appeared to be just above her right shoulder. It took her a second to realise that it was coming through the window behind her.

"There's a light," she said, letting Morgan's legs slide through her arms.

"Hold me up!" cried Morgan. "I've nearly got it!"

"Forget it," said Andry, letting him fall the last few feet. "There's a light out there."

Morgan stumbled and dropped the poker as Andry went over to the window.

"Out where?" he asked as he straightened up.

"Out *there*," said Andry, waving for him to follow, "across the water."

Morgan came to join her, bundling his coat under his arm.

"What *is* that?" he asked, nervousness returning to his voice.

"*I* don't know, do I?" said Andry. "Have you ever seen a light over there before?"

"Never," said Morgan. "It can't be on the other side. It's too bright."

He was right. There was no way that even the most powerful torch or car headlight could shine across the lake with such intensity. It was also the wrong colour. Instead of white or yellow, it had a blueish hue to it, with hints of green and purple. It wasn't moving, but it seemed to throb and pulse, growing momentarily brighter, then dimmer.

"It's like a fire," said Andry. "The kind you get on a gas burner, but bigger."

"It must be coming from the island," said Morgan.

"What's on this island?" asked Andry.

"There's a building," said Morgan. "It's a round thing with pillars." His rising fear caused his voice to crack. "Seriously, what *is* that!"

"Calm down," said Andry. "Whatever it is, it can't get us from all the way over there."

"I still don't like it," said Morgan. "We should go."

"Not yet," said Andry. "We came looking for something, so we can't run away scared the moment we find it."

"*You* said look in the house," said Morgan, jabbing a finger into her chest before turning it on the window. "*That's* not in the house. We need to leave, *now*."

"Just give it a moment," said Andry. "We'll see what happens."

She took hold of his hand, hoping that he thought she was doing it to soothe him, but she was actually doing it so he couldn't run off.

As they stood and watched the strange light, it brightened and dimmed and brightened again, but there was no noticeable pattern to it, which ruled out any kind of mechanical source.

Andry went right up to the window, pressing her nose against the glass and cupping a hand over her brow. She tried to time the gap between the pulses by clicking her tongue at what she guessed were second long intervals, sure that there must be *some* sort of rhythm to it, but she had no luck. She was about to ask Morgan to do the same, when the light gave one last throb, and then died away. She was reminded again of the ring on a gas hob, the flames being gradually extinguished, rather than abruptly turned off with a switch.

"It stopped," whispered Morgan. "Thank *God*."

"It must've happened for a reason," said Andry, "and if we'd been in any other room, we wouldn't have seen it." She took Morgan's hand again and squeezed it. "There's Wyrdness going on right now."

Before Morgan could reply, a sudden, clattering sound came from the floor below them. They both froze, and Morgan's hand gripped so tightly around Andry's that it was as though he was trying to break her fingers.

"They're here," he said, his eyes widening. "They were here all along."

Andry twisted her hand out of his and stooped down for the torch, turning it off.

"We went through the whole place," she whispered. "If they were here, we'd have seen them."

With the torch off, she saw that the stairwell was now bathed in pale, blue light. It wasn't shining in through a window. Instead, it appeared to be coming from the hallway on the ground floor. Just like the one they'd seen in the distance, it pulsed and swelled, casting shadows from the banister rails, before dying back down, only to flare up again, illuminating right to the topmost steps.

There was another clatter, and then a bang, followed by the unmistakable sound of a voice, high and rattling, but not speaking discernible words. A shadow passed across the baleful light, and they heard something coming up the steps.

"Quick," hissed Andry. "Hide."

They backed along the hallway, trying to go as fast as they could without making too much noise. Whatever was coming up the stairs was, thankfully, taking its time. Instead of simply marching straight up, it seemed to be stopping every few steps or so, perhaps even going back down a couple, before ascending again.

"My coat," whispered Morgan, pointing to where he'd dropped it by the window.

"Sod the coat," said Andry as they reached the door to the end bathroom.

"The pokers," Morgan persisted.

"Sod *them*, too," said Andry, pushing him into through the door. "Get yourself hidden."

For whatever reason, Morgan decided that the safest place was in the bathtub, and he clambered into it, drawing his knees up to his chest. Andry began slowly closing the door, but she left just a slit for her to look through. She watched, her heart thumping, as a shape appeared at the top of the stairs. She screwed her eyes shut and rubbed the heel of a hand against them, trying to improve her night vision as much as she could. She looked back towards the stairs and saw that the shape had sprouted hands. They patted against the top step, feeling around across the carpet. It then hopped up and turned, silhouetted against the back wall as it sat on its haunches. Andry very nearly cried out and slammed the door shut, but she managed to hold her nerve.

The shadowy figure then rose to full height, and Andry was surprised to see that couldn't have been any more than four feet tall. It stooped again, then started along the hallway at a crawl. There was no way it'd seen her, its movements were far too casual for that, perhaps even a little eager. There was a rustling when it reached where Morgan's coat lay. It began to sniff, and she heard the coat's zip being run up and down.

"Stincan," it gurgled. "Stincan, stincan, dee-da-dee."

"It's a kid," whispered Andry.

"*Be quiet*," Morgan whispered from the tub.

"It's just a kid," said Andry. "A little one."

"That means the big ones won't be far away," said Morgan.

There was more movement from the hall, and Andry turned her attention back to the gap in the door. The kid creature must have found the torch. She heard a dull, plastic knocking as it tapped it against the wall. The torch then blinked on, and Andry got her first real look at a 'You know what'.

It was remarkably humanoid. Two arms, two legs, a torso and a head. No wings, no tentacles, no devil's horns or talons. What caught Andry's attention the most was its flesh. When she'd seen just the single arm, poking up from behind the bush, she'd noticed how it possessed an almost semi-translucency. Now, however, she saw that, as the beam of the torch passed over the thing, the light went almost straight through its skin, revealing the shadows of thin bones beneath. She also recognised the sheen, the same, petrol on water glimmer which seemed to cover its entire body, for it wore no clothes. Thin, lank hair hung from its head, reaching almost to is shoulders and framing its gaunt face, in the centre of which were large, pale eyes, bulging like goose eggs, and without pupils.

"Sar!" it cried, flinging the torch against the wall. "Yfel fyr!"

The torch didn't go out, but was now laying on its side, pointing directly at the door to the bathroom. The thing seethed and spat at it, like a cat with its hackles up. Andry knew she had to hide herself, but she lingered for just a second longer. As the thing bent down to peer at the torch, she saw something fall from around its neck. A fine chain, with an object dangling from the end, swung back and forth through the torch beam.

"The cheeky bugger's got my pendant," she said. "Only, how could it-"

"Pol! Hwaer meaht thu?" a voice called out from the bottom of the stairs. It was much more guttural than the kid creature's gurgling, meaning Morgan had been right about the adult ones turning up eventually.

"Hwaet!" the kid creature replied, looking over its shoulder towards the stairs. "Ic sum thinge funden!"

Andry couldn't make head nor tail of what came next, but she recognised a parental scolding when she heard one. The kid creature hissed and snarled, slapping its hands against the floor and tugging at the wispy strands of its hair. She wondered if there'd be another argument in this bizarre language later on, where the kid creature would consider dropping the pendant down whatever its kind used as a sink.

It gave the torch one last poke, and then turned away, heading back towards the stairs.

"It's leaving," Andry said to Morgan. She stood up and opened the door a little further.

"What are you *doing*?" whispered Morgan, gripping the

edge of the tub.

"I left the pendant by the stone in the woods," said Andry.

"What pendant?" asked Morgan.

"I bought it from a gift shop," said Andry, "and I buried it by the stone earlier today, but the little 'You know what' was wearing it."

"So?" said Morgan. "Let it keep it. I'll buy you another. Just stay where you are."

"If I left it by the stone *today*," said Andry, leaning in over him, "then how has the 'You know what' already *got* it?"

She left him in the tub to puzzle this over, stepping out into the hallway and walking towards the torch. When she reached it, she knelt and turned it off. She also picked up one of the pokers. When she got to the top of the stairs, she tried to peek around the banister, just in case something was still on the steps. There was nothing, only the strange light flashing up the wall. She saw by the direction of the shadows that it was coming from one of the rooms at the rear of the house, most likely the pantry. She and Morgan hadn't found anything of note in there, but they clearly hadn't searched well enough.

She heard footsteps coming along the hall. Morgan was, at last, following her. He held his own poker out in front of him with both hands, as though expecting something to appear from thin air and attack him.

"We take a quick look," he said, his voice trembling, "and then it's stairs, hall, kitchen, conservatory, out, okay?"

They slowly descended the steps. When they reached the bottom, Morgan immediately made for the doorway to the kitchen, but Andry turned to look down the hall. The light *was* coming from the pantry, and she saw there was a hatch standing open in the floor, just like the one they'd been struggling with, only in reverse. They must've walked right over it during their search. It was from here that the light emanated. It perhaps wasn't the source, but the brightness and intensity of the swelling throbs meant they were getting close.

"There's a floor *below* this one," she said. "A cellar or something."

"We're not going in there," said Morgan. "This is far enough."

"I have to see what it is," said Andry. "I'll go down, and you guard the door. Stay out of the way, though. If I have to come back up fast, I don't want you blocking me."

Morgan protested again, but she ignored him, approaching the hatch and looking over the edge. A set of metal steps led down into the space below the floor. There were seven in total, meaning there'd be more than enough room for her to stand once she was down. She set her poker aside and sat next to the opening. She swung her legs around and dangled them through it, holding her breath in anticipation that something would grab them. When nothing did, she shifted to the side and lowered her feet onto the steps.

She started down them, one hand grasping her poker, the other shielding her eyes. She never would've thought she'd find herself going into a cellar which was too bright, a well-lit cellar being far less frightening than a pitch dark one, but she knew that getting dazzled by light could give something just as much opportunity to have the drop on you as darkness could.

Bare earth covered the floor of the space, but it was packed down flat, evidence that it was used often. Thick wood posts supported the floorboards above, dust motes dancing in the air from where her and Morgan's feet had disturbed them.

There was a lull in the intensity of the light, and she finally got a look at what was producing it. Around twenty feet ahead of her, about where the sitting room would be on the floor above, there was a standing stone. It wasn't quite the same as the one in the woods, it was both shorter and broader, but she saw that it was covered from top to bottom in the same, runic inscriptions as its larger counterpart, and it was *these* which produced the light. It was at its lowest brightness now, and she looked in astonished awe as the carvings glowed and flickered, as though they were the outlets for some internal fire which was burning deep within the stone.

She was so taken aback by this, that she didn't immediately register the strangest thing about it. Her eyes adjusted a little, and she realised that the stone was actually the opening of a passage, almost like a curved door jamb leading onto a tunnel. She took a few steps forward, then stopped and had to rethink. It wasn't a passage or a tunnel. In fact, there was no suggestion of depth to it at all. She was looking directly into what appeared to be darkened trees, the trunks and spindly limbs outlined by the glow of the rune-light.

She shook her head to compose herself, and then took a few more steps forward, this time towards the side of the stone. There was nothing there. She even reached out with her poker and swiped it through the air, sure that it'd hit something, but she was able to make a full circle around the stone without finding anything.

When she was back at the 'Front' of the stone, she got as close to it as she dared. She could hardly believe it. Not only could she *see* the woodland in front of her, but she could feel a breeze on her face, the scent of fallen leaves thick upon it.

She held out her poker and slowly moved it forward. It was met with no resistance. She moved further still, letting her arm go through. With two strides, she was on the other side. She turned and looked back, finding that she could still see into the cellar, but noticed that, on *this* side, the stone was much taller.

It hit her all at once. She was back at the *other* stone. The one Morgan had taken her to. The one with the goat, and where she'd buried the pendant. That was how the kid creature had it already. It must've found it when it came through.

For some, odd reason, her first thought was to wonder what Malcolm the Medium and the rest of that loopy bunch would make of *this*. Magic. Real, right there in front of you, magic. She didn't get long to ponder this, however, as she heard a rustling in the trees off to her right, quickly followed by more to her left.

"Ne gat!" a 'You know what' voice called out, and she was sure she'd been spotted. She dashed back through the stone to the cellar and pressed herself against the side of it.

"Ne gat?" another voice replied. "Thri nihtum, ne gat, ne harran, ne fiscas. Hwaet is to etenne?"

"Briddas?" asked the first voice.

"Nese," the second replied. "Ofermycel faer." It then made a sound which you didn't need to be a master linguist to recognise as mimicking a gunshot. "Boosh-boosh!"

Andry herself didn't have to be a language expert to gather that they were looking for the goat. If she'd left it there, this nighttime sortie would've probably been over much quicker, but then she wouldn't have been around to witness it. It occurred to her that, if the 'You know what' knew the goat was supposed to be there, then maybe she'd been wrong about it being bait. Instead, it was an offering, a 'Sacrifice', meant to keep them from raiding henhouses and the like. It made a strange sort of sense. If you raised sheep, and wanted your lambing season to go well, you couldn't have the process disrupted by any of your animals getting snatched. Therefore, a few old ewes, or, in this case, a goat, left out to satisfy these 'Poachers' was an obvious solution, especially if you didn't have any 'Boosh-boosh!'.

"Andry," Morgan whisper-shouted through the trapdoor. "What's going on?"

Andry heard the rustling in the leaves on the other side of the stone suddenly stop. She crept further around the stone, not daring to go forward and be seen, but also wanting Morgan to be able to see *her* if he somehow plucked up the courage to come down the steps.

The rustling in the leaves started up again, and she wrapped her hands firmly around her poker, meaning to bash anything that came through the stone while she could get it from behind.

"Pol!" one of the voices from the other side called out. "Pol! Cum hither!"

A hand crossed the threshold between the woods and the cellar. Andry raised her poker, ready to bring it down with everything she had. It would've been a decapitating blow, had she not stopped just before she was about to deliver it. The face of the kid creature peeked at her around the stone. They both froze, their eyes fixed on each other's. From this distance, she could see that there *were* pupils in the depths of the thing's pale orbs, fine slits, running from top to bottom.

She did the only thing she could think of. Lowering the poker, she quickly snatched out her other hand and seized the thing by the back of the neck.

"Helpan! Helpan!" it screeched, thrashing and twisting in her grip, like a hooked fish.

"Shut up!" she snapped, trying to get it into a chokehold. Even in the dull glow of the rune-light, she could see that the shimmering, oil slick coating on its skin was rubbing off onto the arm of her jumper. She didn't know if this was some sort of defence mechanism, but it certainly made it harder to keep hold of.

"Faeder! Helpan!" it wailed, digging its fingers into Andry's arm.

"I told you to shut it!" Andry growled into where she guessed its ear would be. "Stop that noise!" It then bit her on the wrist, its small but pinprick sharp teeth piercing through her jumper. "Argh! You dirty git!"

She released her arm from around its neck, but before it could get away, she swung the poker across its belly and yanked backwards, trapping it in a less dangerous hold. She looked over its shoulder and saw the two she'd heard talking now standing on the other side of the stone. These were much taller, as tall as an adult, and maybe a bit more. They both looked horrified. One had its hands clasped at the side of its head, the slits of its pupils wide.

"Take it easy," said Andry. "If you can understand me, stay right there, and I'll let the little fella' here go."

"Ic bidde," said the one with its hands at its head. "Ic …" It twisted its mouth into an awful grimace, like it was tasting something foul. "Be you not pain her. I beg."

It spoke as though it were choking on the words, their very utterance a physical ordeal.

"*Her*?" said Andry, looking down at the cringing creature pressed to her chest.

"Min dohtor," said the adult creature, taking its hands from its head and holding them out imploringly as it took a step forward. "Min maegdencild."

"Stay still!" yelled Andry. "Look, I don't want to hurt *anyone*, but—"

She was cut off by the sound heavy footfalls on the floorboards above.

"What're *you* doing here?" cried Morgan, followed by a thud and a groan as he must've been shoved aside.

Andry spun both herself and the creature around to face the steps. Coming down them, two at a time, was Dennis. He held a revolver out at arm's length and aimed it at Andry and the creature as he came towards them.

"Laet hire gan," he snarled.

"Don't point that at *me*!" yelled Andry and jerked her head at the stone. "Point it at *them*!"

When Dennis saw the stone, his arm bent a little, and his eyes grew wide.

"I *knew* it," he said. "All these years, it was right here. No wonder they never let us in."

"What's going on?" asked Andry. "What've you done to Morgan?"

"Nothing," said Dennis and nodded at the floorboards. "He's up there. His fatha's gonna skin him alive when he hears about this." He aimed the gun back at her. "Get away from it, and I'll put it down."

"No," said Andry and actually hugged the creature tighter to her. "This is some sort of mix up. We're trying to talk it over."

"Doesn't look like it to me," said Dennis. "Looks to me like you've wandered into the viper's nest. What were you *thinking*?"

"How did you know we were here?" asked Andry.

"I followed you half of the way," said Dennis, "but you gave me the slip after the bottom field. I didn't think you'd be stupid enough to come *here*, but it's a good thing I checked."

"Faedrer! Faeder!" the kid creature squealed, starting to struggle in Andry's arms again.

"Give it a rest," she said to it. "I'm trying to save your neck. That thing he's holding, Boosh-boosh!"

It seemed to get the message and went still, but the other two started forward.

"Halt!" said Dennis, turning the gun on them.

"Talk to them," said Andry. "Ask them why they're here. Ask them what all of this *is*."

"It's obvious," said Dennis. "*This* is how they've been getting through. Twenty years ago, the last time it got bad, we were *all* wondering how they got through. Where were they coming from? How were they missing the traps? I've been saying for ages that we should uproot the stones and roll them into the lake."

"There must be another on the island," said Andry. "We saw the light."

"Oh, I *know* there is," said Dennis. "What I *didn't* know was where the third one was. The one that links the other two. If only I'd known that those idiots, Tom and his mad wife, had been sitting on it this whole time."

"Please," said Andry, "talk to them. You speak their language. We can sort this out."

"Don't let my singing fool you," said Dennis with a huff, his gun still fixed on the two adult creatures. "I'm far from fluent."

"*Try*," said Andry, clenching her teeth together.

Dennis gave a laboured sigh, then walked towards the stone, his gun still raised. The pair of creatures winced and threw up their arms to cover their faces, but Dennis raised his other hand, palm out.

He then began to speak to them, but Andry couldn't make any of it out. Not only had the kid creature started up with its keening again, but Dennis and the two others spoke so quickly that she wasn't able to pick out single words.

"They say they used to bring their dead here," Dennis called back to her after a lengthy back and forth, "and the ones before, they must mean Tom's family, would take the bodies in exchange for food." He spoke to the pair again. "Only, *they* ended up …" He shook his head. "It's hard to put into our words. They say, 'Burdened by a death in the skull.'"

"Sounds pretty simple to me," said Andry. "They went crazy."

"I suppose so," said Dennis and turned back to the creatures.

The little one continued its whining and began a fresh round of struggling.

"Oh, alright," said Andry, taking the poker from across its chest. Before it could dart away, she grabbed its arm and pulled it back. "Nope. You stay by me for now." She took hold of the pendant and gave it a tug. "This is *mine*, by the way."

"*Ic* funden," said the kid creature, batting her hand away and closing its own over the pendant.

"I don't give a toss," said Andry. "It was for the stone, not for you."

"Dalcop!" the creature snarled at her, baring its teeth.

"Whatever," said Andry. "I've been called worse."

She heard footsteps on the stairs and turned to see that Morgan had finally decided to make an appearance.

"I couldn't stop him," he said. "He pushed me over, knocked the wind right out of me. I heard screaming, so thought I should come down. Only, you said to stay in the hall, and…" He trailed off as he took in the scene around him. When he spotted the kid creature, he jumped on the spot in fright. "Bloody hell!" he cried. "There's one right there! Watch out! It's got you!"

Andry looked at the creature, and it looked back, its eyes seeming to say, 'What's *this* guy's problem?'.

"Yeah," she said, holding up their clasped hands. "Just look how it's attacking me."

Morgan frowned in bewilderment, then looked towards the stone.

"Oh, no," he said, his voice quavering. "This is bad. This is *really* bad."

"Keep your clamour down, boy," said Dennis. "Think yourself lucky that I didn't bring your fatha' along."

"What are they saying?" asked Andry.

"I'm still trying to figure it out," said Dennis, a pang of frustration in his tone. "I don't think they know we've been eating the dead ones, and *I'm* not about to tell them. Eating too much of it must've been what sent Tom and his wife doolally. Without *those* two here, *these* lot have been jumping through the stones to hunt. They say Tom wouldn't let more than one through at a time, nor would his old man. Apparently, there was some sort of … It's a tricky word again. Grithian. It means an agreement or something."

"*We* can have an agreement," said Andry, marching towards the stone and dragging the kid creature along with her. "Look!" She held up their hands. "See? Best mates."

"Dalcop," the creature hissed again.

"Shut it, you," said Andry.

The adult creatures looked at them, then at each other, and finally back at Dennis before speaking again

"They say they don't trust you," said Dennis. "You might break the grithian." He nodded at the kid creature. "*That* one. They say you killed its mother."

"I didn't!" cried Andry. "I mean, the only one I ever saw before tonight was in the …" She looked at the creature as realisation dawned. It spat a few, harsh words at her.

"It says it saw you there," said Dennis.

"Well …" Andry stammered, not sure which way to go with this. "They broke it, too. The honeymooners. What about *them*?"

"I've been wondering that myself," said Dennis and turned back to the other two.

There was another exchange, the creatures becoming more animated and gesticulating wildly. They seemed very unhappy about something.

Andry let go of the kid creature's hand and took it by the shoulder.

"Listen," she said. "I don't know what your word is for 'Sorry', but it's what I am. Just wait, though. We can do this griff thingy, and no-one else needs to get hurt." She held her arms out at her sides, trying to gesture to the whole house. "*This*, right?" She then patted herself on the chest. "This is *mine* now, but others might come when I'm not here. You need to stay away, so you're safe."

"You're wasting your time," said Morgan. "It doesn't understand a word you're saying."

"It obviously *does*," said Andry, glaring at him. "If only *you'd* tried talking to them, instead of cooking them up in tubs, maybe you'd have gotten this far a long time ago."

Morgan clicked his fingers at the kid creature.

"Oi, you," he said. "You're a soggy, pasty-faced little bleeder, and I hope you fall on a spike."

The creature bit its thumb at him.

"Hinderling!" it sneered. "Unfaeger horningsunu!"

"Wow!" said Andry, unable to keep from laughing. "I'll have to remember *that* one."

"I can see why you get on," huffed Morgan, thoroughly chastised.

"The honeymooners," said Dennis. "They went over to the island, bumped into a few of this lot, then attacked them with a liquid fire. They must mean petrol or lighter fuel. Two of them were terribly burned, and one later died."

"You see?" said Andry. "They were only defending themselves."

"I don't know if I believe it," said Dennis. "I've heard some stories. Back in the old days, you'd hear about them snatching babies out of cradles."

"They're just stories," said Andry. "It sounds to me like the only baby snatching that's been going on is by *us*." She walked up to the stone. "Tell them they need to stay away. Or maybe there's some way I can let them know when it's safe to come, but they can't take people's animals anymore."

Dennis spoke to the two, and they listened, looking at Andry every now and then, before conversing with each other in hushed voices.

The one which had pleaded with Andry stepped forward, almost crossing the threshold into the cellar. It reached behind its back, and she heard something rustling. She now saw that it wore a sort of belt made from woven plant strands, possibly willow bark. A few items hung from it, bones, a short knife and a coil of wire. It brought its hand back around, revealing a small bag, which looked to be leather, or some other such hide.

"Well, I'll be blown," said Dennis. He felt around in his

pocket and brought out his own bag, holding it up for the creatures to see.

"Runas?" it asked.

"Gea," said Dennis, a smile spreading across his face, "runas."

The creature undid the bag and held it out to Andry.

"Ordael," it said, but then twisted its face up, readying itself for another stab at modern English. "You show." It pointed to the still glowing runes which covered the stone. "Never being untruth."

"I might not be so lucky on my second try," said Andry.

"I don't think luck has anything to do with it this time," said Dennis. "It looks like these boys play for real."

Andry reached for the bag, her fingertips touching the runestones within it. They were smoother than the ones Dennis used, probably being stones from the lake. As she felt around, hoping that one of the runes would somehow give her a signal that it was the one to choose, she looked into the creature's eyes. There was caution in them, an apprehension tinged with worry, as though this were a great gamble, perhaps for *both* of them.

One of the runes slid between her index and middle fingers, almost like it was trying to reach her palm, and she knew this was the one. She closed her hand around it and drew it out, keeping it held in her fist until she had her hand back in front of her. She had a feeling that the blank, Wyrd rune was about to make another appearance, but she had no idea if this would be good or bad. Maybe the creatures would freak out when they saw it, deciding that someone who had a link to such an ambiguous rune couldn't be trusted. She slowly opened her hand, and all of them, she, Dennis and the three creatures, leaned forward to look.

The stone wasn't blank. Instead, the marking upon it looked almost like a capital M, or two Ps drawn face to face.

"Mannaz," said Dennis.

"Is that good?" asked Andry.

"In *this* case," said Dennis, "yes, *very*."

The two creatures began debating among themselves, only stopping the flow of their strange speech to look at Andry and the rune she held.

Morgan came up behind her and looked at the rune.

"What happens now?" he asked. "Do they go away?"

"I think I picked the right one," said Andry, nodding from the rune to the two creatures, "but I don't think *they're* convinced."

"What does your fatha' plan to do with this place?" asked Dennis. "I overheard what you said a moment ago. The problem is it's not yours, it's his. You can't strike a deal with these fellas, only for it to fall apart soon after. Something tells me they won't take that very kindly, especially now you've pulled a rune on it."

"It *will* be mine," said Andry. "At some point, I mean. We need them to agree that they'll only come while I'm here."

"That's a heavy burden," said Dennis. "Are you saying, when the time comes, you're willing to live here for the rest of your life? A visit every now and then might sound like fun, but can you stand by the agreement for the long haul?"

"I can think of worse places to live," said Andry. She shot a glance at Morgan. "Besides, there are *some* things I'm growing fond of."

"What about when you die?" asked Dennis. "I'm sorry to put the thought into your head, but it'll happen at some point. What then?"

"Well," said Andry, "I suppose I can train someone else."

She nodded at Morgan. "Isn't that how it's done around here?"

"How about you, lad?" said Dennis, also looking at Morgan. "When you take the reins from your fatha', you'll have a part in this, too."

"I guess so," said Morgan, not sounding enthusiastic at all. "Does it mean we can stop the shares?"

"We'll cross *that* bridge when we come to it," said Dennis. He looked back towards the stone, where the two creatures still stood. The younger one had joined them and taken the rune bag. It was plucking them out and setting them out on the ground in front of it. "When I see them like this," Dennis continued, "after all the shares I've taken part in. I knew something was wrong when we started getting two, three, half a dozen shares in a year. Imagine if it'd carried on, everyone in town crazed by it, like Tom and his wife. I *should've* known that it was something to do with this place, but I was too frightened. The runes kept telling me to stay away."

"I hear you wanted to burn it down," said Andry.

"I thought about it," said Dennis. "More than once. Another year, and I *would've* done, too."

"Good thing I came along when I did," said Andry.

"Aye," said Dennis, giving her a half-smile. "Very auspicious. Cometh the Wyrd girl."

The two adult creatures appeared to have come to a conclusion, and the one which had offered the runes to Andry beckoned her forward.

"Locian," it said, pointing down to where the kid creature had set out the runes.

"I don't know what they mean," said Andry.

The kid creature rolled its big eyes at her and patted a hand on the ground.

"Sona," it said, tapping the first rune in the row. It then tapped along the rest. "Dee-da-dee-da-dee." It stopped when it reached the last rune. "Lange."

"Sorry," said Andry. "I still don't get it."

The kid creature gave a groan and sat down, folding its arms with a tut.

"It's a time spread," said Dennis. "They're trying to see what'll happen between now and sometime in the future."

"Runes can *do* that?" asked Andry. "Why am I only learning this tonight? It could've saved us a lot of trouble."

"It's not always that simple," said Dennis. "Also, it's not complete, is it? You're still holding one."

"Oh, yeah," said Andry, opening her hand and looking at the rune. The kid creature sat back up and pointed at her.

"Thu," it said. It then unhooked the pendant from around its neck. The adult creature to its right took the short knife from its belt and handed it to the kid creature, who began to scratch at the front of the pendant. When it was done, it rubbed its thumb across the pendant, then held it up for Andry to see. It'd carved the same rune that she held. It then patted itself on the chest. "Mec."

Andry closed her hand back around the rune and patted it against her own chest.

"Andry," she said.

"Andry," the kid creature repeated with a nod.

"That's right," said Andry. "Not Audrey, or Mandy, or Annie. Andry."

The kid creature fixed the pendant back around its neck, then pointed to itself.

"Pol," it said.

"Looks like you've made a friend," said Morgan.

"Seems that way," said Andry. "Nice, I guess. I was trying

to throttle it a moment ago."

"Aehta geara," said one of the adults.

"What did it say?" Andry asked Dennis.

"Eight years," he replied.

"Eight years until what?" asked Andry.

Dennis spoke with the creature.

"That's how long the grithian will last," he said. "They'll only come when you say it's safe to do so. After that? Well, let's just hope it's up for renewal, and you've got your affairs in order."

"Ask if we can make it an even ten," said Andry.

"I wouldn't push it," said Dennis. "If they're so desperate to grab hares and chickens every winter, it's probably going to be a hard eight years for them if they can only come when you're here."

"I'll do what I can," said Andry, addressing the three creatures directly. "How can I let you know when it's okay to come?"

The adult creature who had mostly remained silent stepped across the threshold and set a hand against the stone. Andry watched as the shapes of the other two began to fade, as though a curtain was being drawn across the opening. The runes carved into the stone brightened once again, and its face momentarily returned to normal, further runes blazing upon its surface, before it shifted, and a new view was revealed. Several creatures stood there, some adults, some younger. Andry counted five at first glance, but she saw more shapes moving in the distance.

"That's the island," said Morgan. "See? There's the house with the pillars."

When this new throng of creatures spotted Andry, they shrunk back and cried out, some even turning and dashing off into the darkness.

"Wait!" yelled Andry, making to go forward, but the creature on their side stopped her with a raised hand, passing its other across the stone. The view melted away again, and the previous one returned, the kid creature standing right at the middle of the opening, its hands on its hips.

"Sundorwundor!" it declared, flashing Andry a grin of its small, sharp teeth.

"It can be all three places," she said. "All three at once."

"Watch," the adult creature croaked. "Leohtas, we come."

"Watch for the light," said Andry, nodding to show that she understood. "How will you know when I'm here, though?"

"Runa," said the kid creature, patting its hands together and nodding at her.

Andry opened her own hand and looked at her rune. Just like those on the stone, it was now glowing. It wasn't enough to actually cast a light, but the fine lines of the mark gave off the same, blue-green shimmer as the others. The kid creature reached for the pendant around its neck and held it out. There was a glow there, too.

"They shine when they're near the stones," said Andry. To test this, she took a few steps backwards. With each step, the glow on her rune diminished. She looked back at the kid creature, who peered at the pendant and shrugged its shoulders. "But only when *both* are near it. Gosh. They've got this sussed out."

"Which means you don't want to lose that thing," said Morgan. "Looks like I won't have to buy you a new pendant after all."

"No," said Andry, watching the glow of her rune flicker back into life as she returned towards the stone. "I'm gonna keep this safe."

"They must've had something similar with Tom," said

Dennis. "It's a tricky business, being bound to a rune. I hope you're up to the task."

"I *will* be," said Andry, gripping her fist around the rune, as though to manifest her determination. "This all happened for a reason. I'm *meant* to be here."

The kid creature and the other adult came forward into the cellar, and the third passed its hand over the stone, changing it to its neutral state.

Dennis coughed and approached the third creature, speaking to it softly. It twisted its lips, then gave a slight nod and a short reply before passing its hand over the stone once more, revealing the island side. All of its frightened companions had vanished, clearly having been put into flight by the appearance of the Wyrd girl.

"I bet they'll have some explaining to do," said Morgan. "You've just cut off their winter food supply."

"Not if *we* bring them stuff," said Andry. "I found a goat tied up in the woods. People are obviously still offering them things."

"Gat?" said the kid creature, its attention pricked by the word. "Hwaer gat?" It rubbed its belly. "Mmm! Wliteg!"

"I'm afraid I let it wander off," said Andry. "And don't think I'm bringing you *live* goats every time." The creature poked its tongue out at her. "Yeah, yeah. I'm a dalcop, but I'm not a butcher. You'll get what I can give you."

"I can help with that," said Dennis. "If it brings an end to all this craziness, I'm sure I can *acquire* the odd spare fish or fowl."

"Tell them to come again next year," said Andry, "on this same night. We'll do a test run and see how it goes."

Dennis conveyed this to the creatures, and they nodded in agreement. The two adults passed through the stone, but the kid lingered, fiddling with the pendant.

"Min modor," it said.

"That means -" Dennis began, but Andry cut him off.

"Yeah," she said. "I got *that* one. Tell her I'm sorry, there was nothing I could do about it. If I'd known, I'd have tried to stop it. I mean, I *will* stop it. No more traps. No more shooting."

Dennis passed this on, but the kid creature kept its eyes on Andry as he spoke. When he was done, it tilted its head from side to side and waved a hand at her.

"I think that's the best you'll get," said Dennis.

"It's enough," said Andry.

Indeed, it was. She wondered how many of its own kind the kid creature had seen killed in order for it to take the death of its mother so easily. Andry had never had to find out, but she assumed that getting over the death of a parent was *not* among her talents.

The kid creature followed the others onto the island side. The view shimmered, and then became the face of a stone again, the runes slowly dying down until the cellar was plunged into darkness.

Dennis produced a lighter and struck it, the dull, orange flame seeming like nothing after the glow of the runes.

"When you spoke quietly to one," said Andry. "What did you say?"

"I asked it a question," said Dennis, turning around with the lighter held out in front of him, looking for the stairs. "I asked it if it it'd perhaps meet with me again, to share our knowledge of the runes."

"And?" asked Andry.

"It said it'd think about it," said Dennis, "which, in *my* experience, means no." He turned the flame back on the stone. "If *this* is anything to go by, who knows what kind of secrets they have. Secrets we've let escape us. Secrets *I* was ready to roll into the lake."

"We'll worry about that later," said Andry. "First things first, we need to get back to the pub."

"When I saw you two sneaking across the carpark," said Dennis, "your fatha' was only being kept above the table because he had a good grip on his mug. He won't have missed you."

"What about *my* parents?" asked Morgan.

"Your mum looked busy," said Dennis. "I didn't see where Harry was."

"They think I'm in bed," said Morgan. "What if dad went to check?"

"If you come back in with me," said Dennis, "and we get stopped, I can say I caught you necking in the woods."

"Necking?" said Andry.

"Aye, necking," said Dennis. "Snogging."

"You can't say *that*!" cried Morgan. "Think what my mum will do if she thinks I've been snogging guests!"

"Fine," said Andry. "If you think snogging me is so taboo, you can tell them what we were *really* up to."

"We've been gone for ages," said Morgan.

"I'll say it was a very sensual necking," said Dennis.

"This just gets worse and worse," grumbled Morgan.

"Remind me again why I'm getting fond of you," said Andry. "Keep cranking out charmers like *that*, and I might change my mind."

They climbed up through the hatch and headed back towards the conservatory.

"How did you get in?" Andry asked Dennis.

"Same way as you," he said. "I saw it'd been recently busted and knew it was where you'd gone in. How did you get the glass out?"

"I wrapped Morgan's coat around it," said Andry. "It muffles the sound."

"Clever," said Dennis with a click of his tongue. "Where did you learn that?"

"Well, you pick these things up," said Andry with a shrug.

"You really fit through *here*?" asked Morgan, kneeling by the broken pane.

"Now he's calling *you* fat," said Andry, nodding to Dennis.

"I can squeeze through tight spots when I need to," said Dennis.

He dropped down in front of the pane and put his legs through it first. Andry was annoyed that *she* hadn't thought of this, as it made it much easier.

"What if you hadn't been able to squeeze through?" she asked as Dennis twisted his shoulders and slid the rest of the way out.

"I'd have booted the door in," he said, getting to his feet, "and probably torn every muscle in my leg at the same time."

"You could've shot the lock," said Andry, stooping down to follow him.

"Nah," said Dennis. "That only works on the telly. I'd have missed, the bullet would've gone right through the door," he nodded at Morgan, who was scrambling through the gap on his hands and knees, "and the lad here might've wished he *had* been necking in the woods."

"Where are you parked?" asked Andry.

"I'm not," said Dennis. "I couldn't have followed you in the Rover, the whole pub would've seen me."

"So, we're walking back," said Andry. "Perfect."

"What about the pokers?" asked Morgan.

"Leave them with me," said Dennis. "I'll put them in the fireplace when no-one's watching." Andry passed him her poker, and he held it out in front of him, feeling its weight. "You really would've *used* these?"

"I nearly *did*," said Andry. "I was ready to split that poor thing's head open."

"What stopped you?" asked Dennis.

"I don't know," said Andry, frowning to herself as they started along the gravel path. "It was a spur of the moment thing. It didn't feel ... well, it didn't feel *right*."

They scaled the ivy-covered wall again, finding it much simpler with three, and headed back along the bend in the road. Morgan walked beside Andry, and it wasn't long before he slipped his hand into hers.

"You promised," he said when she looked down at it.

"I suppose I did," said Andry, swinging their clasped hand back and forth.

They walked on in silence for a while, but Morgan then turned to her.

"Why do you care?" he asked.

"About what?" Andry replied.

"About any of this," said Morgan. "You've had, like, five opportunities to just turn tail, but you didn't. Why?"

"What's with all these tough questions?" asked Andry. "First Dennis, now you. I don't know why. Does there *have* to be a reason?"

"I think there does," said Morgan. "You're the one who keeps saying that things are *meant* to happen."

"Just because something is *meant* to happen," said Dennis, coming up behind them, "doesn't always mean you know *why* it's meant to happen. Life would be pretty easy if we all knew why things work out the way they do."

"There," said Andry. "What *he* said."

"The Wyrd doesn't choose people," Dennis continued, "but it keeps an eye out for them. If it hadn't been you, it'd have been someone else. Perhaps someone who isn't as understanding as you are."

"Like the old owners of the lake-house?" asked Andry.

"Aye," said Dennis. "There was obviously something at work which decided a change of management was in order." He held out an arm, stopping Andry and Morgan, then leaned down to eye level with both of them. "Never eat it. If they still bring bodies, make them take them away. *That* part of the deal is over."

"How long had it been going on?" asked Andry.

"As long as I can remember," said Dennis, "but times are different. Back in the old days, one or two wasn't a problem. Now, though? Spraying them over fields with machines? It's not the same. It's not meant to be. Our world moves too fast. We're so focused on the future, we forget that some things can't keep up. If you don't believe me, go and talk to the old boys who fought in the war. *They'll* tell you how fast the future comes at you."

"I don't understand," said Andry.

"I think you *do*," said Dennis, drawing his face closer to hers. "No-one can find out. Whatever it is that makes those stones work, whoever owns it *wins*. Would you unleash that on the world? There're now bombs which can destroy entire countries. Imagine how simple it'd be if you just had to wheel one through a stone."

"You're laying this on pretty thick," said Andry. "I only really have to worry about my dad."

Dennis straightened up and gave a laugh, which seemed odd after his philosophical tangent.

"Let's hope so," he said. "Only, right now, I'd be more worried about him slipping into an ale induced coma."

"Happy, boastful, self-pitying," said Andry. "That's his usual drinking routine."

"I left him at happy," said Dennis. "At least, I *think* he was happy. He was definitely smiling."

They continued on, making good time now they didn't have to climb over any drystone walls. Morgan and Andry were still holding hands, but she couldn't tell if there was any genuine, romantic affection in his grip. She wasn't particularly skilled in the practice herself, but during the few times she'd done it before, she'd found that boys with proper amorous intentions held on a little tighter and tried to get much closer than Morgan was, looking for any excuse to bump up against her, or make the jump from hand holding to waist grabbing. She got the feeling that, if she asked Morgan to put his arm around her waist, the shock might kill him.

"You're as deep in this as I am, you know?" she said.

"Am I?" asked Morgan. "How?"

"I want you as my exclusive gamekeeper," said Andry. "We can't have anything getting onto the grounds of the lakehouse and ... I dunno, nibbling the ivy. I'll even make sure you're paid."

"You're offering me a *job*?" asked Morgan, sounding less than thrilled by the idea. "I don't think I want you as my boss."

"You can call me a client," said Andry. "That sounds more official."

"Why do you care so much about the ivy?" asked Morgan.

"God, you're dense," said Andry, giving his hand a tug. "When I say, 'Nibbling the ivy', what I mean is people snooping around. From now on, the only local who goes within a mile of that place is *you*. You're in my personal employ. Your dad will know about this arrangement, and if I hear that anyone's been sniffing around, to find out why the shares have stopped, my dad will blame *him*, and he'll blame *you*. That's how it worked with Dave's chickens, right?"

"You're doing it again," said Morgan.

"Doing what?" asked Andry.

"Flicking that switch which turns you from nice to nasty," said Morgan. "You should give it a rest, or you might break it."

"Yeah," said Andry, "and it might get stuck on the *nasty* side."

She yanked his arm so hard that he almost stumbled.

"Stop it!" he cried. "You're mental, you are!"

"I don't feel you letting go," chuckled Andry.

"Keep it down," said Dennis, his own voice low. "If anyone's out front, they'll hear you."

He was right. They could see the pub now, and anyone walking in, or stumbling out, might not see them, but they were easily within range of even the most booze deadened ear.

"We'll go in at the side," Andry said to Dennis, "and you go back in the front. It'll be like nothing ever happened."

"I'll go first," said Dennis. "I'll make a commotion as I come through the door. It'll make everyone look the other way."

Andry and Morgan hung back as he crossed the carpark. Fortunately, it didn't sound like he encountered anyone.

"How much do you trust that pebble you put in the door?" she asked. "After everything we've been through, it'd be just our luck to be let down by a stone."

"I jammed it in good," said Morgan. "As long as no-one saw it was there, the door should be open."

"Crikey almighty!" they heard Dennis call out as he went into the pub. "If it ain't half cold for this time of year! Terry, you hard-faced old bugger, where's that pint I left?"

"That's our cue," said Andry.

They dashed for the side door, Morgan skidding to a halt next to it and running his hand along the bottom.

"Gotcha," he said, plucking out the pebble as he pulled the door open. "You've got *your* special stone," he clenched the pebble in his fist, "this can be *mine*."

They slipped inside, and Morgan carefully shut the door behind them. There were many raised voices coming from the barroom, some even still singing. Unlike before, Andry was glad that so many of them were willing to devote this much time to drinking.

"We did it," she said, smiling at Morgan in the dim light coming down the hallway. "We actually *did* it."

"Of course we did," said Morgan. "You said it yourself, we're unstoppable."

"I can't believe how brave you were," said Andry, taking hold of both of his hands. "You talk about me having opportunities to turn tail. You did, too, but you didn't"

"If I'd run off," said Morgan, "and you'd gotten out, you'd have killed me when you caught me. I guess I was more scared of *you* than anything else."

"If that's how you want to put it," said Andry, pulling him in for a hug, "then it's fine with me."

They hugged for a long moment, longer than it needed to be, but Morgan then sniffed and pulled away from her.

"Eurgh," he said. "You're covered in the little one's slime stuff."

"There's that silver tongue of yours again" said Andry, thumping him on the arm. She pulled her jumper over her head and flung it at him. "Do something about it. You're the laundry boy."

"We should probably burn it," said Morgan holding the jumper out at arm's length.

"No *way*," said Andry. "My dad got me that from Marks and Sparks, it cost a fortune. He'll go mad if he thinks I've lost it."

"Very well, my Lady," Morgan teased. "I'll have it washed and ironed before you leave."

"You can't *iron* it," said Andry, grabbing the sleeve of the jumper and rubbing it between her fingers. "Feel that. It's Cashmere. An iron will burn right through it. Honestly, you country folk."

Morgan burst into laughter, to the point where he had to clasp a hand to his mouth.

"That's it," he said, stifling another chortle, "I've decided."

"Decided what?" asked Andry. She had no idea what was so funny.

"Whenever you flick the switch to nasty," said Morgan, "I'll just laugh at you. Sooner or later, you'll stop doing it."

"You better pray that it's sooner," said Andry. She wound up to thump him again but stopped mid-swing. "I'm here for one more day. I was thinking we could make it normal, nothing Wyrd."

"I'd like that," said Morgan. "Not sure what my dad will say, though."

"Oh, he thinks I'm the bee's knees now," said Andry. "Didn't I tell you? He says I'm to corrupt you with as much of my fancy, modern, *southern* ways as possible."

"I find that hard to believe," said Morgan. "Speaking of

which," he tugged the front of her shirt, "you might want to turn that inside out before you go through."

"I'm past caring," said Andry. "It doesn't matter if I ruffle a few patriotic feathers at this point."

"That's up to you," said Morgan with a shrug. "I'll see you tomorrow."

"You bet," said Andry, turning to go. When she didn't hear Morgan open the door to his room, she looked back. He was still standing there, wringing her jumper in his hands.

"I was wondering," he said, "if maybe we could … well, *you know* again."

"Nope," said Andry. "You've got to earn it. The jumper clean by the morning, and I'll think about letting you ask me if it's okay to ask me for another kiss."

She headed along the hall to the barroom, having to supress a chuckle herself this time. She knew this kiss currency wouldn't work on Morgan forever, so she intended to make full use of it while she still could and not let him take liberties. It might come in handy later on.

There was still a good-sized group in the barroom, but she saw that her dad had remained in his spot by the fireplace. Dennis was standing next to him and nodded to her when he saw her coming.

"Marty," he said, kicking the leg of her dad's chair, "look who's here."

Her dad raised his head and looked at her through bleary eyes. Instead of her face, the first thing he stared at was her shirt.

"God save the Queen," he mumbled, then reared his head back and gave a loud bray of laughter. "I didn't know she was invited!"

"Hilarious, mate," said Dennis, "but I think it's bedtime."

Between them, he and Andry got her dad to his feet.

"Where did *you* go?" he asked Andry as she slung one of his arms over her shoulder. "You left me all alone for, like, must've been fifteen whole minutes. I was despairing."

"You look like you had plenty of fun by yourself," said Andry. "Dennis is right. Up the wooden hill you go."

They made their way towards the stairs, passing by the remaining drinkers. None of them made mention of Andry's shirt, they were all too busy raising their mugs and tugging their forelocks at her dad, saying, "Thank you, Sir. Good on you, Sir. Many happy returns, Sir."

"We'll be doing *this* again," said her dad. "Only twenty quid behind the bar, and they're eating out of my hand. I'm gonna be a bloody *king* around here." He gave another laugh as Andry and Dennis bundled him into the stairwell. "No safety pins through the nose, though!"

They managed to get him to his room, and Dennis bid him goodnight, refusing his offer of a tip. He shook Andry firmly by the hand in a way she'd never experienced before. It wasn't the casual, dismissive shake that adults often gave to kids. Instead, she felt real meaning in it, a sense that he saw her as an equal, rather than a stupid, southern tourist girl who'd gotten in over her head.

"Thanks," she said, "for everything."

"Don't thank me yet," said Dennis. "There's work to be done. When you next come, things should be different. I'll help as much as I can, but there're going to be people upset about any changes. Don't expect a red carpet to be rolled out for you," he nodded at her dad, who was sitting on the edge of his bed and trying to take his shoes off, "especially not for the new *king* over there."

Andry placed her hand into her back pocket and took out

the rune stone.

"Maybe *you* should keep it," she said, holding it out towards Dennis. "I might lose it or forget it."

"No," said Dennis, placing his hand over hers and closing it. "It's yours. Who knows, there might be something in it that you can use wherever you are. Do what Morgan said. Turn it into a charm or a talisman and keep it close to you. Things like that need life near them. If you lock it away, it might not work when you really need it to."

He patted her on the arm and headed for the stairs.

Andry turned to her dad, who was now locked in mortal combat with his trousers.

"Alright, you," she said. "Bed."

"I didn't …" her dad groaned, struggling to yank his belt from its loops. "I didn't even get to sing a song."

"Never mind," said Andry. "We'll see how much you feel like singing in the morning."

Chapter Eight

SHE TURNED OUT to be absolutely right. The next morning, she couldn't even get her dad to pull the covers from over his head. He moaned and gurgled and told her he *knew* it'd been the beer which had made him sick after all. She asked if he wanted to test this by seeing if there was any of the broth left over from the previous night, but the idea caused him to shudder like he was being stretched on a rack.

Andry, on the other hand, was feeling pretty chirpy. She'd had a great night's sleep, which she hadn't seen coming, and was up and raring to go not long after dawn.

She'd lain awake in the dark for a long time, thinking there was no way sleep would come after what'd happened. When the sound of voices from the barroom below had finally ceased, she'd listened hard. The silence was so utter, it was almost intense. Unlike back in Leicester, she hadn't been able to hear any cars or sirens, no distant yells from late night drunkards, their weekend bacchanal having come to a close. She'd placed her hand behind her head, letting the darkness and the silence envelope her, and fell to thinking that she could get used to living in a place like this.

She left her dad to his misery, deciding that he'd brought it upon himself, and went to find Morgan. She found him with his mum in the small kitchen behind the barroom, busy with dishes from the night before. He'd been true to his word. Her jumper was freshly cleaned. It was still a bit damp, but there was no sign of egg yolk or slime stuff. She rewarded him with a peck on the cheek when his mum wasn't looking.

"Your fatha' put on quite the shin-dig last night," his mum said as Andry stepped away from him, his face blazing as he bent over the sink. "Share or not, I haven't seen everyone in such high spirits for ages."

"He has a way of winning people over," said Andry. "Once he drops his act, he's a sweetheart, really."

"There's not a penny left of the money he gave me," said Morgan's mum. "They got through the lot. I'll have to order new barrels."

"He's a firm believer in supporting local economies," said Andry, trying to think of what her dad would say.

"Well," said Morgan's mum, "he can come and support *my* economy any time he likes." She took a dishtowel from the strap of her apron and tossed it to Andry. "Help him dry, will you? We'll be here all day, otherwise."

"Aww, he's trying his best," said Andry leaning against the sink and grinning at Morgan. "Look how red his face has gone."

"Don't bend so close to the water, Morgan," his mum scolded. "You'll give yourself prickly heat."

"Yeah," said Andry, twisting the towel and snapping it at the back of Morgan's legs, "we wouldn't want *that*."

"Leave off, you two," said Morgan with a sigh. "I hardly slept last night."

"Poor thing," said Andry, dabbing beneath her eyes with the towel. "Let's get this done, and we can go for a nice, relaxing walk."

"I don't want to go for a walk," grumbled Morgan.

"Oh, yes, you do," said his mum. "I promised Mister Watt another jar of Dave Lampard's pickle. You were meant to get it yesterday, but you obviously forgot. Or did you drop *that*, too?"

"Ah," said Andry. "Actually, that was *my* fault. I had it, but I put it down when I was helping Morgan with the eggs. I guess I must've left it there."

"You can go and get another," said Morgan's mum, "but Dave will want paying for both when he next comes in."

"Just don't tell my dad how much they cost," said Andry. "I don't think he knows what anything less than a fiver even *looks* like. Put it in the big book, and he can pay when we leave."

"I hope we'll see you again," said Morgan's mum. "Your fatha' tells me he used to come every year when he was a nipper. You and him can rekindle the tradition. Our house will always be open to you."

"Yeah," said Andry, "I have a feeling you'll be seeing us again."

With the dishes done, she and Morgan left for Dave's house. When they got there, they knocked on the door but got no reply. They walked around to the huge hen shed and found Dave at the top of a ladder, a bucket of whitewash dangling from the top rung. He was painting over the runes which adorned the boards.

"Funniest thing," he explained to them as he loaded his brush. "I had a dream last night. I put a lot of stock in dreams." He pointed the dripping brush at the ground. "I was stood right there, and all the runes were shining, like they'd come to life or something." He pointed towards the lake. "I looked over the water, and *that* was shining, too. Cor lummy, I was frit. I thought it was the end of days. The water broke from its banks and flooded all the fields. It came rolling up the hill, in a big wave, and splashed up the front of the shed, washing the runes away."

"What do you think it meant?" asked Andry.

"That these don't need to be here anymore," said Dave, painting over half a rune with three, broad strokes. "I can't quite put my finger on it, but it's like something …" He tapped the brush on the edge of the tin as he thought this over. He then went back to painting, covering the rest of the rune. "Well, like in the dream, something's been washed away." He dropped the brush into the tin and started down the ladder. "*You* wouldn't know anything about it, would you?"

"Not a clue," said Andry with a shrug. "It's good, though, right? Perfect timing."

"Aye," said Dave, wiping his hands together as he looked up at the side of the shed. "That's what *I* thought."

They got the jar of pickle, as well as a fresh box of eggs, but they didn't go back to the pub straight away, Andry insisting that they went to the lake.

They stood on the shore and looked out at the island and the trees on the far side.

"I've been here almost three days," said Andry, "and this is the closest I've gotten. My dad says it's the biggest lake in England. Is that right?"

"Yep," said Morgan, tugging his coat around himself to block the steady wind which blew in from the water. "It's big."

"How deep is it?" asked Andry.

"Dunno," said Morgan. "Pretty deep, I guess."

"You grew up near it," said Andry, "so you probably aren't impressed by it anymore."

"Something like that," said Morgan.

Andry gave a sigh and dropped her shoulders.

"Okay," she said, "what's wrong? Why have you gone all mopey? You said you'd like doing normal stuff today."

"Well," said Morgan, "you're leaving tomorrow, aren't you?"

"Yeah," said Andry, "but I'm coming back."

"When?" asked Morgan.

"Soon," said Andry. "As soon as I can. There're weekends, and the half term in October, then the Christmas break. I'll bet you do a *great* Christmas here, all pagan and authentic."

"I wish I could come with you," said Morgan. "I don't want to be your *occasional* best friend, *second* best to your *real* ones in Leicester."

"I didn't mean it like that," said Andry. "I can write to you, and send you tapes, and I will. Also, you might've noticed that we have these things called telephones. They're all the rage right now."

Morgan ruminated on this for a moment.

"I don't have a tape player," he said.

"For goodness' sake," said Andry, placing a hand to her forehead. "I'll *send* you one. I'll get you a decent set of headphones, too. Wouldn't want you frightening the locals."

"Yeah," said Morgan, cracking a smile at last, "that'd be a good idea."

"Another thing," said Andry. "I meant it when I said about you coming to visit me. It'd be easy enough to arrange. There're things in Leicester that'll blow you mind. We've got this road called the Golden Mile. It's all Indian shops. Restaurants, jewellers, places that sell saris and wedding gowns. It's like being in a different world."

"Gosh," said Morgan. "I went to one of the big hotels for my thirteenth birthday, and I had a curry, but that's about as much as I know."

"A curry cooked by an Englishman, I imagine," said Andry. "No, mate. You come to Leicester, and I'll show you what the *proper* stuff tastes like."

"I'd like that," said Morgan, his smile broadening. "You promise?"

Andry stooped and started unlacing her boots.

"I'll prove it," she said, tugging off the first boot and rolling the leg of her jeans up to her knee.

"What're you doing?" asked Morgan, frowning down at her.

"We're going to swear on it," she said and nodded at him. "You, too. Get those mud stampers off."

With both feet bare, and her jeans rolled up, she took a step into the water, gasping at the cold.

"You're crazy," said Morgan. "I'm not going in *there*."

"Come on," said Andry, walking backwards until she was almost knee-deep. "Where's my rough, tough gamekeeper?"

Morgan groaned and leaned down to remove his wellies. With his own trousers rolled up, he inched towards the water, curling his toes as it lapped over them.

"Oof, ya bleeder!" he winced.

"Get a move on," laughed Andry. "If you do it quick, you won't feel it as much."

Once he'd waded over to her, she took both of his hands.

"There," she said. "Now it's a *real* promise."

"Would've been just as real with dry feet," said Morgan.

"Nah," said Andry. "This is more symbolic, don't you think?"

"I *think* I'm freezing to death," said Morgan, his knees starting to tremble.

"If you can't handle your tootsies getting chilly," said Andry, "how do you ever hope to go skinny dipping with me?"

"What's skinny dipping?" asked Morgan.

"Never mind," said Andry. "Look." She lowered their hands until the water washed over them. "This makes it solid. I *promise* we'll stay in touch. No matter where I end up, I'll always find a way to get here. Believe me. When I set my mind to something, I *make* it happen."

"I believe you," said Morgan, tightening his hands around hers.

"Okay," said Andry drawing their hands back out of the water. "Do you feel better now?"

"Yeah," said Morgan, "I *do*, actually."

"Good," said Andry, releasing one of his hands and tugging him along by the other as she started back towards the shore. "If only my mum could see me now. All this witchy stuff? She'd be over the moon."

The rest of the morning was, indeed, very normal, but it certainly wasn't boring. Even though it was a Sunday, Morgan still had tasks to perform around the pub, and Andry helped out where she could. They mopped the floors, wiped the tables and built up the fire, noticing that the pokers were back in their usual spot. When the first patrons began arriving, Andry asked if she could try her hand at pulling a pint. She was completely hopeless at it, passing three bemused customers mugs which were mostly foam, saying she'd put them on her dad's tab.

When her dad finally appeared, he sat by the fireplace, sipping at weak tea and attempting to read a newspaper. Whenever someone scraped a chair or spoke too loudly, he cringed and screwed his face up, as though he'd been struck over the head.

"Some holiday, eh?" he said when Andry went to join him. "Me sick for two days. So much for bonding."

"I've been keeping myself busy," said Andry. "The place is really growing on me. Can we come again soon?"

"Of course," said her dad. "If you're still interested in overseeing the refurbishments, I'll need you here as often as possible. I'll even get some sort of contract written up, so your mum can't complain."

"If you write a contract," said Andry, "she *will* complain. If you keep things nice and casual, then she *won't*."

"Yeah," said her dad. "Sorry. Dad, not boss, right?"

Andry saw Morgan lurking by the bar, and she nodded for him to come over.

"Will there be anything else, Mister Watt?" he asked as he sidled up to the table.

"Oh, don't 'Mister Watt' me, boy," said Andry's dad with a frown. "It's Martin. Sit yourself down."

"I've been thinking," said Andry. "What if Morgan was the private gamekeeper for the lake-house?"

"Again, with this gamekeeper stuff," said her dad, narrowing an eye at Morgan. "Look, I know what you're up to. It's no skin off *my* nose if you nab animals that don't belong to you. What I *can't* have is anyone thinking *I'm* involved. It wouldn't look good if you or your old man get nailed, and someone finds out *I've* been paying you under the table."

"Then pay him *over* the table," said Andry.

"As what?" asked her dad. "The place isn't Northanger Abbey. We don't *need* a gamekeeper."

"What about a groundskeeper?" Andry persisted. "We definitely need one of those."

Her dad tilted his head and pursed his lips.

"Reckon you're up to it, lad?" he asked Morgan. "It's a decent trade, good money in it."

"You mean, a gardener?" asked Morgan.

"Nah," said Andry. "Groundskeeper sounds much better. Think how it'd look on a C.V. Someone your age, head groundskeeper on a private estate. You might even be able to turn it into a business one day."

"See?" said her dad, wagging a finger at her. "Now, *that's* thinking. She gets it all from me."

"I suppose it'd get me away from here," said Morgan. "I'm seriously fed up of washing sheets."

"That's settled, then," said Andry. "We'll need to buy you tools and stuff, and new clothes. Tweed. A groundskeeper should wear tweed."

"One thing at a time," said her dad, chuckling as much as his headache would allow. "Also, I guess this means you've let the cat out of the bag. To him, at least."

"Oh," said Andry. "Yeah, I guess I did."

"*Just* to him?" asked her dad.

"Yes," said Andry. She didn't think her dad would be so calm if he found out that Dennis also knew. "Just him."

"Can you keep your mouth shut for a month?" her dad asked Morgan. "Six weeks at the most. I'll come with a small crew, they'll start minor work, and everyone can see I'm not here stir things up. Will you do that for me?"

"Yeah," said Morgan with a firm nod. "I mean, of course, Mister… I mean … well, do I call you 'Boss' now?"

"Apparently, we're not using that word," said Andry's dad. "Martin will do." He levelled a finger at Morgan. "Mind me, though. Tweed suit or not, this isn't a ceremonial position. I'll want graft out of you. You'll take care of every stone."

"*Every* stone," said Andry, kneeing him under the table.

"*Every* stone," said Morgan, a smile tugging at the corners of his lips.

"More in-jokes, eh?" said Andry's dad. "Damn. What've I started?"

"Okay," said Andry, setting her palms down on the table and getting up. "I better go and pack for tomorrow."

"I'll help you," said Morgan.

"Yeah, you *will*," said Andry. "You might be calling *him* 'Martin', but you can call *me* 'Boss' whenever you like."

She, of course, didn't have much to pack, so they spent a while in her room, talking about things. Normal things. Andry told Morgan tales of the stuff she got up to in Leicester, much of which Morgan said sounded terrifying, and he told her more stories about stuck up tourists making his life a nightmare during the summer season. Whenever he mentioned someone who was a real rotter, such as a man who'd run them ragged for a whole week with his demands and then tried to shirk out of paying the bill by saying he was a renowned hotel reviewer, a glowing reference from him supposedly being more than worth the cost, Andry fell about with laughter. She found that Morgan's laughing tactic worked in reverse. If *she* laughed, *he* laughed, and his foul mood was defused.

"It's why we started making people pay up-front," he said. "The cheeky sod. He was proper miffed when we said no."

"If anyone ever gets you down," said Andry, "just do what *we're* doing. Have a laugh about it."

"I might not be able to laugh my way out a kicking from the Stewarts," said Morgan, looking away and biting his lip. "They'll be gunning for me when they see me next."

"If they give you any trouble," said Andry, "tell them the Wyrd fire girl taught you secret, southern fighting techniques."

"And what if they don't believe me?" asked Morgan.

"Go in swinging," said Andry. "You've got a right to defend yourself. Knee the boy between the legs and see how quick his sister backs off. Just try not to miss this time."

Morgan was eventually called away by his dad to do another trail check, but Andry didn't ask to go along. She wanted to see what a more thorough check would produce. She didn't believe the creatures would renege on their agreement, but she worried that the word of it might not have spread right away, and some of them might keep coming through for a while.

She waited in the barroom for Morgan and his dad to return. When they did, Morgan came through the door, all smiles.

"Guess what *we* found," he said, waving for her to come outside.

She followed him out to the carpark, where his dad was standing at the rear of the Range Rover. He opened the boot, and a goat sprang out, landing shakily and bleating.

Andry could instantly tell it was *the* goat, but she tried not to show that she recognised it.

"Where did it come from?" she asked, approaching it slowly, so it didn't get spooked.

"No idea," said Morgan's dad. "It's not got a mark or a tag on it. It was just wandering through the woods."

"What'll you do with it?" asked Andry. She might've been trying not to show recognition of the goat, but it seemed to recognise *her*, and it trotted over, letting her rub it on the ears.

"If no-one claims it by day's end," said Morgan's dad, "it's going in the pot. No share tonight." He sucked his teeth. "Strange. I had the funniest feeling it'd be three in a row."

"You can't *cook* it," said Andry, wrapping an arm around the goat's neck.

"I *can*," said Morgan's dad, "and I *will*. Where do you think mutton chops come from? What did I tell you about country living?"

"Yeah, I know," said Andry. "Muck and blood and stink. Look at its little face, though." She turned the goat's head towards him. "What can you say to that?"

"I'll say it'd look good with mint sauce on it," said Morgan's dad.

"We could keep it for milk," said Morgan. "Mum always moans about how much it costs. This way, we can have our own."

His dad looked at him, then at Andry and the goat, then back at him.

"What spell has she cast on you, Squire?" he asked. "Time was, you'd be dripping at the gob for goat meat." He sneaked a quick glance at Andry, then lowered his voice. "She's not trying to turn you into a vegetarian, is she? Because that's where I draw the line."

"I don't have *that* much influence," laughed Andry. "Go on, keep it. What's better? One night of stew, or a lifetime of free milk?"

"Oh, alright," said Morgan's dad with a resigned sigh.

"It can sleep in the shed," said Morgan, joining Andry in fussing the goat.

"*You're* taking care of it," said his dad. "The moment it stops giving milk," he drew a thumb across his throat, "pot."

He headed towards the pub, and Andry waited until he was out of earshot.

"Nothing?" she asked Morgan.

"Nothing," he replied, standing up and closing the boot of the Rover. "No traps sprung, no fences down, no sign of any animals being taken, nothing."

"This is just the first night," said Andry. "If anything starts again, you call me, okay?"

"Okay," said Morgan with a nod. "Can I still call you if something *doesn't* happen?"

"Of course," said Andry. "How else will I keep in touch with Goaty here? We can work out a code. One bleat for 'Yes', two for 'No', and frantic screaming for 'Help! They're putting me in the pot!'"

"Good thing it's a female goat," chuckled Morgan. "If it'd been a buck, that trick wouldn't have worked."

"I think I know who it belongs to," said Andry, "but do your best to keep it hidden. If he's willing to leave his pets out as sacrifices, maybe he doesn't deserve to have any."

"You'll change your mind when *you* have to start thinking of things to sacrifice," said Morgan.

"Possibly," said Andry, running a hand across the goat's back, "but I'd like to keep this one safe. I think our paths were *meant* to cross."

"It can help me with my new job," said Morgan. "Keep the weeds down. Goats eat anything." He patted the goat on the rump. "It needs a name, though. We can't just call it Goaty the goat."

"Any ideas?" asked Andry.

"Let me think," said Morgan, rubbing his chin. "It turns up where it's not supposed to, tries to make itself useful, but just means more work, does a lot of bleating." He then broke out in a wide grin. "I can call it Andry."

"You think you're dead funny, don't you?" said Andry. "Remember, you work for *me* now, and I won't stand insubordination."

"What *should* we call it, then?" asked Morgan, still grinning.

Andry looked into one of the goats strange, horizontal pupils.

"Audrey," she said. "I'm sick of being called that, so I'll pass it onto something else."

"Who calls you Audrey?" asked Morgan.

"People I don't like," said Andry. "People I'm going to need to deal with when I get home. The battle may be over, but the war isn't won."

"Gosh," said Morgan. "*That* serious, eh?"

"Not if I play my cards right," said Andry. "Forget secretary school, or anything like that. I'm going to study business. *Proper* business. *Law*, even. Yeah, law! We'll see how easily people think they can brush me aside when I've got a few scary sounding letters after my name."

"Good idea," said Morgan. "If there's anything that'll keep people away from the lake-house better than 'You know what', it's a southern *lawyer* living there."

"And a ferocious goat," said Andry. "Come on. Let's go and spruce up its new home. This can be my first stab at property refurbishment."

The rest of the day passed quickly. They kept trying to find things to do, but they knew they were only delaying the inevitable.

The pub started to fill by early evening, but no songs were sung, and everyone seemed rather gloomy. They'd obviously been anticipating a third share night, but when no sweet-smelling steam issued forth from behind the bar, they brooded over their pints and muttered among themselves. A few even got up and left after only a single drink.

Dennis made an appearance, but Andry and Morgan weren't able to get much of a response out of him when they peppered him with thinly disguised questions. He simply puffed at his pipe or nodded and hummed. Whatever he was planning, he was keeping it close to his chest.

When Andry decided to turn in for the night, she went up to her room and, instead of getting straight into bed, looked at the darkened lake. The moonlight skittered across its surface, picking out distant eddies and swells. She wondered if the kid creature, 'Pol' it'd called itself, was somehow also looking across the water from somewhere. Perhaps it looked over waters which were less tangible than that of the lake. Waters which spanned a distance which couldn't be crossed by boat, or even the most desperate of swimmers.

Pondering this made her head hurt, and she thought it best to stop. Finally getting into bed, she remembered part of the conversation she'd had with Dennis and Bernie, which felt like a lifetime ago. Bernie had said that someone could be born *in* a place but not be *of* it. It crossed her mind whether someone could be born *of* a place but not *in* it. She wasn't sure how much she believed of her own talk about things being *meant* to happen, but she hadn't been lying when she'd told Morgan that, when she put her mind to something, she *made* it happen. All this caused her head to start hurting again.

"This could drive me mad," she sniggered to herself. "Law *and* philosophy, maybe?"

The next morning, she and Morgan took her and her dad's luggage to the car. She thought about making Morgan do it on his own, as a farewell present, but she couldn't bring herself to be so cruel.

Her dad paid the remainder of the bar bill. He was happy with his pickle, but he pointed out that there were a few pints on the score that he didn't remember ordering. This was quickly settled when Morgan's mum reminded him that he hadn't been in a state to remember anything on the night in question, which he bashfully agreed with.

She gave Morgan her phone numbers for both Leicester and Manchester but told him the Leicester one would be more reliable.

"Remember," she said, "if you talk to my mum, say something rural and mystical. She'll be dead impressed."

"I'll try to think of something," said Morgan.

They then hugged, Morgan pressing his face hard into her shoulder. Andry looked towards the car and saw her dad sat behind the wheel, looking rather uncomfortable. When the hug had gone on long enough for him to consider it indecent, he honked the horn.

"Put him down!" he called to her. "Come on! The roads are gonna be jammed!"

"I'll call you as soon as I get home," she said to Morgan. "I promise."

"I believe you," said Morgan.

She went to the car and opened the door. Morgan turned towards the pub, and she felt she should add just one thing more.

"Hey!" she yelled. "Stay unstoppable!"

Morgan raised a fist and shook it as she got into the car and her dad started it up.

"I suppose," he said as they pulled out of the carpark, "all things considered, that went pretty well."

"It was a good start," said Andry. "Let's just hope it isn't pitchforks and torches the *next* time we come."

"I don't think so," said her dad. "We had these people wrong. Once I start work on the property, and fire doesn't rain down from the sky, they'll come around."

As they turned onto the first main road, Andry twisted in her seat to get a last look at the lake.

"It's really something, isn't it?" she said.

"Missing it already?" her dad chuckled. "See? I *knew* it'd have an effect on you."

"Yeah," said Andry, facing forward again, "I guess you were right." She drummed her hands on her knees. "Listen. What A-levels do I need to study law?"

"Law?" asked her dad, raising an eyebrow at her. "Where's *that* come from?"

"Just something I've been thinking about," said Andry. "Seems like the right time to bring it up."

"I suppose you're still set against Rossall?" asked her dad. "Doesn't matter. An A-level is an A-level, wherever you get it from. University, on the other hand. If you want to study law, I can help you pick somewhere worth going to."

"As long as it's *help*," said Andry, "not *tell*."

"I have a feeling my telling days are coming to an end," said her dad. "To be honest, I'm glad you're thinking about it on your own. It's like I keep saying, you need to plan for your future."

"I know," said Andry. "I've got a lot to prepare for."

THE END

Thanks for reading!
We hope you enjoyed this book.
If you did then please consider leaving a review or a
rating at Amazon – it would mean a lot to us all.

Afterword

Thank you for reading this story. I sincerely hope that you enjoyed it, and I'd love to hear what you thought of it. I can be found on Facebook at facebook.com/jackcallaghanauthor, and on Instagram at @jackcallaghanauthor.

Now that you've finished reading, I'd like to address a few discrepancies between what are real world facts and what are things that I've made up for entertainment purposes.

Firstly, there are no original bauta or runestones in Windermere. In fact, there are no original bauta or runestones in Britain whatsoever. The discovery of one, let alone three, would be an archaeological marvel and significantly alter our understanding of the Anglo-Saxon era. There are, however, a number of stone circle and menhir sites in the lake district, including Swinside, Burnmoor, Castlerigg, and others, some of which I've had the pleasure of visiting. I encourage you to do the same if you get the chance. Go on the right days, especially on a solstice, and you may even see people holding traditional celebrations.

It can be argued that I could have chosen to use the ancient Celtic religions as the basis for the book, but this is a topic that I have little interest in and, therefore, little knowledge of. The early medieval period is my 'Thing', so it was what I wanted to incorporate into my book.

With regards to my use of the Old English language, my translations are not 100% accurate. I simply used wordings which I felt looked good on the page, and which a reader would be more interested by. For example, 'Nese' could be directly translated as 'Do not let it be', rather than a flat-out

'No', but I felt it was a more interesting word. I also chose to not include special characters, specifically Æ, ð and þ, instead using their Latinised equivalents. Again, this was for ease of reading. When I was composing the sections of dialogue which included the lake creatures using these words, I was aiming for something that comes across as being heavily influenced by the Old English language, rather than a perfect translation.

If you'd like to learn more about Old English, there are numerous resources at your disposal, Oldenglish.info being one of the best. You can also go to YouTube and see a performer named Benjamin Bagby recite the entire Beowulf poem in Old English from memory. It's a great way to hear what this language actually sounds like when spoken. He's also a whizz on the lyre.

The runes described in the story are those of the Elder Futhark. There are also those of the Anglo-Saxon and Anglo-Frisian runic alphabet, but I chose to use the ones which people might more easily recognise. We're living in a time where the symbols and imagery of Germanic paganism are at risk of being hijacked for nefarious purposes. We must, therefore, claim them back. Having an interest in history has nothing to do with modern day political, social or ideological matters. Fortunately, there are many scholars, re-enactors, or just keen enthusiasts, who keep this stuff alive for the right reasons. I'd like to think that my story can play a small part in this, too.

Wes du hal! – Jack Callaghan.

MORE FROM
sci-fi-cafe

Available to buy in paperback and eBook from Amazon
and other good online stores.

Look out for our Audiobooks on
Audible and Amazon too.

Transplant
Greenways
The Tribe
The Seed Garden

Our Paranormal and Paranormal Romance books
are all set in the same world and can
be read in any order or separately.

The Threads Which Bind us
The Wolf Inside us
Into Dust
The Calico Golem

The Threads Which Bind us

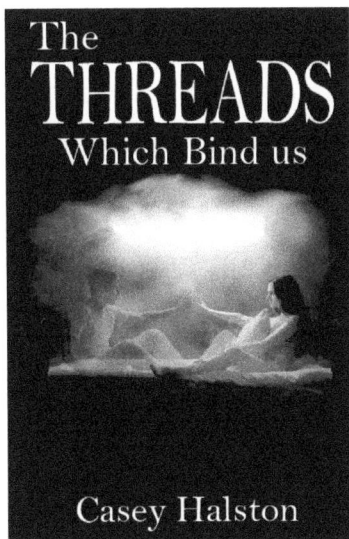

Anna's life is falling apart. She's skipping college, lost touch with her friends and can't face her family. She wakes late to find the ghost of a young man in her room. He has no memory of his past life nor any clue as to why he has appeared here.

In the beginning, she fights to get rid of him, but something about his glasslike sensuality fascinates her as he is drawn towards the only person in his world that can hear him, see him, *touch* him.

As they work to find out who he is, how he died and what is keeping him in the realm of the living, Anna's own recent and tragic past surfaces.

ISBN: 978-1-910779-98-9

The Wolf Inside Us

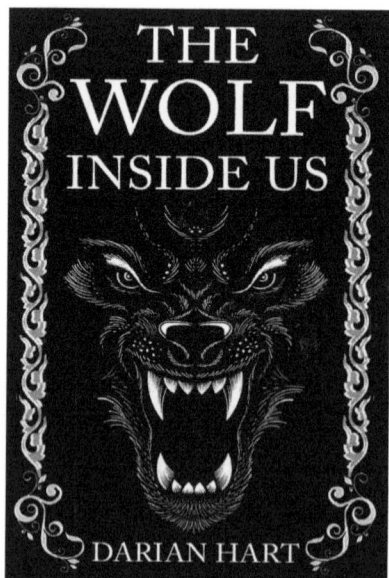

Jake is a reclusive genius shut away in his penthouse apartment where he draws his award winning zombie comics. Kat is one of his biggest fans. She's also his publisher's office manager and each week gets to visit Jake to see his latest work.

Over the years, Kat has developed a soft spot for Jake, so it's not surprising that she's completely thrown when he suddenly disappears. But stranger still, why did he leave a tiny puppy behind, all alone, and where did he get it?

Kat's relationship grows from more than simple puppy love in this sensual werewolf romance where life throws all it has at this girl and her dog.

ISBN 978-1-910779-97-2

The Calico Golem

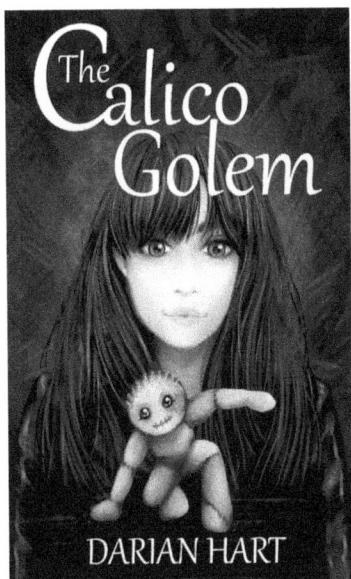

Emily's teenage years had been marred by bullies because she was different. It wasn't just about how she looked, or that she preferred girls to boys. Mads – tall, athletic and delightfully strange too found herself entranced by Emily after a chance encounter in the school shower room and from there the deepest love blossomed.

But troubles pile upon troubles and things seem to happen around Emily that she just can't explain.

Now, living together in a high-rise flat deep in the crumbling concrete estates, an attack by an ancient and mysterious woman leaves the girls for dead in a cold, dark alley.

Emily believes her beloved Mads to have died in the blast, but the appearance of a sinister creature in the darkness suggests otherwise.

What follows is a struggle to cheat death itself and restore life and justice along with some outlandish alliances.

ISBN 978-1-910779-05-7

www.ingramcontent.com/pod-product-compliance
Ingram Content Group UK Ltd.
Pitfield, Milton Keynes, MK11 3LW, UK
UKHW011701101125
464885UK00015B/77